IN *the* SWISH

DAWN GREEN

Red Deer Press

Published in Canada by Red Deer Press, 195 Allstate Parkway, Markham, Ontario L3R 4T8
Published in the United States by Red Deer Press, 311 Washington Street, Brighton, Massachusetts 02135

www.reddeerpress.com

10 9 8 7 6 5 4 3 2 1

Red Deer Press acknowledges with thanks the Canada Council for the Arts, and the Ontario Arts Council for
their support of our publishing program. We acknowledge the financial support of the Government of Canada
through the Canada Book Fund (CBF) for our publishing activities.

Library and Archives Canada Cataloguing in Publication

Green, Dawn (Lisa Michelle Dawn), author
In the swish / Dawn Green.
ISBN 978-0-88995-539-4 (paperback)
I. Title.
PS8613.R42753I52 2016   jC813'.6   C2016-905459-1

Publisher Cataloging-in-Publication Data (U.S.)

Green, Dawn.
In the swish / Dawn Green.
[ ] pages ; cm.
Summary: "Bennett Ryan is one of the region's very best basketball players. In fact, she single-handedly
led her team to an undefeated state championship. But when she is forced to switch schools in her senior year,
she must first fit in with her old rivals on this new team, then face her old team in the most heated play downs
of her young career" – Provided by publisher.
ISBN: 978-0-88995-539-4 (pbk.)
1. Basketball for girls – Juvenile fiction. 2. New schools – Juvenile fiction.
3. High school girls – Juvenile fiction. 4. Friendship – Juvenile fiction. I. Title.
[E] dc23 PZ7.G744In 2016

Also published in electronic formats.

Edited for the Press by Peter Carver
Cover and text design by Tanya Montini

For all the coaches in my life.

And for my fifteen-year-old self,
who looked for this book on the shelf.

Seasons come and go.
Some are calm and predictable.
Others roll in like an unyielding storm
and bring the unexpected.

LAST
SEASON

The tournament program features a picture of a freckle-faced girl with dark chestnut hair and a goofy smile. No matter what I do, I can never smile normally in photos. Say cheese, fuzzy pickles, smile—none of that seems to work for me. My face always comes out looking awkward and ridiculous. A crooked smile, a half smile, a smirk, a snarl, eyes closed, eyes half squinting ... or on my good days, all of the above. My teammates love to make fun of me for it. Most of them have a bad photo of me as a screen saver on their phone. And in this season's team picture, everyone, even our manager, decided to "awkward smile Bennett style" for the camera. My smile has officially become a "thing" on the team.

Lincoln High Lady Lions

PLAYER PROFILE

Name: Bennett Ryan	Year: Junior
Number: 6	Height: 5-10
Position: Shooting Guard/Small Forward	

I am a proud Lady Lion. Everything from my gold shoes to my purple ProWrap matches my uniform. I've been a starting guard for the varsity squad since I was a sophomore. I lead the team in three pointers, assists, and steals.

My best friend Brooke is also a guard. We've played on the same teams for five years. Brooke, Emma, Holly, Morgan, and I make up the Lions starting line-up. All we've wanted, all we've talked about, all we've trained for, is to win the state banner at the end of the season. And it's come to this.

This is the Oregon State Championship game. As predicted, it's come down to the Riverside Storm and us—*A Cross State Showdown*, read the headline in one local sports section. Purple and Gold vs. Blue and White. It's the matchup that everyone waits for. It's what everyone hopes for. It's what the sellout crowd at the championship stadium has come to see.

We've already faced them twice this season—one game went into double overtime. For the record, we won both times.

I like to win. I mean, who doesn't like to win? Losing sucks. And anyone who says they don't mind losing is lying.

Like the others, this game has been a battle, with twelve lead changes. It's everything the local papers predicted and everything the fans have been salivating for all season.

The game clock reads 00:14 and it's a tie game: 62–62. The Storm has called a time out. It's their ball.

All game long I've been battling Teesha Collins. I feel like I've been battling her my whole life.

Riverside Storm

PLAYER PROFILE

Name: Teesha Collins	Year: Junior
Number: 3	Height: 5-11
Position: Shooting Guard/Small Forward	

Teesha is the Storm's best player and, I have to admit it, the girl has got skills. Her first step is a little quicker than mine ... *a little*. She's also (this is difficult to say) a better ball handler. We've traded baskets, traded fouls, traded blows, and even traded blood.

Two years ago, during a select team tryout, she gave me a fat lip in a tussle for a loose ball. Last year, at a preseason tournament, we both crashed the boards for a rebound. I came out with the ball; Teesha came out with a concussion. Any girl will tell you it's just a part of the game. My mom likes to remind me that basketball is supposed to be a noncontact sport.

A "noncontact" sport?! Right.

BENNETT RYAN: PERSONAL INJURY REPORT
- ✓ 2 broken fingers
- ✓ 2 sprained thumbs
- ✓ Unknown number of jammed fingers
- ✓ 3 black eyes
- ✓ 1 concussion
- ✓ 1 bruised tailbone
- ✓ 4 sprained ankles (1 major)
- ✓ Shin splints

We don't try to hurt each other. Things just happen. It's just that more things seem to "happen" when Teesha and I are checking one another.

There's no doubt that they'll get her the ball. She'll drive. It's what she likes to do. I don't need my coach to tell me that, but he does anyway.

Coach Paige has used up all our timeouts. He's drawing out scenarios for everything and anything that could happen in the next fourteen seconds.

Fourteen seconds is a lifetime in basketball.

I'm trying to listen but the gym is incredibly loud. The hardwood court vibrates under my feet from all the cheering fans. Before the game, they announced that we had more fans in the gym than they had for the boys championship—a first in state history.

Coach Paige is trying to yell over the noise. If they score a two, we'll still have time to make a drive of our own. He wants us to take away their drive, make them shoot a two from the outside. They won't go for a three. They don't need a three and they've only shot 2/11 from outside the arc this game.

He continues to yell ...

"BLOCK OUT !"—*Obviously!*

"DON'T FOUL!"—*Obviously!*

"FOUL IF YOU HAVE TO!"—*Obviously!*

Coach Paige thinks we can out-rebound them. *Has he been watching the game?* They have two giant posts and they've been killing us on the boards all night long. If they score—if they don't score—he wants everyone to get the ball to me. *Obviously!* I have a game high 26 points. I'm hot tonight.

HOOORRRRRNNNN.

We cheer—"*LIONS!!!*"—and take to the floor.

Coach Paige is yelling for Morgan and me to run a pick-and-roll play ... I think. I can't hear him over the crowd and my focus is back on Teesha anyway.

I've been working her all game and I know she's getting tired. She gets lazy when she's tired and she usually favors her right side.

Teesha glares at me. She bumps into my shoulder and pushes for position. I push back. We both glance to see if the ref is watching and then trade a few jabs with our elbows. *God, I love this game.*

The ref blows the whistle. Ball in.

PLAY-BY-PLAY

00:14–Teesha Collins runs off a screen and gets the ball.

00:11–Teesha Collins drives right–misses the layup.

00:08–Montana Dunkin gets the rebound. Put back for 2 points.
        62–64–Storm lead.

00:07–Ball in to Brooke Hastings.

00:04–Brooke Hasting passes to Bennett Ryan.

00:02–Bennett Ryan runs off a Morgan Ellis screen. Ryan shoots.

00:00–Bennett Ryan hits the jump shot. 64–64–TIE GAME.

00:00–FOUL called on Teesha Collins.

00:00–Bennett Ryan will shoot an AND 1 for the championship.

I don't even hear the whistle at first. I just know I hit the shot and the gym is going crazy. Morgan is hugging me. Brooke is hugging me. Then I hear the ref's whistle and start to panic. *Oh, shit! Did I travel? Does the basket count?*

It counts. We're tied. A foul was called on Teesha. She must have hit me during the shot—I was so focused, I didn't feel it.

Near the opposite bench, Teesha is flipping out. Members from her team are holding her back. It was her fifth and final foul and she is out of the game.

They get her seated, but she's still yelling that she never touched me. She throws her water bottle and the referee gives the Riverside bench a warning.

There's no time left on the clock.

Both teams are off the court, each standing in a line with their arms linked together.

It's just me at the foul line. And I am shooting for the win ... no pressure or anything!

It's no exaggeration to say that I have dreamt about this moment a thousand times. I've played this exact scenario over and over and over again since I was a little girl. In my room, almost every night, this was my routine ...

My mom has told me to turn the lights off and go to bed. I pull off my socks and wrap them into tight little balls of white cotton. My team is down by one and I've got two foul shots—one will tie it, two for the win. I throw the first sock from my bed ... *swish* ... right into the middle of the laundry hamper. I've tied the game. I get ready to shoot the second. Pressure is on. From down the hall, Mom is yelling at me to turn the lights off ...

I shut out the noise and focus.

Bounce the ball three times. Toss it to myself.

Breathe.

Visualize.

Release.

Hold my follow through ...

Swish.

Game.

Championship.

We win.

The scene in the gym is like the end of every sports movie I have ever watched. I can hear "We Are the Champions" blaring from the speakers. My team is huddled in a group hug, holding our index fingers up to show the world and all the parents taking pictures that we, the Lincoln Lady Lions, are Number One.

We cheer and high-five the Storm. Most of them are in tears. Most of us are in tears as well. It's the way most rivalries end.

When I get to Teesha, she stops and wipes a tear away. "That was a bullshit call and you know it."

"Good game," I smile back. Nothing, not even Teesha Collins, is going to take away the high I'm feeling.

This is the best day of my life. My only regret is that my dad isn't here to see it. He would have hugged me and said, "I knew you were going to ice that shot. I knew it. Your shot was on—I could hear it in the swish."

This is where most sports stories would end.

Championship victory.

"We are the champions ... "

The end.

Happily ever after. Right?!

I wish.

THE PRE-SEASON

CHAPTER

"It's going to be fine."

Parents love to say this, especially when they know that things are going to be anything but *fine*.

"Really, sweetheart," my mom continued, "you'll see. You're getting worked up over nothing. It's going to be better than you think."

I didn't respond. Instead, I clenched my jaw and turned my head toward the car window, watching as beige houses, green trees, and driveways went by. Beige house–green tree–driveway–beige house–green tree–driveway–beige house–green tree–driveway ... I hate it here. And I want my mom to know I hate it here.

"Are you going to be this mopey the entire drive to school?"

"*Yes.*" I hissed it like it should be an obvious fact.

"Bennett, this is no way to start the first day of your senior year."

"You're right, Mom. This is no way to start my senior year."

I may have overdone it on the sarcasm. My mom's hands tightened around the steering wheel. She took a calming breath in and steadied her voice. "Bennett, we've been through this. You belong with your family. You belong with your sister and me."

I flipped down the passenger mirror and looked at the reflection of my sister, Prynne, sitting in the backseat—headphones on as she bopped away to some unknown beat.

Her hair still catches me off-guard. She dyed it midnight black with two chunks of violet blue in the front. She's going through some kind of punk-gothic phase right now. Less than a week ago, her hair was sandy blonde and up in a bunch of tiny pigtails—her indie-rocker phase. Before that, her hair was always down and straight with a cotton headband on top. She wore long skirts and crocheted peasant shirts that she found in our mom's old trunk of clothes—her retro flower-child phase. My mom says that Prynne is searching for her identity right now; that we have to be patient with her. I don't get it. I don't get her. I seriously question that we are genetically related.

Mom glanced in the back. "You see, Prynne is in a good mood. She's at least willing to give this year a chance."

"WHAT?" Prynne pulled an earphone off, yelling loud enough

for the car behind us to hear.

"Nothing, Sweetie. Go back to your music."

Prynne glanced at my mom and then at me, assessing the situation. Thick black eyeliner—that took her about an hour to apply this morning—outlines her squinting blue eyes. "Oh, is Bennett being a bitch again?"

"SHUT UP, LOSER." I turned to hit her.

She stuck her tongue out and scratched her cheek with her middle finger.

"Oh, really mature."

"GIRLS!" our mom barked. "Enough. It's my first day, too, and I don't need this."

I slouched back in my seat and stared out the window again. Beige house—green tree—driveway—beige house—green tree ...

This was supposed to be "The Best Year Ever!" My senior year. A year of driver's licenses, lake parties, house parties, winter formals, the prom, and an undefeated basketball season—this is what I'm most upset about. Upset. Crushed. Devastated. And this is what my mom can't understand. She doesn't get it. Basketball to her is just a sport, but to me, basketball is everything.

My mom has a video of me when I was only two years old. I'm running around the backyard patio. My auburn curls are glowing in the sunlight, and I'm wearing a hot pink basketball tank top that matches a pair of mini Nike high-tops my dad bought me—my first pair of basketball shoes. I still have them. They're hanging off a plastic basketball hoop in my room ... or they were. Now they're in some cardboard box I have yet to unpack.

In the video, I am throwing a foam basketball at a child-sized hoop that I was given for my birthday. I've watched the video hundreds of times, cringing at my form with every shot. Granted, I'm only two years old, but I keep bringing the ball back behind my head like a soccer throw-in and tossing it high in the air. Most times the ball comes back and drops on my head and, from behind the camera, my dad is chuckling and commenting that I already have a natural high arc to my shot.

He played right up until college and he could have gone further, but he enlisted in the army and that was that. For the first ten years of my life, my family moved eight times. The one thing that stayed the same, the one thing that every military base had, was a basketball court.

My dad taught me how to dribble, how to pass, how to fake, how to shoot, how to do a proper layup, how to block out, how to get low on defense ... he taught me everything. We used to spend whole Sundays watching games together. And over dinners, we'd discuss plays, the benefits of man-to-man defense vs. zones, or why a team's pick-and-roll offense wasn't working. It drove my mom and sister crazy.

My mom thinks this is why I am so into basketball. It's

something that I shared with my dad. She thinks it makes me feel like he's still around. I guess, in some ways, she's right. But basketball is so much more than just a game to me. I love it. I love everything about it ...

The court—indoor, outdoor, it doesn't matter, but I prefer hardwood. Give me a court, a hoop, and a ball, and I'm happy.

The sound. The ball bouncing, the cheers, the jeers, the yelling from the coach, the squeak of shoes on the floor—the shoes—don't even get me started on the shoes. I could talk for hours about how much I love basketball shoes ... I *have* talked for hours about it.

The ball—that perfect spherical shape that fits flush to my palm when sitting in my shooting pocket. The black veins that move and groove and give my fingers that little extra control I need, while blowing by my check with a killer double crossover—my signature move.

The swish—not just the sound, but also the feeling. There is nothing I love more than a perfect shot. No backboard. No rim. Just *swish. Swish. Sssswwwiiissshhh.*

Beige house—green tree—driveway ... the drive finally ended as we pulled into a large empty parking lot. My mom wanted to be super early on her first day.

I should be excited for her. I am excited for her. I know this is a big deal, something she's worked toward for a long time. In fact, when she first told Prynne and me that she was finally being made a Principal, I was really excited. I genuinely cheered and said things like, "All right, Mom! Way to go! Awesome!"

Then she dropped the bomb ... her new job meant that we had to move.

Move?

Again?

Now!?

I begged to stay. I actually got on my knees and pleaded with her to let me stay and live with Brooke's family. I had already made all the arrangements. Brooke's family said it was all right with them. They had an extra room for me and everything. I had it all worked out. It would only be for a year, and I could take the bus a couple hours each weekend to come home.

My mom didn't go for it. She didn't go for my second plan, either. It was a bad plan but, in my head, at the time, I thought it could work. I had convinced myself I could get up a few hours early every day and bus across state to school. It would only take an extra hour and thirty-five(ish) minutes each day—in the morning and at night—okay, so three hours. But I could do my homework on the bus, read, sleep ... at least, that was my logic.

It was a crazy plan. I knew she would never go for it, but I needed her to understand how desperate I was to stay. I wanted her to know that this move was going to ruin my life. Actually, literally, for real, one hundred percent, ruin my life.

She didn't care. She just repeated that same speech. "No. My answer is no. The family needs to stay together. This is our team and we are all that we have. Prynne needs you. I need you. I've given up a lot for you and your sister. This is something I need you to do for me, for us. It's not the end of the world, Bennett. You'll adjust. You'll make new friends. Everything is going to be just *fine*."

We pulled into the parking spot closest to the doors, where a shiny new nameplate was mounted on the brick wall.

RESERVED
Principal Jane Ryan

My mom turned off the engine and gazed at her name.

"Awesome, Mom. Check it out. That's you!" Prynne jumped forward. "You're, like, the man!"

Mom smiled and held back a happy tear. I was still pissed off and I still hated life, but this was her moment and, even though I hadn't told her, I was kind of proud. "Yeah, Mom. It's great. Really."

"Thanks." She grabbed her briefcase and quickly checked to see that her eye makeup was still intact. "You two know where to find me." She leaned over and kissed us both on the cheek, the same way she had done on the first day of every school year our whole lives. "Love you both. Have a great day!"

A great day? Yeah, right!

Prynne and I took a few extra minutes to get our bags and get out of the car.

I stood, letting my backpack hang loosely off one shoulder, while eyeing the school entrance.

Prynne nudged me. "Hey, you okay?"

I shook my head.

She looked up at the name above the entrance. "Yep, there's no doubt, this is going to totally suck for you. But hey, have a *great day*!" Prynne slapped my ass, put her headphones back on, and disappeared through the school doors.

I stared at the school logo, letting out a defeated huff of air. "Yep, this is going to totally suck ... BIG TIME!"

Riverside High

HOME OF THE STORM

CHAPTER

Starting in a new school is one thing. Starting in a new school where my mom is the principal is another thing. Starting in a new school where my mom is the principal and it also happens to be the school I've hated most of my teenage life, and the school that houses the team that I helped to defeat in last year's state finals—a team led by my biggest rival—that's not just another thing, that's the worst thing. Ever.

I tried to lie as low as I could before the first bell went. I found a spot to sit off the main foyer and kept my head down, pretending to go over my schedule. I was hoping to sit with my sister, but I hadn't seen her since she left me on the front steps. Left ... she practically ran away from me. *Traitor.*

Every now and then, I glanced up to see if I could spot anyone I knew. So far I had not seen a familiar face—probably a good thing.

Watching the excitement on the seniors' faces as they greeted each other after a summer away made me miss all of my friends at Lincoln. They would be doing the same thing right about now ... without me.

Almost on cue, I received a text from Brooke.

How's the first day? Fraternized with the enemy yet?

I responded:

No. I hate it here. I miss you. I miss everyone.

I looked at my phone and waited impatiently for her to answer. She was probably busy, chatting and laughing with everyone near the outdoor cafeteria tables, where we always sat together. I could picture my whole team there ... without me.

Finally, I could see that she was typing:

I miss you, too. We all do. Not the same without you.

I still can't believe this is happening.

Chat after school?

My reply:

Totally.

I scrolled through my contacts and decided to text my—kind of—boyfriend Nik.

Nik and I had been friends and basketball buddies since middle school, but we hadn't officially become "official" until after the State Championships.

We were at a party a couple days later when he asked if I

wanted to catch a movie with him. When I said yes, I didn't think he was asking me on a "date" date. And I still didn't know we were on a "date" date until he tried to kiss me outside the frozen yogurt bar. It was weird and messy, and not just because my mouth was full of coconut froyo, mini-marshmallows, and chocolate shavings. It was weird because we had been friends for so many years, and I had never thought of him like a boyfriend. He was always just Nik.

Like most of the other girls, I thought he was cute. At six foot seven, he towered over everyone. He played post for the boys varsity but volleyball was his main sport. He already had a scholarship to a major university in the northeast and plans to pursue beach volleyball after. I admired how driven he was. After we kissed, he walked me home and we held hands the entire way. I guess that made us official.

I liked him. We were starting to get serious, but after my mom dropped the job news, and all of my efforts to try and convince her to let me stay had failed, I realized that, like my life, he and I were over. I told him it was never going to work out. He convinced me to stay with him through the summer, and then he told me that he was getting a used car so he could drive across the state to see me all the time.

I had only been in our new place for a few weeks but, in that time, Nik had driven over five times. A few days before school started, I tried to end it again. I had grown up in a military family. I know what happens when people move away. Everyone says they're all going to stay in touch and be BFF'S, but that's never what happens. People move away and they eventually move on. But Nik wouldn't break up with me. He said it was going to be fine and that we'd make it work.

I still had serious doubts about the two of us, but it was nice to know that he was there. It was nice to know that anybody was there.

Me:

How's your first day? Mine sucks.

He responded right away:

I keep looking for you in the hallway.

Wish you were here, or that I was there with you :)

Me:

Me, too.

Nik:

Text me later if you want. Chat tonight?

I'll come and see you this weekend.

Me:

OK. :)

The bell finally went and I thought I had dodged my first bullet. I relaxed, grabbed my bag, and turned a corner to find my first class—English Lit—when I smacked straight into someone else walking down the hallway.

"Oomph," the girl exhaled. "Sorry, chica, I didn't ..."

"Sorry. My fault," I quickly replied.

Our eyes locked. "Holy shit! Bennett Ryan!" She backed away. "It's true. No way. *Holyfuckingshit*. The girls are going to freak out."

She sprinted down the hall before I could say anything else. I recognized her instantly.

PLAYER PROFILE

Name: Camila Cruze	Year: Senior
Number: 1	Height: 5-4
Position: Point Guard	

I knew it was going to happen eventually. I just wasn't expecting it to happen before first period of my first day. Lunchtime maybe, but not now.

When I turned down the next hall, I saw them all standing together—The Riverside Storm.

Camila was standing in the middle of the circle, giving a play-by-play of our run-in. I was so used to seeing them in their blue and whites in the gym, it was strange to see them all out of context.

I tried to slip up a set of stairs before they ... nope. Too late. *Shit*.

A group of heads all turned in my direction. I felt trapped. They looked like a pack of wolves staring down their prey. I had a choice—to let them give chase or ...

"Hey! Lincoln!" a voice called out and I turned.

Shit again.

Teesha Collins emerged from the group. Of course, she would be head of the pack.

CHAPTER

Teesha waved me over. I thought about ignoring her and just going to class, but I knew I was going to have to get this over with eventually. Better to just rip off the athletic tape than pull it slowly.

I waved. "Uh ... hi." I quickly realized how ridiculous I must have looked and dropped my hand mid-wave. My face felt hot and must have gone the same shade of red as my backpack.

"No. Freaking. Way." Teesha and the team circled me. "I mean, we all heard the rumor, but I didn't think you'd actually do it."

Uh, I didn't really have a choice.

"Bennett Ryan in the flesh." I felt like she was sizing me up. They were all sizing me up, and I was doing the same with them.

PLAYER PROFILE

Name: Georgia Oaks	Year: Senior
Number: 12	Height: 6-3
Position: Post	

PLAYER PROFILE

Name: Olivia Franklin	Year: Junior
Number: 7	Height: 5-9
Position: Shooting Guard	

PLAYER PROFILE

Name: Jessica Randall	Year: Senior
Number: 10	Height: 6-0
Position: Power Forward	

PLAYER PROFILE

Name: Tatiana Smith	Year: Senior
Number: 5	Height: 5-8
Position: Guard/Power Forward	

PLAYER PROFILE

Name: Montana Dunkin	Year: Senior
Number: 13	Height: 6-4
Position: Post	

"What's the matter, Lincoln?" Teesha goaded. "Scared without your team to back you up."

She took a step toward me and stood inches away from my face. I didn't back down. I wasn't sure if she was being serious. Did she want to fight me? *Really? Is this how it's going to be?*

"Boo!" She jumped at me and I flinched. My backpack fell off my shoulder and the group started laughing. Teesha was laughing the loudest.

"She's just playin'." A giant black girl with long thin braids stepped forward, picked up my bag, and handed it back to me. "I'm Montana. You can call me Monty."

"Thanks ..."

"But don't call her Dunkin cuz she ain't got nuttin."

Monty pushed a girl in a shiny blue Adidas tracksuit. "And the girl who can't rhyme for shit is Tatiana, but we call her Tats."

"Hey, I rhyme better than you dunk."

"I can't dunk."

"Exactly," Tats snapped back with attitude.

"Whatever." Monty shook her head. She pointed toward a tall, slender blonde whose hair was up in a messy bun. "This is ..."

"Georgia Oaks," I said. They all looked at me. I shrugged. "We call you two 'The Towers.'"

"The Towers?!" Monty questioned and looked slightly offended. I wondered if I had said the wrong thing. "Hell, yeah ... you and me, girl!" She high-fived Georgia.

"Call me Oaks," Oaks smiled.

Camila nodded at me. "Sorry I just ran from you in the hallway like that, chica. I'm Cruze." She put her arm around a stalky, dark-haired girl. "This is O, that's Jess, and you already know Teesha." She put her hand to her mouth, "T-WHAT?"

"T-TIME!" the group shouted in unison.

"T-TIME?" I looked at Teesha.

She shrugged. "I get a little heated sometimes. Might have got a couple of technicals last year."

"A couple?" Tats raised her voice.

"Whatever." Teesha shrugged and the group laughed again.

I laughed with them. I wasn't sure what else to do. The bell had already gone and the hallways had started to clear out. I felt like it was time to end this fake meet and greet and get to class, but I wasn't sure how to make my exit politely.

Teesha snatched the class schedule from my hand. "English Lit, Advanced Calculus, Honors History ..." she looked over her shoulder at the group. "Looks like Lincoln's got some brains."

I snagged my schedule back and quickly put it in my pocket. "Hardly." I don't know why I felt so protective of my academic schedule, but I did. Teesha and I stood staring each other down.

Monty spoke up. "If you've got English Lit with Humphries, you better get to class before the second bell goes. She hates it when students are late."

"Yeah," Teesha nodded. "She does. I'm going that way. I'll take you."

I could see the nervous and quizzical glances that the rest of the team was giving one another. Like me, they weren't sure what game Teesha was playing at.

Monty stepped forward. "I'll take you, I've got French right ..."

Teesha's arm flew up to stop her. "Monty, I said I got this."

Monty looked at me and then shrugged. There was no denying that Teesha was the alpha of the group.

Teesha put her arm around my shoulder and started to lead me away. "We'll catch up with you later."

I went with her but gave a quick look over my shoulder at the group. The looks I got back gave me the sensation that I was being taken to my own execution.

"You know, I could probably find my own way there." I slowed down a bit but Teesha pulled me forward.

"Don't be crazy. This school's like a maze if you haven't been in it before." We walked past a set of stairs and then down a long hallway. The second bell went and, through various classroom doors, I could see students playing first day of class musical chairs.

I kept pace with Teesha as we turned down another long hallway. "Thanks for showing me around," I said, trying to make casual conversation.

"No problem. It's what I do."

We walked by the art room, then the photography and woodworking labs. In my old school, all the trades were in one area of the school. I wondered if it was the same at Riverside and, if it was, I realized that Teesha wasn't taking me anywhere near where I needed to go. "I can probably find it from here. You're going to be late for class, too."

"Nah, I'll be fine," Teesha smiled. "Besides, we're almost there." She opened a door that led to the outside and waited for me to go through. I stopped and gave her a confused look, but she encouraged me to go on. "It's a short cut."

We both knew it wasn't a short cut. I stared at her. She stared right back. Two alphas in a standoff.

I didn't feel like having it out on my first day, so I gave in and took a step through the door. As expected, Teesha slammed it shut behind me.

I turned to open it and, not surprisingly, found out it was

locked. Teesha stood on the other side, smiling triumphantly through the window.

"Let's get a few things straight," Teesha's voice raised with bitterness.

"Okay," I crossed my arms and yelled back, trying to mimic her derisive tone. "Let's."

Teesha crossed her arms and matched my stance. It didn't go unnoticed that she was slightly—very slightly—taller than me. And she wanted me to know it. "I don't like you. I'm never going to like you. I don't know what the hell you think you're doing coming to my school. And don't think I give a shit who your mom is. You are not welcome here and you are certainly not welcome on this team. Some of the girls may buy into having you here, but it won't last long. If I were you, I'd get my sorry ass back to that sorry-ass school of yours, pronto." She turned and took a step, but then paused and turned back, with a finger pointing straight at me. "And that call was bullshit. I know it, you know it, and everyone in the gym that day knows it."

I should have kept my mouth shut, but I couldn't resist. "Maybe if you could hit a layup, that call wouldn't have mattered."

That hit a nerve. Teesha looked like she was going to punch me through the window. "STAY AWAY FROM MY TEAM."

"So this is how it's going to be?"

She smirked and nodded her head up. "This is how it is."

CHAPTER

"Should I even ask?" My mom crossed her hands and glared at me sternly from across her desk.

I hugged my backpack and slunk down in the chair, eye level with a brass nameplate that read *PRINCIPAL RYAN*. The mom/principal title was definitely a double-suck situation for me.

"Bennett?"

"What?" I snapped.

"Do you really need to take that tone with me?"

"No. I don't really need to take this tone with you." Like most girls my age, I have the ability to pull out the snarky-teenage attitude at a moment's notice. And sometimes it comes out all on its own.

My mom closed her eyes and took a deep breath. She was trying to "enhance her calm," a technique she had read about in one of the many leadership books that were piled by her bedside nightstand.

She got up, closed her office door, and went back to her seat. "Bennett, you're not the only one who has to get used to this principal/mom idea."

"Shouldn't it be mom first, principal second?"

"You know what I mean. And you know that it is," she said sharply. "Now, what happened? First day of school and less than fifteen minutes into the first block, and you're sent to my office for mouthing off at a teacher?"

"I wasn't mouthing off."

"What happened?"

"I was late to English because ..." I stopped. I didn't want her to know what had happened–I don't know why, I just didn't. "Because I got a little lost and then, when I finally got there, the teacher ..."

"Mrs. Humphries," my mom corrected.

"Mrs. Humphries," I continued through gritted teeth, "totally jumped all over me for walking in and interrupting her class. I apologized, but then she asked for my name and made a comment about the fact that, just because my mother is the principal, she wouldn't be making any special exceptions for me."

"And?"

"And, I might have mumbled something under my breath–

but there is no way she heard me. Anyway, she completely overreacted and told me to go to the office."

"Is that all?"

"No. I mean, yes." I quickly recovered. I could see that her spidey-mom senses were telling her there was more to it. Before she could dig any deeper, I stood up. "I'm sorry. The last thing I wanted was to wreck your big first day ..."

"You haven't wrecked anything."

A beep on her intercom went off. "Mrs. Ryan, you have a call on line one."

She hit the button. "Thank you, Alice."

"I'll apologize to Mrs. Humphries at lunch." My mom nodded in agreement. "Is that it? Or are you going to give me a detention or something?"

"Not this time. But this ..."

"Isn't over."

"And we're ..."

"Going to talk about it at home. I know." I opened the office door.

"And Bennett ..."

"Be good?"

"I was going to say that I understand this isn't what you want, but can you at least try to like it here? Please."

I put on my best fake smile. "I'll try."

For the record, I did try.

I tried during calculus when Oaks and Jess—I'm sure following Teesha's orders—deliberately got up and moved four rows away from me. I tried during lunch when Teesha, with team in tow, *accidentally* bumped into me in the cafeteria, knocking my cranberry juice out of my hand, conveniently causing it to splash up and stain the bottom of my pants and socks. And I kept trying through lunch, even though no one, including my own sister, would sit or talk to me.

Looking over at a table covered with a mix of knee-high combat boots, leather neck chokers, dark lipstick, and even darker hair, I noticed that it had taken Prynne the morning to merge herself into the punk-gothic crowd. I should have been happy that she was so easily making friends—and in some unselfish place, I was. But at that moment, with the day I'd been having, seeing my sister so happy when I was anything but, just made me feel super-annoyed with her. Didn't she or anyone else care that my life was coming apart at the seams?

Certainly no one in my old life seemed to care. I sent out a flurry of text messages, desperately hoping to hear how things were going back at Lincoln, and received only a single reply from Nik, saying that he would call me later.

At the end of the day, I was done with trying. Done with trying to reach my friends. Done with trying to smile and put on a happy face when I walked by Oaks, Cruz, or any other member of the Storm, who glanced at me like I was a foreign object in the hallway. And done with trying to like it at Riverside. I was done.

I found refuge in the only place that could make me feel like myself again—the gym.

I had played in the Riverside gym two times. Despite its being an opposing team's gym—*the* opposing team—I actually liked playing in it.

It was bigger and newer than the Lincoln gym. And, when they were pulled out, blue stands lined both sides of the court instead of Lincoln's one. A large mural of an angry storm cloud blowing away other school mascots, including the Lincoln Lion, covered an entire wall behind one of the hoops. Painted behind the opposite hoop in bold letters, it read: *HOME OF THE STORM*. A cold shudder jolted through me.

I walked to center court and let out a frustrated exhale as I took in my new surroundings. Pennants and banners lined the walls. Looking at the most recent, a satisfied smile spread across my face.

Senior Girls' Basketball
Oregon State Championships
Second

"I know you," a voice echoed in the gym.

I turned to see a girl sitting on a bench under the *HOME* sign. I wondered if she had been watching me the entire time.

"I know you," she said again. "You're Bennett Ryan. You play, or played, past tense, because you don't go there anymore, you go here, to Riverside now, but you did play for the Lincoln Lady Lions—last year's State Champions. Game MVP. Twenty-nine points, eleven assists, eight rebounds, and six steals."

The girl spoke faster than anyone I had ever heard before, like talking was a race and she was sprinting to get to the end of each sentence.

"That was a really good game for you because, during the season, you averaged 17.4 points, 4.2 assists, 3.5 rebounds, and 2.7 steals. In the finals, I knew you were going to hit that final foul shot to win the game, because you average just over ninety percent from the free-throw line, and you had already missed one previous shot, putting you slightly under your game average."

This girl knew more about me than me. I looked over my shoulder and around the gym to see if Teesha and others from the team were secretly hiding and watching. This had to be a setup.

"What are you looking for?" the girl asked. "There's no one else in the gym right now. Only us. You and me, or me and you."

I walked over to her. She was wearing an old-school Chicago Bulls T-shirt and a pair of Air Jordans that I would have killed for, but she certainly did not look like a basketball player. A pair of round glasses framed her big eyes, and she sat nervously twirling a long braid. When I got closer, I noticed a basketball-shaped backpack that I would have liked in grade school, sitting at her feet. It was clear that something wasn't quite right about her.

"Wanna sit?" She smiled at me.

"Umm, sure," I said hesitantly and sat beside her. *Of course*, I thought. The first person to talk to me would be a social outcast.

"My name's Matti—double T with an I but no E. I don't like E's. It's short for Matilda, which was my great grandma's name."

"You don't like E's?" I questioned.

She shook her head. "Fifth letter of the alphabet. No."

"I've never met anyone who doesn't like E's before. In fact, I've never met anyone who doesn't like a particular letter."

"You must have a letter you don't like," she said matter-of-factly. "Everyone does."

"I don't know. I've never thought about it." She looked at me, waiting for me to say more. Well, she kind of looked at me. Her eyes were focused slightly to the side of where I was sitting, which was a little unnerving. "I'm Bennett."

"I know. Bennett—double N, double T."

Yep, something was definitely not right with this girl.

"That's a strange name," she continued rapidly. "I don't

know any other Bennetts." She looked at me (again, to the side of me) like she wanted me to explain.

"Well, my mom used to teach English and she loves to read. She's a freak about ..." I stopped, not wanting to offend Matti in some way. "She really loves English literature, and she got my name from a character in *Pride and Prejudice*, Elizabeth Bennet. But there is only one T in her name ... anyway, my younger sister Prynne got her name from Hester Prynne in *The Scarlett Letter*."

"So, you and your sister are named after storybook characters?" Before I could answer, she continued, "That's cool. I like being named after someone real. But I like your name, too. It's unique, like me. I'm unique."

"You certainly are," I laughed. I hadn't meant it to be cruel, but Matti looked at me like I had offended her. I quickly tried to recover. "How come you know so much about me?"

She looked toward center court. "I like basketball. It's my favorite sport. It's my favorite thing ever, actually. And I'm good with statistics. I'm good with all numbers. My mom says it's a gift, but really it's because I have autism."

"Autism?" Everything made so much more sense. Even though I hadn't said it out loud, I felt bad about the social outcast thoughts.

"ASD—Autism Spectrum Disorder. I was diagnosed when

I was four. They call me high functioning. Functioning, like operational, like a machine. I like the word spectrum. It's like a rainbow. When I was six, my mom told me to imagine what color I was, and I picked purple because that was my favorite color. Still is. Do you have a favorite color?"

I was struggling to keep up with the pace of her words. "Well, it was purple, but I don't know anymore."

"Is it because purple and gold are Lincoln High colors and you're not a Lady Lion anymore?" I nodded. She shrugged, "Blue's a nice color, too. It's my second favorite color."

I couldn't help but smile and laugh.

"Was that funny?" she asked seriously.

"No. It's just that you're right. Blue is a nice color, too. I like your shoes, by the way." I nodded at the Jordans.

"Thanks." She proudly tapped her feet on the hardwood. "They were an early birthday present from my grandpa."

I checked the time. My mom was probably waiting for me and, after our talk in the office, I didn't need to give her the extra ammunition to nag at me over dinner with. "I gotta go. Are you okay by yourself in here?"

"Yep. I'm just waiting for my mom. She meets me here."

"Okay." I stood up. "It was nice to meet you, Matti with no E." They weren't just words; I actually meant it. Talking with her had been the highlight of my day. "You know what?" I added, "I'm not sure that I'm such a fan of P's."

"Sixteenth letter of the alphabet." She smiled. "I'm happy you're here, Bennett–double N, double T."

"Thanks," I smiled back. *I think you're the only one.*

CHAPTER

Propped up on my bed, hugging a pillow with my laptop resting on my shins, I watched Brooke adjust the screen on her computer so she could paint her toenails and talk to me at the same time.

The family dogs, two English Bulldogs named Slam and Dunk—my dad let me name them—were sprawled out like lazy lumps of dough on the sheets beside me. The rest of my room was covered in clothes and half-open boxes I was too lazy to unpack or put away. A small part of me was holding out hope that my mom would suddenly realize this was crazy, or she would hate her job, and we would have to pack up and move back.

I scratched Dunk's head while I waited for Brooke to chat. "I hate this."

"Sorry, I'll just be a second."

"No, not that. *This!* Having to talk to you on the computer,"

I said, waving at the screen. "I should be there with you. Not here. I hate it."

"Agreed." She sat back and opened a bottle of light violet nail polish, "Okay. Tell me everything. Did you see anyone from the team? Are they as bitchy in person as they are on the court? Did it totally suck? Spill it."

"Yes, I saw the team. Yes, it totally sucked. No, they aren't ... well, they're not all bitches. Teesha, maybe. She definitely let me know that I'm not welcome on her team."

"Oh, my God. Did you two fight?"

"No, we didn't fight. But she does *not* like me."

"Well, can you blame her?" she said, while attempting to paint her little toe.

"Thanks."

She looked up at the screen. "No. I don't mean ... it's just that we don't like them and they don't like us. It's not personal; that's just the way it is."

"Yeah, well, I happen to be one of *them* now."

"You haven't made the team yet."

"You don't think I'll make the team?!" I sat straight up. The thought of *not* making the team had never crossed my mind. I'd never *not* made any team before.

Brooke shrugged. "I just don't think it's a given. You're not exactly welcome there. Maybe the coach won't want to rock the boat. Have you met her yet?"

"Coach Kelley? No." I shook my head and leaned back against the wall.

"I wonder if she's as scary off the court as she is on."

"I hope not." I only knew Coach Kelley from what I had seen on the court. When she wasn't barking at her players, she was usually crouched at the end of the bench, looking stern while banging a coach's white board or throwing an erasable marker on the floor. The only words she had ever said to me came during the handshake at the end of the championship, when she told me, "You sure can play the game."

"I heard she played professional ball overseas for a few years."

"In Spain and Germany. I googled her," I confirmed. "You really think I might not make the team?"

"I don't know. Do you really want to?"

"What do you mean? Of course I want to."

"It's just that I don't think anyone would blame you if you sat out this year. I'm sure you'd still get scholarship offers. You could train on your own, play for the club teams, plan for next year."

Brooke was focused on her nails as she offered me her unwelcome advice. She couldn't see how angry her words were making me. It was true. I already had a few scholarship offers—not the ones I wanted, but they were respectable enough. "So, you actually think I should just sit out the year?" I baited back.

"I don't know. Maybe."

"I can't believe you right now!" I threw the pillow.

"What?" She looked up, surprised at my outburst.

"Could you do it? Not play for a year?"

"Chill, dude. No need to get so defensive. I just think, if you're not wanted there, why would you want to play for ..."

"Because it's basketball!" I shouted.

"But it's Riverside! Let's be honest ... you're not one of them."

"Okay, let's be honest. You'd love it if I didn't play."

"Please. This isn't about me. It's about you." She dipped the brush into the paint bottle. "Besides, even with you, it's not like they can beat us anyway."

My jaw clenched. Now it was on. "You don't think Riverside will take Lincoln this year? Did you guys get some all-star transfer I don't know about, because I think we'll take you by twenty." It was the first time I had said "we," including myself with Riverside. Brooke tried to hide a sly smile. "Brooke?" I said flatly. "Who'd you get?"

"Oh, no one."

Now I was interested. "Who?"

"Just these two six-foot power forwards from Australia. Twins. Their family moved here over the summer. I haven't seen them play yet, but Coach Paige is really excited about them." Brooke looked to see my reaction. She was trying to make me jealous.

I didn't like where this conversation was going. "I don't want to talk about basketball anymore."

"You always want to talk about basketball."

"Tell me how school went."

"It was good. Emma dyed her hair platinum blonde."

"She did?"

"It doesn't look very good. I like her better dark."

"Did you see Nik?"

"Yeah. I have Bio with him. Haven't you talked to him yet?"

"For a few minutes after school. He had volleyball practice. I just feel so out of the loop with everyone. I tried to text you during the day."

"Sorry. I saw your text but things were crazy busy. You know how it is. Getting the summer gossip from everyone. Besides, didn't you meet anyone at Riverside? What's it like having your mom as head honcho?"

"Oh, awesome," I said sarcastically. "In fact, I got sent to her office today."

Brooke looked up. "You did not."

I nodded. "I totally did. Sent to the principal's office on my first day. It was complete bullshit. The English teacher has it out for me."

"Your mom must have hit the ceiling."

"She was pretty pissed."

"Wow! You did have a shite day."

"I did meet this one girl, though. Her name's Matti and she knew some crazy stuff about me. She's got ..." For some reason I didn't feel like telling Brooke about Matti. I already knew what she'd say—something about me committing social suicide on my first day. "It doesn't matter. Tell me more about your day. Did Holly talk about her trip to Europe? Last I heard, she had met some guy in France and ..." I heard a buzzing sound and watched Brooke reach over and grab her cell phone. She smiled and laughed at whatever she was reading. "What is it?" Brooke ignored me and laughed again. "Brooke?"

"Huh?" She looked up. "Oh, it's nothing. Just Emma, she's ..." Her phone buzzed again. She giggled and started to type something back.

"I better go. My mom's calling me." It was a lie, but I was annoyed and wanted to end the conversation quickly. "Brooke?"

"What? Oh, you gotta go. Are you sure?" She looked down and continued typing on her phone.

"I'm sure."

"Talk later?"

"Sure."

"Okay." She finally looked up at me. "Miss you."

"Yeah," I said halfheartedly. "Miss you, too."

CHAPTER

There is something awesome about a gym. Or, to be more specific, there is something awesome about a gym, 90's jock jams, and a ball.

Everyone has *that* place. And if they don't, they should. That place that is uniquely theirs—literally, metaphorically, whatever—where they can go and just shut the world out. Shut out the noise, the hateful glares, nagging, enemies, frenemies, the unanswered texts, the answered texts, the unwanted notes slipped into bags and lockers that have pictures of slaughtered lions and say things like: *Go back to the den you came from ...* yeah, that happened. Twice.

The gym is my place.

It didn't take a psychologist to figure out why. Although my mom had made me see one when I was fifteen, because she was concerned with the, as she put it, unhealthy amount of time I was spending alone in the gym. The psychologist told my mom that the gym was a constructive outlet for me to deal with the traumatic death of my father. The gym was where he and I spent the most amount of time together, so it made sense that was where I would want to be, where I felt closest to him. That was the psychologist's diagnosis. I just knew that the gym made me feel better. Or feel less.

I was already pretty good at most sports WD. But it was PD when I started to excel in basketball—my sister and I use the acronyms WD and PD when referring to our lives. WD = With Dad. PD = Post Dad.

It makes it easier for us to talk about certain things. Like, mom was a lot more fun to be around WD . PD , mom focused on work, I focused on basketball, and Prynne focused on herself. The family has never felt the same PD . I'm not sure we ever will.

There were a lot of times PD when I just couldn't be at home anymore, so I would grab a ball, put my earphones on, set the playlist to 90's dance, and turn up the volume. Brooke and the rest of the team used to make fun of my music selection. Most on the team prefer Eminem or Hip Hop, but there is nothing like a little C+C Music Factory or Snap! to get me in the gym and out of my head.

I came to school with my mom most mornings. She had to be (or she wanted to be) earlier than everyone else. It was too early for Prynne. She opted to sleep the extra hour and take the bus. Not me. I wanted the gym time.

My mom knew that something was up. The first few mornings we drove together, she tried to nonchalantly start a conversation about how I was feeling and how school was going. When she got frustrated with my one-word answers, she started asking direct questions about how I was adjusting to the new surroundings and how the basketball girls were treating me. Having once been a teacher and now a principal, she was overly concerned with the idea of bullying and was worried that it was going on. I laughed. In another world, maybe. But in my world, this was just basketball.

"Bennett, don't laugh. Bullying is a serious issue."

"I know it is, Mom."

"And you would tell me if you felt someone was bullying you or anyone else."

I wanted to hug her right then. I really did. For being so darn cute ... and naïve. "No one is bullying me, Mom."

"But you would tell me if they were?"

Sure, Mom. Sure. "Of course I would."

"I'll never understand why this basketball thing is so important to you."

Then you'll never understand me. "It just is."

"Things will get better, once the season starts," she said, trying to comfort me.

Maybe. Maybe not. I smiled and nodded back.

I had between forty-five minutes to an hour of gym time before I had to change and get to class—depending on if I had to get to English first block or not.

Being late to Humphries's class the first day was enough to make sure that I was always one of the first students, book open, pen out, eager and waiting, when she started to write the day's notes on the board.

For some reason, and I knew it went deeper than my just being late to her class, Humphries had it in for me. My mom said that within the faculty, she had a reputation for being a strict "old school" teacher, and that I shouldn't take it personally. But it was personal. There was a particular disdainful look she gave to me and no one else. If she did a homework check, mine would be the first desk she came to. A tough question no one wanted to answer, my name was the first off her lips. She was trying to catch me off guard. But English had always been my best subject—my mother's daughter and all that—so it was game on, Humphries. Game on.

Forty-five minutes wasn't enough time to break a sweat, not that I wanted to do that before class anyway, but it was enough time to get in some dribbling drills and do some shooting.

About halfway through some stationary dribbling, I looked up to a second level corner window overlooking the gym. As usual, Matti's face was glued to the glass, watching me.

The first time I noticed her, I felt weird having her eyes on me. But now I was not only used to her, having her interested little face in my peripheral gave me some strange sense of comfort. I'd seen her in the hall a few times, but we hadn't talked since that first day.

I waved. She waved back.

Turning away from the window, I bounced the ball on the floor and was going to get back into dribbling, when I came face to face with Coach Kelley. With my headphones on and music blaring, I hadn't heard her come in. I jumped and clutched my chest ... I might have let out a surprised scream as well. Not exactly the first impression I was hoping to make.

"Sorry," I muttered quickly and pulled my headphones off.

"I'm sorry I scared you." She reached down and picked up my loose ball.

"That's okay." I took my ball from her outstretched arms. "Thanks."

"I'm also sorry that I haven't officially introduced myself yet." She held out her hand and I shook it. "I'm Kate Kelley. You can call me Kate, or Coach, or Coach Kelley. Most call me Coach K."

"I'm ..."

"The girl who helped put that banner up in my gym," she said, pointing to the second-place banner.

She looked back at me and crossed her arms. I wasn't sure what to say. "I know exactly who you are, Bennett Ryan. Heck, anyone following high school girls' basketball knows who you are."

I felt the heat from my cheeks flaming red.

"When I heard your mom was going to be our new principal, I wasn't sure if that meant you were going to come here as well. To be honest, I didn't think you would. Switching schools, switching teams in your senior year, that's a pretty big deal."

"Tell my mom that."

"I take it coming here was not something you agreed to lightly?"

It wasn't something I agreed to at all. "Not really." I shook my head.

"You in here every morning?"

"I usually come in early with my mom."

"I wish half my team—heck, a quarter of them—were as motivated as you. Have you met any of them yet?"

I nodded but kept my mouth shut.

Coach K laughed. "I guess that answers my next question. If they were welcoming or not?"

"They all seem ... really nice."

"Do they?" She raised an inquisitive eyebrow. "I bet they gave you warm fuzzy hugs and everything."

I didn't respond.

"Well, look. If you get to know me, you'll find out that I'm a pretty straight shooter, so I'm just going to cut to the chase. Are you planning on coming out to tryouts?"

My response came angrily and uncontrollably out of my mouth. "Why do people keep asking if I'm planning on playing this year? Of course I'm going to play. It's basketball!"

Coach K nodded approvingly. "Well, all right then." She turned toward the gym doors and then quickly spun back around. "Oh, by the way, my daughter really likes you."

"Your daughter?"

She glanced up to the corner window. Matti dropped out of sight when I looked up. "Matti's your daughter?"

Coach K nodded. "She's taken a real liking to you. She's always been a fan but, now that you've talked to her, you're all she likes to talk about. I think she was more excited than anyone when I told her you were coming here. I'm telling you because I want you to know that she's ..."

"Autistic. She told me."

"And sometimes she doesn't have a filter. So, if she's coming on too strong or starting to bother you, just come and talk to me. And if you don't want her watching you, I can tell her to ..."

"No," I interrupted. "It doesn't bother me. If she wants to sit in the gym while I practice, or if she wants to come and play a bit, that would be cool."

At first Coach K smiled, but there was something sad in her eyes. "Matti loves basketball. She might love it more than anyone I've ever known, and that's saying something. The thing is, she can't handle loud noises very well. They can ... set her off. She can be around a bouncing ball for a little bit, but not too long. When we have home games, she watches from my office, up there."

"What about away games?"

"She usually stays home. Watches the game tape later that night. Anyway, Matti likes you. She's a pretty good judge of character, so I'm going to let that whole scoring on us in the championship final go for now." She smiled and winked. "I'm not so sure the girls will be as forgiving. As I like to say, it's a matter for the court. See you in a few weeks, Bennett Ryan."

I don't know if Coach K said something—I think she did—but the next morning as I was doing up my laces, Teesha came into the gym, dramatically announcing her presence with the hard thud of her gym bag.

I looked over at her.

She pointed toward the hoop in front of me. "Your half," she pointed to the one in front of her. "My half."

"Whatever." I wanted to sound like I didn't care.

I continued to tie my shoes, glancing a few times in Teesha's direction. She looked at me. We both slid on headphones at the same time and took to our own side of the court.

I stood in the circle of the key and started my stationary dribbling drills. I could see Teesha doing the same thing. She turned to face me. I did the same.

Every time I pounded the ball on the floor Teesha matched my dribble and then did it again—a little harder, a little faster.

I switched to cross overs. She switched to cross overs.

Our eyes were locked on one another.

Dribble—cross—dribble—cross ... like a mirror image, Teesha matched me dribble for dribble.

I upped the intensity. *See if you can keep up with this!*

Dribble—cross—cross—dribble—cross—cross ... right hand, then left, back again ... a challenging grin formed in the corner of her mouth—*anything you can do, I can do better.*

She jumped to dribbling between the legs. So did I—*I can do anything better than you.*

I'm not sure how long we kept the game (if that's what it was) going. At some point, my hamstrings and calves started to burn and twitch, begging me to stand and get out of the crouched position I was in. I could see a sheen of sweat forming on Teesha's forehead, and I knew she was feeling the same pain.

Give up. Give up, already.

After another couple of minutes (felt like hours), I could see her legs starting to shake. I wondered if she saw mine doing the same thing.

And then I lost the ball. It bounced off my toes and rolled down the gym toward her.

Teesha continued to dribble with her right while reaching down and picking up my ball with her left. Without missing a beat she began to dribble both balls simultaneously. *Point, Teesha.*

I smiled and nodded, conceding defeat.

And this is how it went most mornings after that. We acknowledged each other's existence but we didn't talk. School life was the same. The team still ignored me, but the notes and bumps in the hallway stopped. I don't know if it was that they were beginning to tolerate me more, or if Teesha had something to do with it.

Each morning we met, a new challenge was extended and accepted. We didn't plan the competitions, they just happened. I'd hit a three. She'd hit a three. I'd hit another one. She'd hit another one. And so on and so forth, until one of us missed.

I will never admit this to her, but I looked forward to the mornings, to the competition.

CHAPTER

It took a lot of complaining and convincing, but my mom finally gave in and got me a used car—a small blue hatchback—on the understanding that she knew where I was at all times and that I had to help drive my sister around. Really, I think she got the car more for her than me. Being principal was demanding, and my having a car made things a lot easier ... for all of us. For me it was the freedom to drive back home—it was still *home* to me—and I couldn't wait to get back.

Brooke was throwing her annual Halloween party. She had started hosting them when we were in the sixth grade. Back then, it was all about cute witch costumes, scary movies, sleepovers, and sugar hangovers. Now it was slutty witch costumes, less innocent sleepovers, and a very different hangover.

My mom had three non-negotiable conditions. 1. I had to

take Prynne with me. 2. No drinking. 3. We had to be home by midnight. Number three was meant to ensure that we followed number two. And number one was to ensure that I followed two and three and made sure Prynne did the same.

Getting back home by midnight meant that we would have to leave the party around 10, 10:30 at the latest, which wasn't ideal, but it was also non-negotiable. Post-Dad Mom was really strict and liked to use words like non-negotiable with her conditions. Prynne and I might not have agreed but we understood.

Prynne leaned over and turned on the AC. "Do you mind? I don't want my makeup to get all runny." We had left the house forty minutes later than I wanted to because she had to apply the perfect shade of corpse-white for her gothic-zombie-bride costume. I went as Buffy the Vampire Slayer. Classic. Simple.

"I don't mind," I said, focused on the road ahead.

"And can I change the station?"

"Sure, whatever."

"Okay!" Prynne turned in her seat. "What the hell is up with you? You didn't get mad at me for making us late and you never let me change the station."

"Huh?"

"Are you nervous about seeing all your old friends or something?"

"Or something."

"What's up?"

"I'm breaking up with Nik tonight."

Prynne laughed.

"What's so funny?"

"Nothing. I called it. I told mom you'd end it any day now."

"How would you know?"

"Basketball season is about to start."

"So?"

"So, you always end things with guys before the season starts. It's what you do."

"I do not. And besides, Nik's my first real boyfriend. I was never that serious with Nolan or Grady."

"You never let it get serious. You ended it with both of them right when the season was about to start."

I thought back. Was that what I did?

Prynne checked her makeup in the visor mirror. "It's not like I care. The guy's a dud. All he cares about is volleyball, but I guess that could work because all you care about is basketball. It's not like you two were really hot and heavy, anyway. I mean, really, I'm surprised you stayed with him this long."

"Tell me how you really feel."

"Please, you were never that into him. When's the last time you saw him?"

It had been three weeks. He had come to see me. We went

for a drive to a lake and he wanted to fool around, but I kept pushing him away and wanting to talk about how awful things at Riverside were going.

Prynne was right; I was never that into him. The distance between us wasn't helping. And trying to schedule Skype dates around his volleyball schedule was getting annoying.

I should have ended it when we were at the lake, but something in me didn't want to. Even though Nik and I weren't really anything, ending it with him meant letting go of another part of my connection to Lincoln, which was starting to feel farther and farther away.

Prynne split from me as soon as we walked in the front door. I yelled at her to make sure she met me back at the car around 10, but Michael Jackson's "Thriller" drowned my voice out.

Standing in Brooke's house brought back a wave of memories. From the front foyer, I could see into her living room. Basketball trophies and pictures of the family covered the fireplace mantel.

Brooke's older brother Jaydon had graduated as a basketball god from Lincoln. He got a full scholarship to Kansas. A blue jersey and a Jayhawk pennant were framed prominently for all to see as they entered the home.

"BENNY BEAN!" a voice screamed above the music. Only one person called me that.

I stood on my tiptoes and saw Brooke dancing her way through the crowd. "Hey, girl, you came." She hugged me, spilling some green-ooze-colored punch on my shoulder. "Ohhhh, I miss you." Her outburst of love and glossy eyes gave away that this was her third or fourth glass of punch. "Come, come," she tugged on my arm, "the girls will be psyched that you're here."

As she pulled me through the congested room of costumed partygoers, I got nods and high-fives from familiar faces who seemed happy to see me. It felt good. I realized just how much I was missing being around people who genuinely wanted to be around me.

"Have you seen Nik?" I yelled over the music.

"Yeah. He's around somewhere."

Our journey through the house ended in the kitchen. "Look who I found!" Brooke said triumphantly.

"HEY!" Arms and punch-filled plastic cups were raised in the air as members of my old team greeted me. The whole group of them was wearing 80's head and wrist bands, short (really short) red and white striped shorts, knee-high gym socks, and blue basketball jerseys strategically cut off just below their breasts.

"We're the Harlot Globetrotters. Get it?" Brooke drunkenly smacked me in the arm.

"I get it." I smiled. Not that I wanted to wear ass-hugging

shorts and a stomach-exposing crop top, but I was a little hurt that I hadn't gotten the memo.

Two Athena-looking blondes stepped to the front of the group. Identical sun-bleached blonde hair, tanned skin, blue eyes, six-foot frame—what I imagined every teenage boy's fantasy to be. They smiled and handed me a drink.

"You must be the famous Bennett we've heard so much about." The one on the right spoke with an irresistible Australian accent. I could feel them sizing me up. "I'm Hanna, and this is my sister Hayley."

I left Lincoln for Riverside and this, THIS, is what replaced me?!

"Nice to meet you." I absentmindedly took a sip from my cup and quickly spat it out. "Whoa! That's just vodka," I said, stating the obvious. The Aussie goddess laughed. "I'm driving home tonight. I'll pass."

"What?" Brooke pouted. "You're not spending the night?"

"Mom's orders. Have to be home by midnight. And Prynne came with me."

"Brooke sad," she said, referring to herself in the third person. A definite sign that she was about to drink one too many.

"You know my mom."

"No-fun Jane? I know her."

"Tell us about Riverside," Emma interrupted. "Brooke said they're all bitches."

I hadn't made friends with any of the Riverside players yet, and yes, one could argue they had their bitchy moments with me but, standing in the kitchen, I felt strangely defensive. "They're actually not that bad."

"So this is the big rivalry, right?" Hanna, or maybe it was Hayley, asked. "You're playing for the team everybody has a hate on for?"

"The team we beat in last year's State Championships!" Emma yelled.

"YEAH!" The group held up their drinks and yelled in unison. For the first time ever, I didn't celebrate with them. Brooke's eyes surveyed my non-reaction from the top of her plastic cup.

"Well, that has to be a bit awkward," Hanna looked between Brooke and me.

"It is," Brooke said, sounding bitter and surprisingly sober. "And it will be when we kick your ass this year."

"Back-to-back championships!" Emma encouraged the group. "Undefeated season, woop woop!" They turned toward one another and started to sing and dance victoriously in a circle.

It was suddenly very clear to me how we must have looked to someone walking in. The group of *them*, dancing in a circle in the middle of the kitchen, and me. The two Aussie girls were the newbies but I was the outsider.

Brooke turned to look at me and I got the sense, from the

anger in her glare, that this is how she wanted me to feel.

"You know this wasn't my choice, right? I didn't want to leave the team."

She shrugged. "But you did." She turned back to the circle and continued to dance and chant. "Cham-pi-ons. Cham-pi-ons. Cham-pi-ons ..."

No one noticed as I left the kitchen and disappeared into the party. My cheeks felt hot and tears threatened to escape my eyes.

I didn't used to cry ... ever. I was known as the tough kid. The one who could fall off a bike, scrape my knee, bang my head ... not a single tear. But then my dad died and it was like someone opened the floodgates on my tear ducts.

I hate emotions sometimes. *Stupid tears. Get it together, Bennett.* I gave myself a pep talk and scanned the room for Prynne. Who I saw was Nik.

He was dressed as a vampire and sucking face with some redhead I recognized from a younger grade. *Perfect.*

Yes, I was about to break up with him, so seeing him nibbling some random girl's neck shouldn't have stung. But it did. And it fueled an inner rage that had been ignited in the kitchen.

I snagged a half-full cup of some blood-red drink out of the hand of a guy dressed as a pirate and marched over to Nik.

"Nik!" I waited for him to turn around, but he was too absorbed in his conquest. "NIK!"

As soon as he turned, I threw the drink in his face. Red juice splattered over his face and down his shirt. The girl he was kissing screamed, and everyone in the room stopped to look at us.

"What the hell, Bennett!"

"What the hell, Nik!" Seemed like an appropriate comeback.

"That. Is. Awesome!" Prynne cheered and took a photo with her phone.

"Let's go." I pulled her by the arm toward the door.

"But we just got here. Do you know how much time this makeup took?"

"I don't care. We're leaving." I didn't want to wait for anything Nik had to say. I didn't want to wait for the cheers and clapping from the drunken partygoers. And I definitely didn't want to wait for Brooke and her Harlot Globetrotters to come out from the kitchen and see what had just happened.

THE
WARM
UP

CHAPTER

Tryouts: Day 1

"Let me be perfectly clear. No one is guaranteed to make this team. No one." Coach K paced in front of twenty-four anxious bodies standing on the baseline. "I don't care if you were on the team last year ..."

A few of the girls glanced briefly at one another.

"And I don't care who you are or how good you might be ..." That was directed at me.

Teesha raised an eyebrow and looked over to make sure I had heard it.

"If, at the end of these tryouts, I don't think you're right for the team, your name will not be one of the final twelve. That means half of you won't be standing here next week. If you want on this team, you have to earn it. You got it?" We all nodded.

Some people look forward to their birthdays, or Christmas, or the summer—their favorite day or time of year—because they get to be with family or their loved ones, or they like being outside, enjoying what that particular time has to offer. For me there are only two real seasons of the year—basketball season and not basketball season. And yes, with club teams, select teams, and skills camps, one could technically argue (as my sister has) that basketball season is really year-round. But those people (Prynne) don't get it.

There is nothing like the actual start of a new school season. A zero wins–zero losses clean slate. It doesn't matter what happened the previous year. Last season is in the books, engraved on the trophies, reminisced about in the locker room—it's done. A new season means new teams, new games, and the optimism of the unknown. And *that*—the unknown—is the only thing that matters because it means that anything is possible.

This is my favorite day of the year.

I couldn't concentrate in class. Humphries caught me off guard and unprepared to answer a question about *Hamlet*. My lack of focus could be attributed to nerves or the fact that I hardly slept the night before. Too many thoughts about missing a tryout or arriving late kept me awake.

I hadn't been this nervous since my first junior-high tryout.

I threw up then. As I stood on the line, staring down sideways glances from Teesha and others, I felt like throwing up now.

And then Coach K said the words that no basketball player wants to hear. "You don't need a ball." A collective groan emanated from the group as basketballs were tossed to the side.

I felt a familiar pair of eyes on me and I looked up to the coach's corner office window. Matti waved down at me. I smiled back.

"Let's see how many of you are coming into the season ready to play." She measured out and set down four orange cones twenty meters apart. "I think you're all familiar with Beep Test."

Shit.

A much louder, almost choreographed groan echoed off the gym walls.

I had faced the evilness of the Beep Test five times before. Coaches like to use it to measure the fitness levels of their players.

I'm convinced that if hell exists, somewhere down there, large groups of sinners are running an infinite Beep Test.

"Cruze has got this." Cruze stretched her body like she was in an 80's exercise video and then started to punch the air as if she was a boxer warming up. "Ain't none of you slow-ass turtles gonna catch me." Everyone laughed.

"Careful, Cruze," Oaks joked. "It was the turtle, not the hare, that won the race."

"Pshhhh," Cruze waved Oaks away. "All I know is you best call me Professor Cruze, cuz I'm about to school y'all. Lesson one: How to eat my dust." She bent down like a sprinter waiting for the gun to go off.

We all kept laughing as we got ready on the line and waited for the familiar and unwanted melodic beeps that signaled us to start running.

The Beep Test is all about pacing, but Cruze took to the front, with Teesha staying close behind her and a few steps ahead of me.

At about level seven, I could feel my lungs beginning to burn. One by one, as the running pace continued to increase, girls started to drop out. Teesha looked unfazed.

Level eight—Cruze was still cruising but I could see Teesha slowing down. We were even in our stride.

Level nine—only myself, Teesha, Cruze, Tats, and O remained.

Level ten—Cruze, Teesha, and me.

Level eleven—I wanted to quit. I really wanted to quit. But Teesha was fading and there was no way I was going out before her.

Still level eleven—now it was on. The twenty-one others who had dropped out and were sucking their water bottles on the sideline cheered Teesha and Cruze on.

Level twelve—this was a personal best for me, which should

have been enough, but it wasn't. I tried to push, but my legs felt like logs and refused to listen ... I want to die. I was done. But so was Teesha. I didn't see her, but I felt her drop out and it was enough to push me a couple of beeps further. *Point, Bennett.*

Cruze was in front. "Hey, Lincoln, you might be a Lion but I'm a Cheetah." She yelled as she ran. "Never gonna catch me." I could barely breathe let alone respond.

Still, level twelve—there's a point when an athlete thinks they are done. And then there's a point when they are actually done. This time I was *done* done. Overdone. I doubled over with my hands on my knees, gasping for air.

Cruze sprinted by me. "Like a Cheetah," she yelled. "Like a Cheetah. Woop woop."

The group cheered loudly—not because Cruze was the last one left, but because I wasn't.

Tryouts: Day 2

Each girl walked into the gym doing the familiar penguin waddle of day-two tryouts, our muscles shrieking in pain from the abuse they had endured the day before.

With every step I took, I felt like my hamstrings and calves were waging a secret battle against me. My sore and tired muscles crying out: *Don't make us do that again. We hate you. We hate you so much. Please, be nice to us today.*

The Beep Test was only the beginning of rigorous conditioning exercises that included suicides, wall sits, pushups, and countless defensive drills. We hadn't touched a ball until the last twenty minutes, and that was to do a timed full-court layup drill. When we didn't hit the fifty-basket target set by Coach K, we had to do it again. And again. And again, until finally Coach K blew her whistle and walked out of the gym, waving her arms in disgust.

There is a scene in the *G.I. Jane* movie where the recruits who can't cut the hardcore Marine training go and ring a bell to signal they are voluntarily dropping out. I know because Prynne had put the movie on while I sat and iced my legs on the couch after tryouts.

"I thought you could relate," she joked. "And maybe use the inspiration. Just don't go shaving your head."

"Very funny," I winced back. I ended up skipping some homework to watch the entire movie. Prynne even made popcorn. I needed all the inspiration I could get.

The way Coach K was running tryouts, there should have been a bell like the one in the movie by the change-room door. As it was, only twenty-one girls returned for day two. But maybe that was what she wanted, for only the strong to survive.

After stretching my legs, I grabbed a ball and went to a

hoop for warm-up shots. As I entered the key, the four others shooting—Oaks, Jess, Monty, girl I didn't know—all scattered like I was patient zero of the zombie plague.

When one of my shots rebounded wide and bounced to the next hoop, I called out to Cruze—the nearest person—to pass it back. Not only did she not answer me, but she actually had to step away from the ball to avoid it hitting her. Then she turned back to shooting like I wasn't even there.

So this is how it's going to be. I thought back to *G.I. Jane* and Demi Moore doing one-handed pull-ups ... *It's okay. I can handle this.*

Coach K went a little easier on us. We did some ball handling and then went to partner activities. With twenty-one players, it doesn't take a genius to figure out who was the odd girl out. Every. Single. Time.

But for clarification—this girl right here. Me.

That was me now—the outcast loner that no one wanted to play with. At Lincoln and almost every club team I ever played on, I was always the first person others wanted to pair up with. And I am aware how that sounds, but it is also the truth. This was uncharted water. Uncharted and shark infested.

"Bennett?" Coach K's voice echoed loudly off the gym walls. "You can find a group or use the wall for this next passing drill."

Everyone tensed and looked away—the official "don't pick me" stance. "It's okay." I moved to a spot near a wall. "I'll go here."

As I bounce-passed off the wall to myself, I glanced up to the corner window. Matti, her face lit up, waved down at me wildly. At least someone was happy I was there.

Tryouts: Day 3

When I got home I let my school and gym bags fall to the floor and then limped to the freezer and pulled out two Ziplocs of ice. A quarter of the freezer space was dedicated to icepacks just for me.

I tied a bag to my ankle and another to my knee. My mom turned from the pot of boiling pasta she was stirring and looked me over. I heard her tsk.

"What?"

"Bennett, you're all bruises. You look like you've been in a bar fight."

Ha, I thought. A bar fight would be a cakewalk next to what I had gone through. "I'm fine."

She reached into a cupboard and pulled out two ibuprofen pills and then poured me a glass of water. "How are tryouts going?"

"Fantastic!" I said sarcastically.

"Are the girls taking to you yet?"

The irritable look I gave conveyed my response. "When's dinner ready?"

"Fifteen minutes."

"I'll be up in my room."

"Bennett?"

I stopped in the hall but did not respond or turn around.

"I know basketball was something you and Dad shared. But you can talk to me."

No, I can't. "I know," I mumbled and then hobbled up the stairs.

When I got to my room, I saw Slam and Dunk curled together on my bed. "Hi, guys." Their tails wagged but neither made any attempt to move or even lift their heads. "I know how you feel."

I slumped into my beanbag basketball chair just as I felt my phone vibrate. Brooke's name and face flashed up on the screen. *Interesting.* I hadn't talked to her since the Halloween party.

"Hello?"

"Hey," came a tentative voice. "It's Brooke."

"I know it's you, loser."

"How's it going?"

"Just peachy."

"You sound crusty."

"I feel crusty."

"Is this a bad time?"

"No. I'm just ... it's nothing. What's up?" I tried to lighten my voice and my mood.

"Nothing. I just wanted to call." She paused. "We're in the middle of tryouts."

"Us, too." I didn't hear anything on the other end. "You still there?"

"I miss you."

I must have been overtired or about to get my period (or I was just being me) because I instantly felt like crying. I pushed it back down. "I miss you, too. Are the Aussie twins living up to the hype?"

"Yeah. Hanna's better than Hayley but they're both pretty solid. It's not the same without you there."

"I know what you mean. Can we not talk about basketball?"

I could sense Brooke's relief. "Totally. Let's not."

"How's Nik?"

"Whatever happened at my party? One minute you were there, and then the next I heard everyone reacting like you slapped him. And then I saw the picture Prynne posted—"

"I didn't slap him. I saw him sucking face with this girl and I threw some punch on him."

"Awesome. So, you two are over?"

"Were we ever really on?"

"Good point. Do you think you'd still be together if you stayed at Lincoln?"

I thought about Prynne's comment, that I always break it off around the season. "Maybe. Probably not."

"How's Prynne? Is she still in her gothic-punk phase?"

"Sadly, yes." We both laughed. It felt good to laugh.

We talked until my mom called me down for dinner. Neither of us brought up basketball again.

Tryouts: Day 4

I quit. I'm done. I'm out. Where's the bell because I want to ring it.

After the tryout, I went up to Coach K's office and knocked on the door. Maybe I was being rash. I should probably have let myself cool off before I did something I would regret, but I didn't think I could take it anymore.

So what if I don't play anymore? It has to end sometime. I can play for fun. Grab a ball, head to the outdoor courts, and find some pickup games. I'll have way more free time. My grades will get better. I can join a club or something. Maybe I can go back to soccer or find something else. I could even look for a boyfriend, a better one. I don't need basketball. It's just a sport ...

Matti opened the door. She looked happy to see me. "Hi, Bennett–double N, double T. Come in. Are you here to see my mom? She's not back yet. I think she's doing some photocopying or ordering some new uniforms or something in the office. I can go get her if you want. Come in, come in. There's a couch, it's super comfy. Sometimes I fall asleep here. So, do you want me to?"

As usual, it took my ears a minute to adjust to the speed of Matti's speech. "Do I want you to what?"

"Go and get my mom?"

"Oh, no. That's okay. I'll wait." I stepped into Coach K's office.

With just enough room to fit a desk, two chairs, and a small couch pushed up against the window, it was a tight squeeze. I imagined Matti on the couch, sitting on her knees, and watching a practice or game through the glass.

There were pictures of past teams and players tacked up on the walls, trophies symbolizing past wins on a shelf above the desk. I stepped up to an older photo of Coach K. It was an action shot of her playing days in Europe. She looked like she would have been—probably still was—a tough player to guard on the court.

"That's my mom when she played in Spain. It was before I was born. She can speak Spanish and a little German, you know."

"No, I didn't know."

"She could have played in the WNBA, they asked her to, but she decided to coach instead."

"That's cool." I turned to look at the rest of the office. A giant classroom-size whiteboard took up the entire wall behind the door. It was covered in mini basketball keys and courts, with hundreds of lines, arrows, and tiny X's and O's. It looked like the creation of a mad scientist, trying to figure out an impossible basketball equation. "Are these plays?" I looked closer.

"I like to come up with different offenses and sets. Some of them are things I've seen other teams do during a game or from watching games on TV with my mom. Sometimes I think they could be organized better, more efficiently, so I ..."

"You did this?" I asked surprised.

Matti turned red and grabbed an eraser. She seemed agitated and started to clean the board.

"What are you doing?"

"You think it's stupid and that I'm dumb. You think because I have ASD and I can't be in the gym that I don't understand the game, but I ..."

"Matti, no. I don't think that at all." She stopped and looked at me. "I think it's great ... awesome, actually."

"You do?"

I nodded.

She smiled and put the eraser down. "My mom uses some of my stuff sometimes. She does, really." Matti jumped on the couch. "I was watching you today. But you know because you saw me watching. I like it when you look up here. You hit seventeen of twenty-eight three-pointers today. That's just under sixty-one percent."

"I did?"

Matti nodded. "And I watched the scrimmage. Cruze should have passed to you in that last play."

My jaw clenched. "Yes, she should have." But she didn't. Instead, she tried to drive herself, got rejected by Monty, who sent a long outlet to a fast-breaking Teesha for an easy game-winning layup.

"Maybe she didn't see you."

"Maybe," I shrugged. *She did.* I looked at Matti's board. "So, is it because of your mom that you like basketball so much?"

"I don't know. I just like it. I love it."

"But you don't ... I mean, you can't ... the noise ..." I didn't know how to ask what I wanted without offending her.

"Sometimes my mom plays with me. I've even played with other autistic kids like me. I'm better than most of them, though."

"But I thought ... doesn't the bouncing bother you?"

"Sometimes it does. And sometimes it doesn't. But when there's a lot of balls and people and cheering and whistle and horn," she put her hands over her ears and started to shake her head, "loud, loud, too LOUD. It hurts." She dropped her arms. "But I like it up here. And I get a better view of the court. Best seat in the house."

"Do you ever wish you could play?"

"I do play."

"No, I mean do you ever wish you didn't have autism and you could play on the team?"

"But I do have autism."

"I know but ... if you didn't?"

Matti looked confused. "I stay up here and watch. It's who I am. You play down there. It's who you are."

It's who I was, I thought to myself. Matti looked at me—directly at me—and I saw her expression change. She looked like she was concentrating on solving a really tough problem. I felt like she was trying to look through me. It made me uncomfortable.

"What do you need to talk to my mom about?"

She knew. Did she know? How did she know? "I ... umm ..."

"What's your favorite thing about basketball?"

"What?" Talking with Matti was like trying to watch a pinball being batted around the machine, fast and all over the place.

"Your favorite thing?"

"Well, there isn't any one thing. I like ..."

"Yes, there is. What is it?"

Suddenly I felt like I was in the middle of an intense interrogation. Matti was relentless. "I don't know ..."

"Yes. You do."

I ran my hand over my head and ponytail. "What's yours?"

"Foul shots. I like watching them. The gym gets really quiet.

They seem simple but they can mean so much. They should be easy but they're not. No defense, time to shoot, but even the best shooters have trouble scoring. Think too much. Feel the pressure. You can see it in their face. Everyone has a different look, a different routine. You, Bennett Ryan, like to step to the line, left foot then right, take three bounces—one, two, three—and then toss the ball so it bounces back to you. You look at the hoop and take a breath. Then you shoot."

That was exactly what I did.

"What do you think about when you look at the hoop? You always look like you're thinking about something, and I always wonder what it is. Are you saying something to yourself? Are you seeing the ball go in the hoop? My mom says good players vis-u-al-ize"—she struggled to say the word—"their shot. Or are you ..."

"The swish," I said quickly, trying to get a word in.

"The what?"

"The swish. I think about the sound of the swish my shot will make when the ball goes in. I guess that's visualizing. It's also my favorite thing about basketball, since you asked."

"Swooiiishhh, *swooiiishhh*." Matti tried to shape her mouth and make the sound. "That sound?"

"Yeah. That sound," I laughed. "My dad once made me close my eyes and listen to it. The sound of perfection, he said. When that ball is let go and flies, with just the right arc to drop into the hoop without hitting the rim. Swish. That's when everything is right. Sometimes, after a game, I'd ask him if he saw this shot or that shot that I had made, and he would just shake his head and say no. He didn't see it. He closed his eyes and heard it. And he knew if it was a good shot or if I was having a good game because he could hear it in the swish."

Matti looked mesmerized by my story. "In the swish?"

"In the swish," I confirmed.

"Cooooool," she smiled. "Swwwiiiisssshhhhhhhhh!"

"Bennett?" Coach K's voice startled me as she walked into the office. "Sorry. If I knew you were waiting, I would have hustled. What can I do you for?"

"Uh, n-n-nothing," I stuttered. "I better get home. See you later, Matti."

"Did you want to talk to me about something?"

"Nope," I said, sprinting past her and out of the office before I could change my mind. "Nothing at all."

Tryouts: Day 5

This was it. The last tryout. And I had come for blood.

I attributed my flirtation with quitting to a temporary moment of insanity.

I had let Teesha and the team get to me. They had almost

taken basketball away from me. Almost. But thankfully, Matti—whether she meant to or not—helped me see the light. They couldn't take anything away unless I let them. And that wasn't going to happen. I felt guilty for even considering quitting, like I had betrayed basketball in some way. But I was back. And I was going to make it up.

Eighteen of us stood on the line awaiting instructions. Matti waved at me from the window. I waved back.

We were split into two teams for a final scrimmage. No surprise that Teesha stood on the opposite side. Coach K wanted to see us battle and I was not going to disappoint.

I stood next to Teesha and waited for the jump ball. She tried to push me out of position.

Until now, I had let her run things her way. I didn't want to step on Riverside toes, so I had stayed off to the side, stayed quiet, gone to the back of the line, and let myself be pushed. I hadn't played my game. But things were different now.

I pushed back. *Game on.*

If the team didn't want to pass to me, that was their problem. They couldn't stop me from rebounding, stealing, and taking it to the hoop myself. And the first half of the game, that's what I did.

When Teesha played close, I drove. When she backed off, I shot. And I wasn't missing.

Teesha knew that something in me had changed. She tried

to drive, tried to respond, but I wasn't going to make it easy. I played her tight. I made her work to get open. By the time she got the ball, she was tired and easy to read. If she managed to get open and get a shot off, it was with pressure. Her shots rimmed in and out. Her layups stubbed under the hoop. Her game was off.

The first two quarters had gone by much the same as the first four days of tryouts. It didn't matter if I was open; the girls weren't passing me the ball. But I passed to them. The better I played, the more help-side defense came to Teesha's aid. I drove, drew the defense to me, and dished up wide-open layups and shots.

At halftime my team led by 16.

In the third quarter something happened.

I had stolen a pass and dribbled down the court in a two-on-one breakaway with Cruze at my side. I passed her the ball and got into position for a rebound, but the defender (Teesha) stepped toward Cruze and she passed it back to me. It was the right play and, in any other circumstance, I would have been expecting it, but Cruze hadn't passed to me through the entire tryouts, so I was nowhere near ready when the ball came at me. It hit me square in the chest and dropped into my hands. I finished with a power layup and a high-five from Cruze.

She didn't say anything, or even look at me after. She just ran back down the court and got on defense. But from that moment on, something had changed.

I passed to the team and the team was passing back. Instead of playing with them, I was playing *with* them, together. And I wasn't just playing basketball—I was having fun.

I should have been expecting it.

My team was up by 30. There was no way we were going to lose the game.

I wasn't missing my old team. I wasn't thinking about the new team, or about tryouts, or even about Teesha. I was playing basketball.

I received a back-door pass from Oaks and went for a left-handed layup. Teesha was too far back to recover and defend, but she jumped at me anyway. I saw her coming but I was already in the air. There was no way I could defend myself, so I prepared to take a hit. And a hit came.

Teesha slapped the ball down but she took me out with it. I heard a whistle blow as my body slammed into hardwood. I rolled and skidded to a skin-screeching stop, inches before hitting the wall.

Ouch, that fucking hurt.

My knee was pink and raw from where a layer of skin had been taken off. I was definitely going to get a nasty bruise on my hip but, other than that, I was fine. I started to stand when I heard Cruze's voice.

"What the hell was that, T?"

"What?"

"You know what." Cruze was standing body to body with Teesha. She had a finger in Teesha's face. The rest of the girls stood watching the altercation.

Teesha pushed the finger away and looked at me. "She's fine."

"That was low, and you know it."

"I got the ball, didn't I?"

"You'd be out of the game if you pulled crap like that on the court."

"It's okay," I said. "I'm okay."

Coach K walked into the middle of all of us. "I think that's it for today." She looked from me to Teesha. "The team list will be posted on my office door Monday morning."

No one moved.

She blew the whistle. "I said we're done. Unless you all want to run a few sets of lines?" And with that, we quickly dispersed and walked off the court.

Going our separate ways, Teesha and I shared one last hateful glance. She may have taken me out, but we both knew who had won that round.

I was exhausted and sore when I got home. There was a dark purple bruise making its presence known on my hip and outer thigh. When I limped into the kitchen, my mom greeted me with a fresh icepack in her hand.

"Thanks," I gladly accepted and wasted no time applying it to my throbbing knee.

"Well?"

"She's posting the list on Monday."

"Did you leave it all on the court?" It was something my dad had always asked after every tryout and game.

I nodded and lifted the icepack off my knee to show the damage. "Literally."

"That's all you can do." I saw something white fly into the air behind her.

My sister stood at the island tossing a ball of dough into the air. The counter was covered in cut veggies and grated cheese.

"Prynne wanted to make the pizza tonight." My mom raised her eyebrows and gave me an expressive look that said: *Your sister is trying to do something nice for you. So, be nice.* "And," she continued, "look what I managed to dig out of the DVD box." She held up a tattered cover of *Love & Basketball.* "Prynne and I thought we'd join you for girls' night in."

It was tradition. At the start of every season, the night after the last tryout, I got to order my favorite pizza and watch my favorite movie. With all the changes and the intensity of tryouts, I had completely forgotten. I was happy my mom and sister hadn't.

"Thanks." I smiled and stole some funny-tasting cheese. I hadn't realized until this moment just how much I needed this. Ever since we had moved, each of us had been adjusting to our new surroundings in our own busy way. We all needed this.

Prynne threw the hard ball of dough into the air again. "Isn't it supposed to be flat and round," I joked. My mom nudged my arm. *Be nice.*

"I'm using a gluten-free all-natural flour. It's better for us. Plus, I got some organic veggies and dairy-free cheese."

I scrunched up my nose. "That's why it tastes off."

My mom nudged me again. "Don't you need to shower?"

"Uh, yep. Yep, I do."

"Ben," my mom whispered just outside of Prynne's earshot. "Don't worry, I already put in an order for a double-pepperoni-stuffed-crust with Pizza Palace. And I bought some vanilla ice cream and root beer."

"Mom! What will Prynne say?"

She shrugged and smiled slyly. "I'll tell her it's organic."

Sometimes, my mom could be just that awesome.

CHAPTER

RIVERSIDE STORM
Senior Girls' Varsity Basketball

1. Tatiana Smith
2. Georgia Oaks
3. Nikki Michaels
4. Montana Dunkin
5. Jessica Randall
6. Bennett Ryan
7. Taya Owens
8. Camila Cruze
9. Maya Hernandez
10. Olivia Franklin
11. Jazmin Johnson
12. Sierra Hampton

I'm not sure what my brain registered first, the fact that my name was on the team list, or the fact that Teesha's wasn't.

I looked over the names again. And again. Twelve names, no Teesha Collins.

"Holy shit." Cruze's familiar potty mouth summed up how I was feeling. "Holy shit. Holy shit."

"I know," I said flatly. "Do you think she made a mistake?"

"Coach K doesn't make mistakes."

"Hey guys!" Jess greeted us and turned to the list. "Sweet!" Smiling, she looked at our bewildered faces and then realized something was wrong. She looked back over the list. "O ..."

"... MFG!" Cruze finished. "Has she seen it?"

"I don't know."

"She's going to lose it," Cruze shouted as she ran down the hall. "I have to find her."

Jess ran after her. "I'll go with you."

I stood, staring at the list. What was Coach K thinking? There were at least ten girls that Teesha was better than, but that didn't matter; the team was going to blame me. They were *definitely, one hundred percent* going to blame me. This wasn't right. It just wasn't right.

I knocked on the door.

"Come in," Coach K's voice called.

I entered and closed the door behind me.

"Yes?" Coach K was going over paperwork on her desk. She didn't bother looking up.

I stood there waiting. "Umm ..."

"Bennett, say what you have to say." She set her pen down and crossed her arms.

I took a breath. "You can't do this."

"I hate to pull the head coach card, but I will. This is my team and, like I said at the beginning of tryouts, I picked the players that I feel deserve to be on the team."

"Teesha isn't just one of the best players in the school, she's one of the best in the state."

"Being good and being good for the team are two different things. And to be honest, Bennett, I thought you of all the players would understand my reasoning."

"What I understand is that the girls are going to hate *me* for this."

"Is that what you're worried about?"

"Yes. No. She ... she should be on this team."

"Perhaps the girls will blame you for a little while. And I am sure they will blame me as well. But I think they will eventually realize that Teesha did this to herself. I've warned her about her attitude countless times. With her actions during tryouts and that last play of the game, she sealed her own fate."

"You're wrong." It came out of my mouth before I could stop it.

"What did you say?"

I shook my head and lowered my voice. "I disagree."

"Disagree or not, what's done is done. Twelve spots, twelve girls. Who would you have me kick off?"

The first name that came to mind was Nikki Michaels. She was in Grade 11 and she was the least skilled. "Me," I swallowed.

"Do you really mean that?"

No. "Yes."

"You should know that Teesha has already come to see me. When I asked her the same question—which player should I kick off for her—just who do you think she said?"

Me, of course. Why the hell was I fighting for her? "Teesha deserves to be on this team. It's her team. And hothead or not, the girls play for her. They won't play for me." I could be wrong, but I thought I saw Coach K smirk.

"Do you have plans to play after high school?"

"What?"

"University. College. Do you want to continue to play basketball?"

That's all I want. "Yes."

"Where? You must have some schools in mind." She continued before I could answer. "Let me guess. Tennessee? UConn?"

Any girl who plays basketball knows that the Tennessee Lady Vols and the UConn Huskies are the pinnacle of women's college basketball. Their head to head matchups were and still are one of the highest rated sporting events on TV.

When I was seven, my dad came home from a garage sale with a box full of old VHS tapes. My mom thought he was crazy. VHS was out. DVD was in. But he was so excited. He said the woman selling them had a daughter who was interested in sports and, growing up, she had taped every women's sports event she could find on TV. It had been ten years since her daughter went off to college, so she was selling the entire box for five dollars. My dad haggled her down to two and dug out our old VHS player.

Together we watched game tapes of the Tennessee vs. UConn match-ups, Final Four Finals, and highlights from the '96 and '00 Olympic Games.

There was one tape at the bottom of the box that wasn't a game. It was a documentary *(In the Game)* of the Stanford Cardinals women's basketball team and their 1990 season. I must have watched that tape every night for a month. There was something about watching the team, their chemistry, the fun they had, and the passion those women shared for the game together. Somewhere it planted a seed in me. If that documentary hadn't been in the box, or it had been about another team at another school, maybe I wouldn't have wanted to go there. But it was in the box and it was about Stanford—the only school I've dreamed of playing for since I was seven.

"Maybe Stanford?" Coach K raised a knowing eyebrow.

"How did you know?"

"I did my homework. Every talented player I have ever coached had those same aspirations. Guess how many got recruiting visits from any of those schools?"

Zero.

"I've coached good players and some great ones. And lots have gone on to play for excellent Division I schools. But never have I coached one talented enough to make it there. You, Bennett Ryan, have the talent but, more importantly, you have the passion. Are you willing to give that up?"

Was I? Was I really?

"Look." Coach K stood up and leaned forward on her desk. "She can't have your spot. I'm not going to let you fall on the sword and sacrifice yourself for Teesha. If you quit this team, it will be because *you choose* to quit. You can't put this on me, on the team, or on Teesha. It's your choice. In or out? I'll give you until tomorrow's practice to think about it."

I didn't need to think about it. "In," I said firmly and opened the door. "You actually think I have the potential to play for Stanford?"

"If you're going to play for me, you should know a couple of things: One, I don't say things if I don't believe them. Two, I hate the word potential. All it really means is that you're neither here nor there. And in my mind, you either have it or you don't."

"Is there anything else I should know?"

"The rest will come," she smiled. "And you're late for class."

Shit. I was. And, of course, it was Humphries's English class.

CHAPTER 10

It took a bit of convincing, but Cruze finally gave in and told me how to get to Teesha's house. "It's your funeral," she said, handing me the address.

I'm not sure what I expected Teesha's house to look like. She was rough around the edges, played a bit like a street baller, and (yes) black, so—as racist as it sounds—I thought she lived in some kind of project. I blame my ignorance on watching one too many basketball movies.

As I nervously waited on the front step of a mini-mansion in the middle of Mini-mansionville, it occurred to me that apart from her player profile and her temper, I knew absolutely nothing about Teesha "T-time" Collins.

The door opened and a severe-looking woman wearing a blue pencil skirt and matching business blazer stared back at me. "Can I help you?" she asked sharply.

"Hi, Mrs. Collins ..."

"It's Ms. Rainer."

"Oh, my name's Benn ..."

"I know who you are, Bennett Ryan," she said coldly and opened the door for me to come in.

I cautiously stepped in. "Is Teesha home?"

"TEESHA?"

"YEAH, MOM?" Teesha bounded down a winding set of stairs. When she saw me, she stopped. Her face dropped. "Oh."

Her mom bent down and picked up a briefcase. "Lupita put dinner in the oven. I'll be home after eight. Did you finish your history essay?"

"Almost."

"Teesha, you were supposed to have that done by now so you could study for math."

Teesha looked at me as I stood there awkwardly—the way one does when listening to a parent lecture a child.

"I only have the conclusion left."

Her mom nodded. "I'll read it when I get home." She looked at me and then to her daughter. "You have homework. Don't visit too long."

"We won't," Teesha said through gritted teeth.

"Pleasure to meet you, Bennett."

"You, too." I'm not sure if either of us really meant it.

When the door closed and we were alone, Teesha came down the rest of the stairs. "Come here to gloat?"

"I came here to talk."

I followed her through the house and into her kitchen. I felt like I had walked into a department store or furniture showroom. The rooms were giant and immaculate, straight out of a *House & Style* magazine. I never understood what color matching was, or why it even mattered, until now. Everything seemed brand new and like it had a specific place to be. It looked nice but it felt … cold. The opposite of how a home should feel.

Teesha must have seen me gawking. "Have you never been in a house before?"

"Not one like this."

"What? Did you think I lived in the projects or something?"

Was I that obvious? "No."

"Yes, you did."

"Maybe I did."

"Whatever." She pulled out two bottles of water—the good kind, in the fancy green bottles—and jumped up so she was sitting on the marble counter. "What do you want?"

"WHAT IS THAT?" I set my bottle down and went over to a giant window overlooking the backyard. There was a full-size basketball court with a blue and white rubber surface. "You have your own court?"

"You don't?" She joked. I think she was joking.

"I wish," I said, salivating. Really. I may have drooled a little.

"Aw, dude. The windows!"

I stepped back and saw two perfect handprints on the glass. Teesha was there with a spray bottle and paper towels before I could say sorry. "Your mom's a little uptight, huh?"

"You don't know me and you certainly don't know my mom."

"Sorry."

She finished with the window. "Forget it."

"What does she do?"

"She's a lawyer. A good one, or so I'm told." She put away the spray bottle and jumped back to her place on the counter.

"What about your dad?" I was making small talk but I sensed I had hit a sore spot. I asked it without really thinking. I, of all people, knew better than to ask that question.

"He's an investment banker. He lives in Seattle with his new family. He built that basketball court for me two weeks before he told my mom he was having an affair. She hates it. Every time she looks at it, she thinks about him." She waved her hands in the air. "And that's all the information you get on this round of 'Get to know Teesha.' Why are you here, Bennett?"

"You know why I'm here."

"You're going to give me your spot on the team?" Wide eyes

and a sarcastic grin covered her face.

"No." I shook my head. "Coach K won't let me."

"You talked to her?"

"Apparently, so did you."

"It's done. I'm out. You're in."

"A) That's not the reason you didn't make the team, and B) I don't think it's done."

"You don't know Coach K. When she decides something, there's no changing her mind."

"If someone would have told me a month ago that I'd be here, in your ridiculously big house, fighting for you to play on the team, I would have said they were crazy. Literally, crazy. But here I am. We both know ... everybody knows, including Coach K, that this team would be better with both of us on it." Teesha gave me a doubtful look. "Let's be honest. I didn't want to come to Riverside any more than you wanted me to come to Riverside. But I'm here. And I don't want to take your spot or your team away from you. I just want to play basketball. Do you?"

"Yes."

"We both know that we'll never be besties. We don't even have to like each other that much. But we do need to play together, because I know that this team is better with you than without you. And you might not want to admit it, but this team is better with me, too."

Teesha took a minute to think about what I had said. Like it or not, she knew I was right. "You kicked my ass the other day."

"Uh, I have this that proves otherwise." I pulled my pant leg down and flashed my nasty plum-colored hip.

Teesha cringed. "I really didn't mean to hit you that hard."

I shrugged. "I'll survive."

"Okay, but pull your pants up. No one needs to see your white ass. It's blinding." We both laughed.

"Hey, it's hard to get a tan when I'm in the gym all the time. And I only kicked your ass because you took yourself out of the game. You started to play me instead of playing the game."

"I don't need you telling me how to play." That famous temper started to flare.

"Okay. You're right. I'm sorry."

She looked like she wanted to keep fighting but held back. "So, what do we do?"

"First, you have to accept that I'm here to stay." She tensed. "At least appear to accept it."

"Fine. But you have to accept it, too."

"What do you mean?"

"I mean stop playing like you wish you were playing with your old team."

I wanted to object but (it pains me to say it) Teesha was right. It was a truth I needed to hear. "Fine."

"And second?"

"We have to let Coach K know that your not playing on the team is not an option."

"How?"

"Just come to practice tomorrow and be ready to play."

"Coach K is going to kick me out the minute she sees me."

"Maybe. Maybe not. Are we good?"

Teesha nodded. "For now."

"Awesome. So, can I stay for dinner? Maybe play some hoops after?" I was messing with her and she knew it.

She played along, talking like a teen character on a California reality show. "And maybe after we can, like, paint our nails and have, like, a slumber party."

Our smiles faded into an awkward silence. "I'm going to get out of your house now."

"If you don't, I'll have the butler kick you out."

"You have a butler?" She smiled. "Oh. Now you're messing with me."

"Couldn't resist."

"Does that mean you're warming up to me?"

"Don't push it." She walked me to the door. "You got balls coming to my house like this, Bennett Ryan. I'll give you that."

"Coming from you, Teesha Collins, I'll take it."

CHAPTER

11

I was feeling pretty good when I got home. I was officially on the basketball team and soon (hopefully) Teesha would be on it, too, and all would be right in this alternate universe I was living in.

Speaking of alternate universes, Prynne—I think the girl sitting on the couch was my sister—called to me. "Warning: Principal Mom is pissed and on the loose."

I came closer to get a better look. She was wearing a floppy knitted beanie and her black and pink hair was back to its normal sandy blonde. Gone was the dark eyeliner, replaced by a pair of thick-framed glasses. I'd never known my sister to need glasses. Topping the whole ensemble off was a beige sweater two sizes too big and a pair of skinny jeans. She was watching a documentary on climate change. It was official. Prynne the punk-goth had been taken over by Prynne the eco-hipster.

I was too used to her changing styles to make a comment. "I like your hat."

"Thanks. Laynie took me to this cool vintage store after school."

"Who's Laynie?"

"This girl in my French class." Her voice was indifferent. "She's an exchange student from Germany."

What amazed me the most about Prynne's changing styles was how her whole persona, attitude, and group of friends changed with her. She was still a brooding teen but, with the dark clothes and choker necklace gone, so was the edgy attitude. Now she seemed more blasé in a "to care or not to care" kind of way. My sister was an anthropologist's dream.

"BENNETT?!" My mom's voice beckoned from the kitchen.

"What did you do?" Prynne asked.

"I was late for Humphries's class ... and then I might have skipped detention."

"Oh. Have fun with that."

"Thanks."

"Hey," Prynne called. "Did you make the team?" I nodded. "Knew you would."

My mom was waiting for me with her hands on her hips. Prynne was right; she was in her Principal Mom pose. I took the innocent approach. "Hi, Mom. What's up?"

"Oh, you tell me."

"Okay, I was late for class because I was talking with Coach K."

"Did you make the team?"

"Yes."

"Good. Now then, what was so important you had to be late for the one teacher that you can't be late for?"

"Well ..."

"And then you decide to skip the detention she gave you."

"Yeah, but ..."

"So then, guess who comes into my office, telling me in no uncertain terms that if I can't control my own daughter, how can I be expected to control a school."

"And you took that? Can't you just fire her or something?"

"I dealt with her ... carefully. Now, back to you."

"I didn't ask for you to be my mom and my principal. You did that."

"So that's what this is about? Because I don't recall ever having to deal with any disciplinary issues at your old school. Unless I missed something, it seems like you are doing this on purpose. I might have expected this kind of acting out from a five year old, but you're seventeen ..."

"Oh, my God, Mom! I'm not acting out and this isn't about you."

"Then what's it about?"

"Teesha didn't make the basketball team so I ..."

"Don't tell me this is all because of basketball?"

Prynne walked in to get a glass of water. "You two need to chill out."

"PRYNNE!" we barked at the same time. "OUT," my mom finished.

"Okay, relax. But there's bigger issues, like global destruction, happening in the world right now." She left us, but I knew she was listening intently from the other room. I usually did.

Prynne probably loved this. She was almost always the one fighting with our mom. It was like watching Bruce Banner turn into the Hulk. She could be happy and content one moment, but borrow the wrong sweater or say the wrong thing, and she morphed into a total bitch-monster the next. Here I was, doing the same thing.

I knew the next words out of my mouth were going to hurt and I said them anyway. I think I wanted them to hurt.

"Yes, Mom. This is about basketball. If Dad were here, he'd understand."

My mom sat down like I had slapped her. Emotionally, I had.

"I'm sorry." My tone said the opposite. "But Dad got how important basketball is to me. I know you think it's just a sport. But it's not to me, and he got that. He got me." As I stormed off, my mom spoke up.

"You have recycling detail every day before school for two

weeks." Recycling detail was the "new" garbage duty. Going around to every classroom, collecting and sorting through their sticky, fruit-fly-infested recycle boxes. It was gross.

"But I go to the gym ..."

"And you're grounded for a week. No car. If you're not at school or practice, you're here. Do you understand?" I was down the hall and almost at my room. "DO YOU UNDERSTAND?"

"I UNDERSTAND!" I slammed my bedroom door and threw my bags on the floor. The noise made Dunk jump off my bed and hide in the closet. Slam came over and nuzzled my leg. "It's okay, buddy. I'm not mad at you."

In the corner of my bedroom mirror was a taped picture. I had a trophy in my hand for winning a shooting competition. My dad stood with his arm around my shoulders, a big proud smile on his face. If he were here, I know exactly what he'd say.

You're angry, but your mother didn't deserve that.

I know.

She misses me, too.

I know.

CHAPTER 12

My mom may have grounded me from the car, but she let me catch a ride with her for my first morning of recycling duty. We hadn't said more than a few words to each other since our fight the night before.

"Are we out of milk?"
"I'm buying some after school."

"Where are my lucky red shorts?"
"In the dryer."

"Has anyone seen my keys?"
"They're by the coffeemaker."

"I'm sorry."

"Me, too."

"I love you."

"I love you, too."

Pᴅ it was a family rule that we never left angry and without saying goodbye. It should have been a family rule wᴅ. It should always be a rule.

I went to report for recycling duty and was surprised to see Matti standing with a clipboard. She was handing two boys—Grade 9's by their hairless and scrawny yet-to-hit-a-growth-spurt size—a large clear bag and directing them to start on the east side of the school, near the parking lot.

"Nice jersey," one of them mocked and then hit his buddy.

"Thanks," Matti said proudly, unaware they were making fun of her. "It was my mom's."

"I like your headband," the other one said. They laughed at their unfunny inside joke. "Was that your mom's, too?"

"No. I got this at the dollar store. I don't know why they call it a dollar store, because it actually cost a dollar fifty-seven." The laughing continued.

Matti was still oblivious to the intention of the boys' questions and laughter. I stepped closer, making my presence known. "Actually, I think your headband and your mom's jersey are really cool."

Her face lit up. "Hi, Bennett!"

"Hi, Matti." I was older and taller than both of the boys. They saw the aware and angry glare I had in my eyes and stopped laughing.

"Bennett, this is Hanson and Kris. Kris spells his name with a K. Bennett spells her name with two N's and two T's. She plays on the basketball team."

"Oooh," they mocked.

I stepped closer. "And my last name is Ryan, as in Principal Ryan, who just happens to be my mom. This is her sweatshirt, in case you want to say anything about it." It wasn't her sweatshirt, and I had never pulled the mom/principal card before, but I couldn't resist. The terrified look on their faces was priceless. "Shouldn't you two get started?"

They nodded in unison and tripped over themselves as they left the room.

"Do Hanson and Kris help with recycling a lot?" I asked.

"Together they've been here eleven times. Kris has come two more times than Hanson. They like to smoke marijuana and laugh. I only let them go around the outside of the school and pick up extra bottles and garbage. They don't get to go into rooms and sort. That's my job. I like my job."

"Does it bother you when they laugh?"

"Laughing makes people feel good."

"Does it make *you* feel good when they laugh?"

She shrugged and wrote something on her clipboard. "Laughing is laughing. Put these on." She handed me a plastic apron and latex gloves. "It's going to get sticky."

I know it was the autism—well, actually, I don't know. I can't know. But Matti amazed me with the way she didn't let things bother her. She had this ability to make really simple things sound really profound, like a mini Buddha or Yoda. Maybe it wasn't what she was saying but how I was hearing it. Either way, I don't think she had any idea the impact her words had.

She looked at her watch. "Aren't you usually in the gym right now?"

"Usually. But I'll be here with you every morning for two weeks."

She leaned over to whisper. "Did you get caught smoking marijuana, too?"

I laughed. "What? No. If that happened, I'd be dead, not doing recycling. I just missed detention. How about you? Did you get caught smoking marijuana?" It was a joke but Matti didn't see the humor.

"No. Marijuana is bad, Bennett. I'm here three times a week. I'm in charge—Captain of the Green Team. I like recycling. Everything has a place to go. Plastic, juice boxes, pop cans, water bottles, glass, paper. I like it when things have a place. Everything should have a place. I can show you. I mean, you can join me ... if you want."

I finished tying up my apron. "I'm yours to command."

Matti took me through all of the classes, working like an efficient little recycling robot. I wanted to help but I felt like I was in her way most of the time. She directed me where to stand and how exactly to hold open a large bag as she dove into the mess of empty cartons. As I learned, there was a very specific way to hold open a bag. There was also a pattern to the way her arms moved, and an intricate Matti system in how she sorted through the stacks of recycling.

I tried to make small talk and ask her what she thought about Teesha being left off the list, but she was mumbling something and too focused on the task to answer me. Instead, I did as she asked. Holding open and carrying full bags from the rooms to the back of the school. While I waited for her to finish with each sort, I watched her work.

Paper was mixed with cans. Garbage was thrown in with juice boxes. Plastic bottles were thrown in with garbage. There were half-eaten pudding packs and cans with pop still in them. It was a mess. And from what I could see, Matti enjoyed it. The more disorganized it was, the more intensity she applied. After each room was complete, she would take a satisfied step back and admire her work.

Over my school life I had seen a few students with autism, Asperger's, and other issues. Every now and then there was one or two in my classes. I knew their names, but not once had I ever really gotten to know any of them. I had seen outbursts and seizures and I didn't understand them. I never wanted to understand them. I was usually too busy playing sports, hanging out with my friends, and feeling lucky that I wasn't like them.

"Okay, that's it for today. Did you put everything where I told you?"

"I think so," I nodded.

"Did you leave three bags of cans and bottles behind the bin?"

"Yes."

"Three bags? One-two-three? Behind the green bin, not the blue?" She seemed very concerned that I had done it in this specific manner.

"Yes. Three bags. Behind the green bin. I still don't get why they don't go in the bin with the rest of ..."

"Because they don't. That's just the way it's done. I think Teesha's name should be on the list."

"What?"

"You asked me. I was counting. When I'm counting I can't talk about basketball. But we're done now. I like Teesha. She's my friend but I saw her push you. She shouldn't have done that, but she gets mad sometimes and my mom doesn't like it."

"Did your mom talk to you about why she didn't put her on?"

"Yep."

"What did she say?"

"She said ... I can't tell you."

"Can't tell me? Or can't tell anyone?"

"I can't tell you that, either."

"What? I'm confused."

"Me, too. My mom's confusing sometimes. I'm hungry. I have a banana in my locker and I need to get it before class. I like bananas, lots of potassium, good for the heart and muscles. Thanks for helping with the recycling, even though your mom made you do it. I'll see you at practice later. Bye."

Matti was a fast talker, and sometimes it was hard to follow the flow of her conversation—I thought that was the autism. But now, I suspected that she had strategically changed the subject on purpose to avoid any more questions I had about Teesha and the team. *Sneaky, Matti. Very sneaky.*

That afternoon I stood with twelve other girls at center court, waiting for Coach K to walk in.

"She's not going to go for this." Teesha bit down nervously on her nails.

"She's going to make us run suicides until we die," added Monty.

Cruze punched my arm. "If this goes wrong, it's on you, Lincoln."

"Thanks," I said sarcastically. "Can you not call me Lincoln? I'm one of you now."

"We'll see."

The gym doors opened and Coach K walked over to us. The group pushed me to the front.

She looked at all of us—at Teesha. "What's this?"

I tried to make my voice sound confident. "Coach K, we all think that Teesha should be on the team. And ... if you don't let her play, none of us will." She stared me down. I swallowed an anxious ball of saliva building in my throat.

"Really?" She crossed her arms and waited for a response. I couldn't tell if the smirk on her face was anger or amusement, so I crossed my arms and held my ground. "I told you that I only have twelve spots."

"But you could take more," I petitioned.

"I could. But that's not how I run my team, and only twelve can dress. League rules."

"Only twelve can dress," I repeated. I was hoping she would say that. "But thirteen could practice? We can all be on the team, and you can select the twelve you feel deserve to play for each game." At Lincoln, Coach Paige took fourteen, selecting a new twelve each game. He said it was to make us all more competitive at practice—but I wasn't going to share that with the team. "Dress twelve and the thirteenth can manage or keep stats. If one of us gets injured, you'll have an extra body and ..."

She raised her hand to make me stop talking. I shut my mouth and waited for her response.

"Do you all feel the same way?" Thirteen heads nodded. "And you all agree to let me dress twelve a game. No arguments when it comes to who I choose to dress?" We nodded again. "Fine."

"Fine?!" I repeated, confused. "Just like that?"

"Teesha, don't pull that crap you pulled ever again or you'll be off the team, for good."

Teesha nodded.

"And Bennett, don't pull *this* crap ever again."

I nodded.

"Good. You two are team captains."

Wait. What?

She blew the whistle. "Enough talk. We've wasted enough time already. Let's get started. I want two lines under the hoop. Ball on the left side ..."

As Coach K barked out orders, Teesha and I looked at one another.

"Huh. That was easy," I said suspiciously.

"Too easy," Teesha confirmed.

"Do you think ..."

"Yep," Teesha nodded. "We just got played."

Up in the window, Matti was looking down, giving me two enthusiastic thumbs up.

THE
SEASON

CHAPTER 13

Every year before the season begins, a sports reporter for the state newspaper writes an article about his pre-season predictions. Last year the headline read: *Lions Set to Pounce*. And pounce we did. This year's headline: *A Storm's Brewing*.

Tats sat down at the lunch table with the paper in her hand. There had been no official invite, but ever since I had made the team—and stuck my neck out to get Teesha back—there was an unspoken understanding that I was welcome at the team table. We weren't having late night chats or braiding each other's hair, but it was nice to have a place to eat. It was nice to have a place. Teesha and I sat at opposite ends, of course.

"The players may have changed," Tats read the article aloud, "but the game remains the same. And the two teams slated to do battle yet again this season are archrivals, the Riverside Storm and the Lincoln Lady Lions. The courtside drama heats up this season with last year's championship MVP, Bennett Ryan, making a shocking switch to join Riverside. With Ryan added to the mix of talented guards like Teesha Collins and Camila Cruze, and height on the inside with Montana Dunkin and Georgia Oaks, many would have thought the Storm to be a shoo-in for this year's State Championship ..."

"Yeah, we are!" Cruze cheered out.

Tats raised her hand. "But don't count out the Lions just yet. With six returning players, including all-stars Brooke Hastings and Emma Finnerty, and the addition of Australian twin powerhouses, Hayley and Hanna Taylor, the Lions might just be ready to roar again."

"Like hell they are." Cruze hit her fist on the table.

"Do you know anything about these Australian twins?" Oaks asked and everyone looked at me.

I nodded. "I met them at a Halloween party. They're both six feet. I don't know how they play. Brooke says they're okay, and that one is a little better than the other. That's all I know. I swear."

"Anything else?" Teesha asked Tats.

She skimmed the article. "Some stuff about Westview or Southlands maybe being a dark horse this year."

"Westview was pretty scrappy last year. We almost lost to them in league," Teesha said.

I agreed with her. "And they were mostly juniors last year. They'll be tough. And the Spartans have that six-foot-four monster."

"I thought she graduated." Oaks looked at Monty.

Monty shook her head. "She was only in Grade 10 last year."

"What? She's a junior?"

Monty nodded. "And I heard she already has full-ride scholarship offers to Baylor, Gonzaga, and Texas A&M."

Cruze sat back. "Shit."

"There's more on Bennett," Tats said. "With her late game heroics and Championship-clinching free throw ..." all heads turned to me as I tried to disappear into my seat, "... all the bleacher gossip is focused on Bennett Ryan and what she can accomplish with the Storm this year. Lincoln's head coach, Mark Paige, has said he was sad to see his star player go. 'She's a special player,' he said. 'Riverside is lucky to get her. With or without her, we still plan on cutting down the hoop at the end of the season.'" She dropped the paper. "Not if we have anything to do with it." The table grumbled in agreement. She continued, "Early rumblings from the court indicate that all is not well between Teesha Collins and Ryan—and with the blood spilled on the court last year, who could blame them? But if Coach Kate Kelley can find a way to harness her two star players, it could just be that this season a storm's rolling in that no team will have the power to stop." Tats turned the paper over. "Look at the picture they got of you two."

I recognized the moment instantly. I'm sure Teesha did, too. It was from the finals, right after the last timeout and just before the ball was to be thrown in. Teesha was standing, ready to pounce. I was crouched ready to defend the inbound. It must have been before the referee handed the ball to Jess, because we were staring at one another with a look to kill. It was the perfect picture to sum up how we felt about one another. Since the start of practices, things between us had been ... I can't say better, but they weren't worse. Which was something. I'm not sure what. But it was something.

Having thirteen players vying for twelve spots made everyone up their game and be on their best behavior.

To make things more interesting, Coach K had made the team run her own personal fitness test. We had to run three miles in under twenty-seven minutes. She said that the professional team she played for in Germany made them run it in under twenty-three, so she was letting us off easy. *Gee, thanks*. I'm curious about what her version of hard is. Actually, scratch that; I don't want to know.

Each girl that didn't make the time had to run it again each week until they did. Thankfully I got 24:47 my first try. I doubled over and practically collapsed on the ground, gasping for air when I finished, but I still did it. Cruze was first, easily finishing around 22:33–trash talking everyone as she ran by, of course. Six girls had yet to complete it: Sierra, Taya, Monty, Oaks, Nikki, and Jess. With an icebreaker tournament fast approaching, Coach K told the six of them that anyone who didn't make the time wouldn't dress. If we played with seven players, so be it. And *if* they all managed to make it, she was going to sit the slowest time.

Coach K meant business. She was the most intense coach I had ever played for. I say this, remembering that one of my summer club team coaches once threw a tantrum worthy of a two-year-old by dropkicking a basketball into the stands, then going on to throw/kick every water bottle sitting on the sideline (all fourteen of them), and finally picking up and throwing a garbage bin onto the court while storming out of the gym ... all because he didn't agree with the referee's travel call.

Every coach has their own unique way of showing their ... displeasure–feels like the right word. Coach Paige, at Lincoln, pulled players out of the game if we didn't run a play right or if we did something he didn't like. He also made us run, A LOT. Sometimes, when he was really angry, he just wouldn't talk to us. We spent a few uncomfortable halftimes sitting in complete silence in the locker room. He said it was our time to think about how we were playing and what kind of player we wanted to be in the second half. It was awkward, but weirdly effective.

When Coach K was displeased with us—because we didn't run a play right, because we didn't take care of the ball, because we didn't rebound, because we weren't listening, because we weren't hustling hard enough, because we weren't in defense stance, because were weren't in the right defensive stance, because we weren't in deny or help-side defense, because we just weren't playing defense at all, because we missed a cut, because we missed an outlet pass, because we forced a pass or made a bad pass, because we didn't look up the court, because we took a bad shot, because we didn't shoot, because we didn't take the right shot, because we weren't talking on defense, because we just didn't get it—she let us know. She definitely let us know.

When she was angry, Coach K had this specific way of yelling where her voice started with a normal volume but gradually gained momentum until people outside the school and in the parking lot could hear her.

Whistle—"How are you going to rebound if you don't BOX OUT!"

Whistle—"We can't run the play if you don't CUT TO THE BALL!"

Whistle—"How are you going to stop the screen if you don't TALK ON DEFENSE!"

Whistle—"Nobody is going to pass you the ball if you DON'T GET OPEN!"

Whistle–"Box out. Box out. BOX OOOUUUTTT!!!!"

It was when Coach K's voice sounded calm that we knew the eruption was coming. And for the most part, we deserved her wrath. She was harsh but never mean. She pushed us, just far enough, and then a little farther. She knew the game. She had been in the trenches. And the girls, myself included, respected her for it.

She yelled at Oaks, Teesha, and me the most—me a little more than Teesha or Oaks.

With Teesha, it was because she wasn't listening—because she was saying something under her breath, either to me or about me—or it was that she decided to take the ball on her own instead of running the play.

Coach K–"Teesha, that was a nice shot."

Teesha–"Thanks, Coach."

Coach K– "You know what would have been nicer? If you passed the ball, set the screen, AND RAN THE PLAY!"

Oaks usually got yelled at because she wasn't hustling enough, because she wasn't fighting to get around her check, or because she wasn't rebounding. Usually it was because she wasn't rebounding. Oaks might be one of the nicest people I have ever met. But there is no room for nice in the post.

Coach K–"Oaks, I'm curious. How did Tats get that rebound?"

Oaks–"Umm ..."

Coach K–"How tall are you?"

Oaks–"Six foot three."

Coach K–"Six-three. Maybe six-four with your shoes on?"

Oaks–"Maybe."

Coach K–"How tall do you think Tats is?"

Oaks–"Five-eight."

Coach K–"On a good day. Let's do some calculations. Six-three. Five-eight. SIX-THREE. Five-eight. Who should be getting the rebound?"

Oaks–"Me!?"

Coach K–"YOU. Not maybe. Not sometimes. EVERY. TIME. YOU!"

With me, she yelled about pretty much anything and everything. I wasn't passing enough. I was passing too much. I wasn't moving my feet quick enough on defense. I took too long to get water. I wasn't running the plays right ...

I'm not complaining or saying I didn't deserve some of the yelling. Coach K ran a completely different offense to the one I was used to and I was struggling to get the plays down.

Coach K–"BENNETT!"

Me–"Yes."

Coach K–"Where are you supposed to be?"

Me–"On the wing?"

Coach K—"Is that a question or an answer?"

Me—"An answer?"

Coach K—"Girls, can anyone tell Bennett where she is supposed to be?"

Teesha—"At the top of the key."

Coach K—"AT THE TOP OF THE KEY! And Bennett. Why did Teesha beat you at the other end?"

Me—"Because I reached."

Coach K—"BECAUSE YOU REACHED. And what happened when you reached?"

Me—"She beat me."

Coach K—"And then?"

Me—"She scored a jump shot."

Coach K—"So, what are you NOT going to do next time you're on defense?"

Me—"I'm not going to reach."

Coach K—"GOOD ANSWER!"

CHAPTER

My two-week recycling sentence had ended, but I still dropped in to help Matti a couple of days a week. Matti would say that she didn't need my help, but I wanted to make sure that no one was bothering or making fun of her. Also, I just liked hanging out.

Now that I had been helping her for a few weeks, we were twice as efficient as we had been on my first day. She even let me do some of the sorting myself, which doesn't sound like much but (according to Coach K), it was a big step for her.

When we finished early one morning, leaving exactly three bags in exactly the right spot behind the green recycling container, I asked her if she wanted to shoot around with me in the gym. By the expression on her face, you would have thought I'd asked her to go to Disneyland.

As I tied up my basketball shoes, Matti grabbed my earphones and iPod from my bag. She was wearing her favorite Air Jordans and a pair of basketball shorts that were about three sizes too big and looked like capris on her.

"How come you're always listening to music when you warm up and shoot?"

"It puts me in the mood. Gets me in the zone."

She put my headphones on and pressed play. Suddenly her face cringed and she shook her head, throwing the headphones to the ground.

"Hey, I saved three months to buy those headphones."

Matti's hands were around her ears. "What was that?"

I looked at the screen. La Bouche, "Sweet Dreams." "What? That song is awesome. It's from the 90's. Matti waved her arms for me to stop. "Okay. What kind of music do you listen to?"

"Classical pop."

"What the heck is classical pop?"

"It's where they take popular pop songs but they play them with violins, pianos, cellos. Music with words bothers my head. But I like listening to instruments. The violin is my favorite. My mom said it used to calm me down when I was upset. But she used to play Mozart and Beethoven. They're old dead guys and I like them, too, but I really like classical pop. Just go on to YouTube and type it in. You can listen to it for free. Sometimes my teachers let me listen to it while I'm doing my schoolwork.

But I'm not supposed to tell anyone. So don't, okay. Don't tell anyone."

I shook my head. "I won't."

"Promise."

"I promise."

She breathed a sigh of relief. "Okay."

I gave Matti a ball and she started to dribble it as we walked over to a hoop. Her dribbles were a bit high but she was pretty good, surprisingly. She could even put it between her legs and do a decent spin dribble. I think she was trying to show off.

"Okay, Matti. You shoot and I'll rebound."

She hit a bank shot on her first try. Then she hit another one. "You have a nice shot. Good follow through. Did your mom teach you how to shoot?"

She nodded. "When I was little, she used to take me to shoot around all the time. But then she had to put me in a special school and it cost a lot of money, so she had to work more. We still played but not as much. I think she wanted me to be like her, but then we found out that I had autism and things changed. I think she was sad. She could have played in the WNBA. Really, she could have. They asked. But then my dad left and she had to take care of me. She says that she never misses it, but she takes me to games sometimes and I can tell. I can see in her eyes that she misses it. I tried to play. I tried to be like her but, when there are too many people and too much noise, I get ... confused sometimes. My counselor says I get overwhelmed with too much stimulation. That's why I like it in her office. I can see everything from the window but it's quiet. One day I want to be a coach, too."

I smiled. "I think that would be awesome." I couldn't help feeling sad for Matti. I hated that she had autism. It didn't feel fair. I wondered if Coach K knew how much her daughter wanted to be like her.

"You know what?" she whispered.

"What?"

"I think you're awesome. You're my favorite player. But don't tell anyone else."

"I bet you say that to all the players," I joked.

"Sometimes. But with you I mean it. I liked watching you at Lincoln, even though you were a Lady Lion and I wasn't supposed to like you. I wasn't even mad when you hit that foul shot. Don't tell my mom or the others, but I wanted you to hit it."

"No, you didn't."

"I did. I really did. Not because I wanted Riverside to lose but because Lincoln deserved to win. You had the better percentage of play. You were ahead in every category but defensive rebounds. My mom said it had nothing to do with the numbers, that in the end, you wanted it more. I don't know what that means, but she must have been right. And you know what else? When you came to Riverside, I knew we'd be friends, because I know what it's like to be the outsider on the team."

"All the girls like you."

"They like me. But they know I'm not like them."

"Matti ..."

"It's okay. I'm not." She took another shot and missed the hoop.

In that moment, I realized that all Matti wanted was to be a part of the team, a real part of the team. Not just the coach's autistic daughter who watched the game from the window. I got the rebound and passed her the ball. She took another shot and missed.

"Bennett? Can you let me hear a swish?"

I nodded. "Sure. I can try."

I told Matti to stand behind the hoop and close her eyes. I hadn't warmed up and I hit the rim on my first three attempts. I stood at the foul line, took a breath, and went over my routine. I held my follow through and ... *swish*.

Matti's eyes were closed but she smiled really wide. "Do it again."

I laughed and went back to the line. *Swish*.

She opened her eyes and looked up at the hoop and then at me. "That *is* an awesome sound."

"Right," I said nodding. "The best."

I was walking back to the foul line when Matti asked a question that echoed throughout the silent gym. "Where's your dad?"

I turned to her. "He died."

The normal reaction when I said that was usually a shocked-sympathetic expression followed by an awkward I'm sorry. But Matti simply asked, "How?"

"He was a police officer, and one night he went to work— New Year's Eve night—to do road checks." I could tell Matti didn't understand. "It's when they stop cars in the street to make sure people aren't drinking and driving. We don't know exactly what happened, but they told my mom that he was checking a car when another car, driven by an elderly lady, sped up instead of slowing down. She swerved into three officers and hit a police car, but my dad was the only one who died. He got pinned between the two cars. They told us he died on the way to the hospital, so we never got to say goodbye."

"Was the lady drunk?"

"No. She was just old. She got confused when she saw the police lights and hit the gas instead of the brakes. It was an accident."

"Oh. My dad didn't die but he left. I didn't say goodbye, either." She closed her eyes. "Can you shoot another swish?"

"Sure." And I shot four more before the bell went.

I knew I didn't have time to change, so I left my basketball shoes and gear on and sprinted to Humphries's English class, hoping to make it before the second bell. I did not. I was only ten seconds—give or take—late. But that was enough.

Humphries tipped her glasses down and gave me a disapproving scowl as I snuck into my seat. "I will see you after class, Miss Ryan."

I nodded and fished out an 826-page anvil of a book ironically titled—at least I thought it was ironic—*A Brief Venture into the World of Poetry, Prose, and Essays.*

Good times, I thought to myself.

"As I was saying, class," she glared at me again, "turn to page 344. Miss Ryan will read out the title, the author, and start us off." I fumbled to find the page. "We're all waiting for you, Miss Ryan."

Yep. Really good times.

When I was the last student in the class, I approached Humphries's desk and waited for my *admonishment*—fittingly, it was a word used in the poem I had just read out.

"Mrs. Humphries, I'm really sorry. I was in the gym and ..." She held a finger up and I instantly stopped talking. *Here it comes. Detention? Principal-mom's office? An essay? Let me have it.*

"The Mustang Classic Icebreaker Tournament is this weekend, is it not?"

Oh, God, I thought. Please don't take basketball away from me. I swallowed nervously. "Yes."

"Last year Riverside had an unfortunate loss to Southlands in the semi-final and we only came third. I say unfortunate but, really, it was a disastrous second quarter and a very bad call on Montana Dunkin that fouled her out in the fourth that cost us the game. I'd say that referee needed glasses, but he had some on, so that buffoon really had no excuse for calling a foul when it was clear to myself and everyone in the stands that her rejection on that girl was clean."

Wait. What? Grumpy, gray-haired, long-skirt-and-flower-blouse-wearing Humphries knew what a rejection was.

"I expect that this year's tournament will have a much better result. Don't you think so, Miss Ryan?" I didn't answer. My brain was still catching up with what my ears were hearing. "Miss Ryan?"

"Uh ... I think we could win it."

"Could? I believe you should."

"Well, Westview is on the other side, and they're supposed to be pretty good this year."

"Yes, they were tough last year. And mostly juniors. A good three-point shooting team but, if I remember correctly, no real posts. With Montana and Georgia, I don't see how they can stop you in the middle."

It still wasn't computing that Humphries—who had seemingly hated me since the start of the year—was talking basketball with me. "Yes, but Oaks ... I mean Georgia, might not play this weekend."

"What?" she asked, genuinely outraged.

"She and three others haven't run a sub-twenty-seven minutes on the three-mile fitness test. And Coach K said ..."

"Well, I suggest you help her," she said sharply.

"Yes, but ..."

"You'll find a way."

I could feel the class starting to fill up with her second block, and I had to get to calculus, but I was still too shocked to move. "I didn't know you cared about basketball. I thought you hated me."

"Miss Ryan, I may look old. I may be old. But I will have you know that I was captain of my basketball team and All-State two years in a row. And long before Coach Kelley took over, I coached the varsity squad here."

Aha, now it all makes sense. My eyes widened as it dawned on me. "You do hate me."

"Hate is a very strong word. But, when it comes to the purple and gold, you are not far off. Where you have missed the mark is with the 'do.' I *did*, not *do*."

"Because I'm on the team now?"

She looked sternly at me. "It will be nice to see you in blue and white, Miss Ryan. Purple and gold are a dreadful color combination."

"But ..." I paused. "You still pick on me all the time."

She took a deep breath. "Yes, well, I have to admit that I might not yet be over the sting of last year's championship."

I couldn't help but smile and laugh. "So, this is about basketball?!"

"Riverside hasn't seen a banner in nine years. I'm an old lady nearing retirement, and before I go, I'd like to see the *State Champions* raised one last time." She shuffled a pile of papers on her desk. "Play well this weekend, Miss Ryan. And know that I still expect to see your final Shakespeare essay on my desk Monday morning—before the second bell goes."

When I sat down in calculus, I was still trying to envision a young Humphries dribbling and shooting a basketball. I couldn't do it.

"What's up with you?" Oaks asked.

"Did you know that Humphries used to play basketball?"

"You didn't?" I shook my head. "She's a super fan. She's at, like, every game we play. She's pretty hard core, too. She brings a cowbell and sometimes paints her face."

"She does not paint her face."

"She totally does."

Class had started but, thankfully, we had a substitute who wrote up a bunch of textbook questions on the board and then sat down and read a newspaper. Subs like this were my favorite.

They didn't know what they were teaching and, because they didn't want us to know that they didn't know what they were doing, they usually just wrote work up on the board and left us alone. We could listen to music, chat, or even do work for another class. If we didn't bother them, they didn't bother us.

Oaks, Jess, and I pulled our desks closer and opened the textbook.

"So, when is Coach letting you run the three-mile again?"

"Ugh ... tomorrow morning," Oaks complained. "And if I don't do it in the morning, she's going to give us one last chance after practice."

"I was thinking about maybe running with you."

Jess looked up from the text. "Are you crazy? You want to run it for fun?"

"Not for fun. I was thinking about helping you pace it," I said looking at Oaks. "You know, cheer you on and stuff."

"Forget that." Jess put her earphones in. "I just barely made it last time. I never want to set foot on another track." She turned up her music and tuned us out.

"You'd do that for me?" Oaks asked.

I shrugged. "We need you this weekend. Besides, I know you can do it."

"I don't know. I don't want to make you do that with me. It sucks. Do you think Coach K will even let you?"

"You're not making me do anything. Besides, it's good conditioning, and what's she going to say? No, you can't run the three-mile again?"

Oaks thought about it. "Well, maybe I can help you get the plays down."

I smiled. "It's a deal." I looked up at the sub. His head was still hidden behind the newspaper. "Can we start now? I have no idea what's going on with Indiana."

She flipped to a fresh page in her notebook, drew a basketball key and a three-point line, and we spent the rest of class going over the full-court/half-court offenses, the inbounds, and the sideline plays. Some things are just more important than calculus.

CHAPTER 15

In the morning, I kept my word and met with Oaks at the track. Nikki, Taya, and Sierra were there, too. I told them I just wanted to run it for fun—which got me a lot of eye rolls and anger glares—but I didn't want to tell them the real reason. It's not that I didn't want the others to pass the test. It was just that none of them was six-three and could do as much damage as Oaks under the rim.

I'm not saying they weren't as important, but the harsh reality of any team is that some players play a bigger role than others. And if you're six-three, and a girl, and in high school, and (hopefully, if you're that tall) playing basketball—even if you can't dribble and you kind of suck—you'll still be a "big" player for the team. When it comes to basketball, height may not be everything, but it matters. It just does.

Oaks didn't suck. She was actually pretty agile and a decent ball handler (for a tall girl), and if we were going to win the icebreaker tournament, we needed her. Which is exactly what I told her when, between heaving breaths, she asked me, "Why are you doing this?"

I looked at my watch. We were slightly ahead of Nikki and Sierra but, at 18:58 at the end of mile two, we were behind the time. "Come on, Oaks. You got this." I tried to push her.

"I hate this," she huffed. "I hate you."

"You don't hate anything," I laughed. "You're Oaks. You're too nice."

I could hear the footsteps and hard breathing of Nikki and Sierra as they slowly gained, and then eventually passed us. Oaks started to slow down. "No. You CAN STILL DO THIS."

"I can't," she puffed. "I can't."

Nikki and Sierra finished with 26:12 and 26:47. Oaks crossed the line with 27:36.

"That's it, Oaks." Coach K shook her head disapprovingly. "You got one more shot or you'll be riding the pine this weekend."

"Did you do it?" Jess asked Oaks during calculus.

She gave her a grumpy glare and shook her head.

"But you still have one more try after practice today," I said positively.

"It's done. I'm not playing this weekend. I'm the only one who can't do it."

"Oaks, first of all, you can. Secondly, it's not done. If you beat twenty-six forty-seven you'll be in and Sierra will sit out."

"But I don't want to make Sierra miss this weekend."

"Oaks, stop being nice," I said sharply. "If you beat her time, you'll deserve to dress this weekend."

"What does it even matter?" she complained. "Coach K is already mad at me. Face it, big white girls can't run. I hate basketball." She got up and stormed out of the room.

"Should we go get her?" I asked Jess.

"Nah. Let her cool off. She gets like this sometimes."

"What do you mean?"

"I mean, every year she says she hates basketball. But every year the season starts and she loves it again. Just give her some time."

Oaks was still upset when practice came around. She was slow, missed easy layups, and got out-rebounded by nearly everyone. It felt like Coach Kelley laid into her every couple of minutes.

"Oaks, if I have to tell you to BOX OUT ONE MORE TIME!"

"Oaks, move your feet. Get position. SEAL HER!"

"Oaks, play DEFENSE!"

"OAKS! HUSTLE!"

"OAKS!!"

At the end of practice, I found Oaks in the locker room packing up her bag. "What are you doing? You still have to run the three-mile."

"No, I don't," she said, defeated. "I can't do it, anyway. Besides, I don't think Coach K even wants me to."

I sat down beside her. "Did you mean it when you said that you don't even like basketball?"

"Yes."

I picked up her phone. The cover was like the leather skin of a real basketball. "Really?" I said, holding up the phone.

"Give me that." She grabbed it and sat on the bench, twirling it in her hands. "You know, I didn't even pick this sport. My parents just put me in it because they didn't know what else to do with me."

"What did you want?"

"I don't know. To dance, sing—I like acting." She looked at my surprised face. "And see, that expression you just gave, that's the same look that all my dance teachers had when my parents brought me to class."

"I'm sorry. I'm just trying to picture you as a ballerina."

"I don't mean that. I like hip-hop and contemporary."

"Are you any good?"

"I'm okay. I'm six-three, so I don't exactly blend in on the dance floor. I was always made fun of because real dancers were "five-two and tiny ... and bitches."

"Whoa." I'd never heard Oaks swear before.

"They used to call me names like Iron Giant and Big Foot, and I used to come home crying all the time. That's when my parents enrolled me in basketball."

"But Oaks, you are kind of built for it. I would kill to have your size."

"No, you wouldn't. Being this tall sucks. Nothing fits and I'm taller than most of the boys. Nobody wants to date a girl who's that much taller than them."

I'd never thought about it that way before. I'd always been so jealous of how easy it was to get a rebound. "Do you remember last year's Winter Ball tournament?"

She nodded. "You ... I mean, Lincoln beat us in overtime."

"Well, I remember this one particular play. I had just finished this spin move to get by Teesha, then another move to go by Cruze, and I thought I had an easy layup after that. But then this giant shadow and huge arm came out of nowhere and rejected the ball into the stands." She smiled. "And you smiled just like that when you did it."

Her smile turned into an evil grin. "I remember that."

"So do I, because you apologized after."

"I did?"

I laughed. "Yep."

"Monty always gets mad when I say sorry. I can't help it. It just comes out."

"I have a hard time believing that you don't love this game. And maybe you didn't pick it. Maybe it chose you. And maybe that's okay."

She looked down at her shoes. "Coach K is so mad at me right now."

"She's not mad. She yells a lot, but I think it's because she expects more from you. You could be better ..."

"Thanks a lot."

"I was going to say, you could be better IF you let yourself be. If you love this game, it will love you back—something my dad once told me. What's your favorite thing about basketball?"

"What?"

"Your favorite thing? Matti asked me once when ... when I was feeling like quitting and ..."

"You? Quit?"

"I wasn't exactly welcomed here. I'm still not sure I am."

Oaks looked guilty. "True. I guess my favorite thing is right before the game when we're in the locker room. Someone puts on some music and we have a little pump-up dance party. Everyone's laughing, cheering, we're all together, and excited for the game. The team. Being together. That's my favorite thing. Oh, and I also like blocking shots."

"I bet you do," I laughed. "Are you really willing to miss that this weekend? Because you couldn't run thirty seconds faster?"

"Actually, it's fifty seconds if I have to beat Sierra," she corrected me. She pulled her running shoes out of her bag and started to tie them up. "Okay, let's do this."

When Coach K yelled out that we had completed one mile, I looked down at my watch—8:51. We were on pace but still needed to speed up. "Come on, Oaks." I tried to push her.

"I'm trying!"

"Remember those bitchy dance girls calling you Iron Giant and Big Foot? Well, maybe they were right."

"What?!"

"You run like an Iron Giant." Our pace increased. "And maybe you were right. Big girls can't run."

"You ... are ... trying ... to make ... me ... mad," she huffed out between breaths.

"I thought you didn't get mad," I continued. "You're too nice. In fact, I don't think you have what it takes to be a basketball player. Those other posts are going to eat you alive. Coach K thinks you're too nice. She thinks you're soft. But I mean, you are a little soft. Who says sorry after rejecting the ball?"

"I ... still ... rejected ... you."

"And I still won the game."

Two miles—17:48.

"We're not ... going ... to make ... it."

"You're not going to make it," I said coldly. "You're going to miss the tournament, the pregame dance." I looked down at my watch. "Are you really going to let me beat you ... again?" Oaks was too tired to respond. "Maybe you should just stick to dancing."

"Three miles!" Coach K yelled out.

Oaks held a cramp in her side while her chest heaved up and down. I wasn't much better. Leaning over with my hands on my knees, sweat dripping down the side of my face.

Coach K walked up to us. "Not bad, Oaks. Who knew you could actually move that fast?"

We looked up, eager to hear the final time.

Coach K held up the stopwatch as she walked away. "Twenty-six flat."

I gave Oaks an exhausted high-five and we both collapsed on the track together. It was just starting to rain and the cold drops felt good on my face.

"You know," Oaks said. "I thought you were a bitch last year."

"That's okay," I heaved back. "I thought you were a bitch, too."

CHAPTER 16

I stared at myself in my bedroom mirror. A stranger wearing a blue Riverside Storm jersey stared back.

"Blue and white. White and blue." It didn't matter how I said it, it still didn't feel quite right. I had last year's Lincoln team photo taped on my mirror. That didn't feel right either.

I took the photo down and put it in a shoebox along with my purple basketball shoes and all the medals I had won with Lincoln. I even shoved in a small stuffed lion that Brooke and I had each bought together and brought to all our games. I looked around my room to see if there was any more Lincoln memorabilia and then pushed the shoebox under my bed. If I was going to do this, if I was going to be a member of the Storm, I was going to do it right.

"Bennett?" my mom's voice called. "Are you ready? You're

going to be late."

I looked back at the player in the mirror. *Yes,* I thought. *I'm ready.*

Westview High hosted the Wild Mustang Icebreaker Tournament. It was a two-hour drive from Riverside, and Coach K had decided that it was far enough away that we would all go in a team bus and stay the night at a hotel.

I knew Lincoln wouldn't be in the tournament because they hosted their own icebreaker tourney that Riverside was not invited to; a relief because I was nowhere near ready to see my old team.

We all spread out with our own seat on the bus. Teesha and Cruze had claimed the back with Monty and O. I grabbed a seat near the front. Oaks was behind me and Coach K was two seats ahead.

I was hoping Matti would come with us, but she told me that away trips were too loud and she missed sleeping in her own bed. She then went on a rant about how awful hotel bathrooms and bedspreads were and about the high percentage of bedbugs found in hotel mattresses—which creeped me out. She had a million excuses why she couldn't come, but all I saw in her face was that she really wanted to. I told her I'd text after each game and that seemed to make her happy.

The start of the ride was pretty quiet. Everyone either had

their head down in their phone, in a book, or like me, they were listening to their music. Every now and then, I would look up and to the back and see Teesha playing a game on her phone or laughing about something with Cruze. Sometimes our eyes would meet and we would quickly look away, pretending that we weren't just checking in with the other.

Coach K had made Teesha and me captains but she couldn't make us friends. We got changed at opposite ends of the change room. Took our warm-up shots at opposite ends of the gym. Kept our water bottles on different benches. When we knew Coach K was watching, we both put on a decent show, passing to one another, talking on defense, sometimes even doing a two-person drill together. But when we knew her back was turned, evil glares were given and returned, elbows were thrown during one-on-one drills, and box-outs under the hoop were set with more force than necessary.

I tried not to think about Lincoln, but I knew that yesterday night, the night before their first game, Brooke's family would have hosted the players and their families with a pasta dinner at their house. And that today, they were about to play the home opener in front of the entire school, that would be let out of their classes early to watch and cheer. And I wasn't there. I was here. On the bus. With Riverside.

"Are you okay?" Oaks leaned over the bus seat.

"Yeah. Why?"

"You look ... nervous or something."

"I just get like this before a game."

"What are you thinking about?"

Everything. "Nothing."

"Are you thinking about Lincoln?"

How did she know? I nodded.

"It must not be easy." I just smiled. She was the first and only one who said that to me. "You know what I think we need?" She quickly kneeled on her seat and addressed the rest of the bus. "You know what time it is?"

Almost as if it was planned, Tats jumped out of her seat and pointed at her. "I know what time it is." Then she swung around and pointed at Cruze. "Do you know what time it is?"

Cruze popped up next. "Hell, yeah! It's time to dance!"

The next thing I knew, Macklemore and Ryan Lewis's "Can't Hold Us" was blaring out from the bus speakers while everyone's arms and hands went up– *"Because the ceiling can't hold us."* The music blared out, O started to rap with the lyrics, and players got out of their seats to take a turn dancing down the aisle with a specific dance move.

At first I felt uncomfortable. Like we shouldn't be doing this. Coach Paige would have yelled at my old team to sit down, be quiet, and focus on the game, but Coach K just sat at the front like she couldn't hear any of it and wrote down notes in her coaching binder, seemingly oblivious to how loud we were being.

It had never been in my nature to be loud or get up and dance, especially in front of a group. I always admired anyone who could be that free. I stayed in my seat, watching and clapping in awe as Oaks and Cruze grooved together in what seemed like a choreographed routine. And then, out of nowhere, Tats jumped on my seat and shook her booty in my face. "Come on, Lincoln, get crazy!" I broke out laughing and slapped her on the ass. Out of the corner of my eye, I saw Teesha watching me. She was smiling and laughing, too.

The rest of the ride continued this way. I couldn't bring myself to dance but, with each song, I started to feel a little less nervous. I turned to Oaks, "Do you guys always do this?"

She nodded with the beat. "Welcome to Riverside!"

CHAPTER 17

Our first game was against an all-girls private school named St. Anne's. It was a team I had never played before, but Cruze said it would be a "cupcake stroll." I asked her if she meant cakewalk and she responded, "I always mean what I say ... and cupcakes are better than cake any day."

When we got to Westview, the first thing I did was find a bathroom and throw up. Tats was fixing her hair in the mirror when I came out.

"Damn, Lincoln, you eat some bad cookies on the bus or something?"

"No." I rinsed my mouth in the sink. "This happens sometimes." *When I'm nervous.* "I'll be fine in a minute."

"Okay," she said, slightly disgusted. "Coach K wants us to meet in the locker room."

I nodded.

One of the things that I equally love and hate is a coach's pregame talk. It helps me get my head in the game, get focused, but I also just want to stop the talk and get to the court. Sometimes I'm so anxious to get things started, I sit with my legs bouncing up and down, hearing the music booming from the gym, hearing the fans, hearing the other team cheering in their own locker room, hearing voices in my head–hearing everything but what the coach has to say.

Every coach has a different style, a different approach to psyching-up his or her team before a game, but it's usually the same stuff: stay focused, defense first, come out strong, don't let the other team think they have a chance, BOX OUT, then some team strategy, offense, defense ... it's all the same. In the end, they want us to go and play basketball. And that's all I want. Lincoln, Riverside, Purple, Blue, all the changes and challenges in my life will go away the minute that whistle is blown and that ball hits the court. *The gym is my temple and basketball is my Zen.*

Coach K went on about how this was the first game of the season and how this was the time we set the tone for the year ... blah, blah, blah ... and then she announced the starting line-up– Cruze, Teesha, Tats, Oaks, Monty.

What?!

Teesha smiled and looked for my reaction. I tried not to have one but I was freaking out inside. I've never not been a starter—not for as long as I can remember. I always start. I fought for Teesha to make the team. I helped Oaks pass the three-mile fitness test. And now they are starting and I'm sitting on the bench?

This is bullshit.

Coach K must have seen my face or read my mind because after the team cheer, as everyone ran out the door to warm up, she grabbed my arm and held me back.

"Bennett, you okay?"

No, of course not! "Yeah, Coach. I'm fine."

"No, you're not. You want to punch me in the face right now."

I looked at her, clenched my jaw, and held back the *"yes, that's exactly what I feel like doing."*

She continued, "I know you want to start. You should be starting but you can't. They're not ready for it yet." As mad as I was, I understood. "A coach once told me that it shouldn't matter how many minutes I got, it only matters what I did with them. You get me?"

"I get you," I nodded.

And I did get her. I just didn't like it.

For the first few minutes of the game, all I could think about was how I wasn't playing. Each second, each whistle, each shot taken ... it was torture to be on the bench and not on the court.

We got off to a strong start. Only five minutes into the game and we were up 18–0. Six minutes, 24–0. Seven minutes, 30–4. Teesha was playing well and easily had about half the team's points. Toward the end of the first quarter, St. Anne's started to fight back, but it was clear we were the much stronger team.

Start of the second quarter and my ass was still riding the pine. Jess went in before me. Then O. After a little while—I'm not sure exactly when—I stopped counting the minutes that I hadn't played and found myself cheering for the team. I'm not sure if this is what Coach K was waiting for, but it was at that point that she called my name and sent me to sub in for Teesha.

When the whistle blew, I called Teesha's name. She ran by me to the bench, leaving my high-five hanging in the air and ignoring my question, "Who are you checking?" I didn't even care. I was in the game.

The first time the ball hit my hands, I was behind the three-point line on the baseline. I pulled up and took the shot—which was ballsy of me, coming in cold, no real warm-up, no dribble, no matter—*swish*.

And just like that, all felt right in the world.

At the half, we were up 48–11. Starting the third quarter, Coach K kept Teesha off and me on. I must have had some pent-up shooting energy from sitting on the bench for so long. In eight minutes of play, I went six for six from the three-point line.

Both Teesha and I sat for most of the fourth quarter—at opposite ends of the bench, of course. It was a good game. Everyone got in to play. I finished with 22 points. Teesha had 28.

Final score: Riverside 88—St. Anne's 21.

The win put us into the quarter-finals that same night against the Pearson Park Panthers.

I didn't start—again—but I did go in for the second quarter.

We took an early lead. Pearson was a little tougher than St. Anne's, but they were young and their guards couldn't handle our full-court press. Actually, it was Cruze they couldn't handle.

She was like a maniacal little hummingbird—which I know doesn't sound very threatening, but hummingbirds can be vicious—and I really don't have another way of describing how she moved on defense. If a guard even tried to put the ball down and get by her, Cruze somehow—I couldn't see how because her arms and legs moved so fast—popped the ball out and, by the time the player even realized they lost it, she was already down the court in the process of doing a layup. Being Cruze, her steals were usually accompanied by some snappy nonsensical trash talk like, "Ding, ding! You keep dishin' it up and I'll keep cleaning the plate. It's like a serve-yourself all-you-can-eat buffet down here!"

Having personally had the ball stripped from me a couple of times last season, I can honestly say that being on the receiving end of Cruze's defense and trash talk sucks. But it was fun to watch—if you were on her team.

At the half it was 38–20.

By the end of the third quarter, it was obvious that we were going to run away with the game. It was also obvious that Coach K was deliberately avoiding playing Teesha and me together. *Fine by me.*

I ended up with 21 points—Teesha 17.

Final Score: Riverside 73—Pearson Park 36.

I've always found it interesting how differently coaches and players view a game. We had two dominant victories. We had advanced into the semi-finals the next morning. We all celebrated in the change room as if the games had gone well, because, in our minds, they did. But then Coach K walked in and started going off about lazy defense, poor shooting choices, too many fouls, plays that hadn't been run right, missed box outs ... it was like she had been watching a different game. But then the more she ranted on, the more we all started to see the game through her eyes and, okay, she might have had some valid points. It was the start of the season and we did have a lot of work to do.

We did a final team cheer and everyone started to file out toward the team bus. Coach K told Teesha and me to stay behind. We received looks of sympathy and concern from the girls as they left.

This can't be good.

We sat on opposite sides of the change room. Coach K stood in between us, looking from one side to the other. She raised her arms in frustration. "Are you two kidding me with this?" She paused. It was so silent in the room that all I could hear was a dripping faucet. "Take out your jersey and put it on. And before either of you complains about how sweaty they are—I don't care. Put them on and stand up."

We did as we were told.

"Oh, look at that. Blue and white. Both say Riverside Storm. They do match. I wanted to check, because by the way you two played out there, you wouldn't know it was for the same team. And I bet you're both dying to make a comment about how I didn't actually play you together."

I *was* thinking it, but I would never dare to say it out loud.

"Let me ask you this. Teesha, in two games, how many times did you give Bennett a high-five?"

Teesha looked down at her shoes and didn't answer.

"And Bennett," Coach K turned to me, "how many times did you cheer for a good play or a good shot that Teesha made?"

Now I was looking at my shoes.

"Teesha?" Teesha looked up. "How many points did Bennett have the first game?"

"Twenty-two."

"How many points did you have?"

"Twenty-eight."

"Bennett? How many points did Teesha have the second game?"

"Seventeen."

"And you?"

"Twenty-one."

"Do you know how many points Monty had? Or Cruze? Or the team?"

We shook our heads.

Coach K put her hands on her hips and looked to the ceiling like she was searching for divine intervention. "I tried. I've been patient. I got inventive. I made you captains. But the thing that really gets to me is that you two are too pigheaded to see how good you are for each other. You have an opportunity to take your game to a completely different level. But all you see when you look at the other is competition. And before either of you can point a finger and say it's her and not me, know this—there can never be just one stubborn person in a room, or in this case, on the court." She stopped and took a deep breath. "Speaking of rooms. You

— 172 —

two are bunking together at the hotel tonight."

We both looked up in protest. Neither of us opened our mouths. We knew better.

"I'm going to be dropping off a questionnaire and it will be your job to interview the other person. In the morning, there will be a test. And no, I'm not kidding. If you get even one answer wrong, you'll be running—both of you. You can't leave the room. You can't invite other team members into the room. In fact, if I find out you left or had anyone come in, you and the entire team will be running suicides until you wish you had never heard of the game of basketball. Clear?"

We nodded.

"Good. Oh, and it's not just the room tonight. You will sit together on the bus—yes, on the same seat. You will eat together. You will change beside one another. You will sit together on the bench. Your water bottles will be side by side. If I look at either of you, at any time, and I don't think you're joined like Siamese twins, you'll be running suicides—with your ankles tied together like it's a three-legged race. And no, I'm not kidding. You two are going to learn to be teammates or you're going to kill each other. Either way, problem solved."

She walked to the door and then spun around with one more statement to make.

"You're not just on the same team now, you're on my team!"

CHAPTER 18

The chatter on the bus fell silent as Teesha and I stepped on and walked down the aisle together. No one said a word as we sat next to each other. I didn't even bother asking for the window seat.

Dinner went pretty much the same way. We talked—just not to each other.

At the hotel, we got off the elevator and started to walk down the hall toward our room. Teesha started to quicken her pace so she was a step ahead. Then I did the same. It turned from a walk, to a race-walk, to a jog, and finally to an all-out sprint with each of us elbowing for first-place position. I won.

We put our bags on our beds and then took turns having a shower. Teesha went first. I waited and read my text messages.

Matti:

My mom told me about you and Teesha. Just

don't suffocate each other with pillows while you
sleep. Those pillows are disgusting.

I texted back:

LOL

Then she asked:

Did you check for bedbugs?

I responded:

Your a bedbug.

She wrote:

First of all, it's you're not YOUR, it's YOU'RE. I thought
you were good at English. Second, no I'm not.
Third, I'm serious. You should check.

I was laughing at Matti's text, but I still got off the bed and did a bedbug check.

I just checked. It looks like there are some. But
only on Teesha's bed so no biggie.

Her response came quickly.

WHAT?????

I heard the shower turn off.

Matti, I'm kidding. No bedbugs. Except for you.
Gotta go.

When I came out of the bathroom, Teesha was sprawled out on her bed watching sports highlights. She held up two sheets of paper. "Coach dropped these off for us." She threw a page and pencil on my bed and turned the TV off. "Let's get this *Remember the Titans* moment over with."

I picked up the sheet and smiled. "Hey, I was thinking the same thing. Good movie."

She rolled her eyes. "Look at that. We like the same movie. We're besties already."

"Well, you don't have to be a bitch about it."

"You're the bitch."

I slammed the paper down. "WHAT is your problem?"

"YOU."

"Me? Just me or ..."

"Admit that I didn't foul you."

"OH, MY GOD. Are you still pissed about that call?"

"It was all ball! I never touched you."

"Teesha, what does it matter? I didn't make the call. The ref did. And it's in the past. It's over. Even if it was a bad call, it wouldn't make any difference."

"So you're saying it was a bad call?"

"I'm saying ... GET OVER IT!"

Teesha took her sheet and sat cross-legged on her bed, facing me. "Let's just do this. First question ..."

"Why do you get to ask the first question?"

"Are you serious? Because I do. You can ask the next one."

"Fine."

"How old were you when you started playing basketball?"

"Two."

"You weren't two?"

"I was. I have the little high-tops to prove it." Teesha just stared at me. "Fine, I was eight when I played on my first team."

"I was seven."

I felt like she was trying to one-up me, but I kept my mouth shut and wrote down her answer. "Question two," I read before she could beat me to it. "Who do you think is the best female basketball player of all time?"

"That's easy. Maya Moore."

"What?" I countered. "No way. Sheryl Swoopes."

"Who?"

I dropped my pen. "What do you mean, *who*?"

"Never heard of her."

"WHAT?" I quickly got to my knees. My hands were on my head in shock. "She's the Michael Jordan of woman's basketball. Three time WNBA MVP—in fact, she's the first woman to sign in the WNBA and the first woman to have a shoe named after her—Air Swoopes."

"She had a shoe named after her?" Now Teesha was interested.

"Only the best shoe ever." I grabbed my phone, pulled up an image, and handed it to her. "I still have a pair of them that I bought off the Internet. My mom wonders why I didn't just throw them out. They're a size too small, the soles are all worn down, and the leather is cracking, but they're my favorite pair of basketball shoes. And you don't just throw something like that away. You just don't."

"No, you don't." She shrugged and gave me back my phone. "They're cool and all, but Maya Moore is still the best, or Diana Taurasi."

"Okay, I'll give it to you, Taurasi is awesome. But Moore is not the best of all time."

"Not yet," she said with attitude. "She will be."

"Not better than Candace Parker," I mumbled.

"What?"

"You heard me." I looked down at the sheet. "I guess I know your answer to question three. Tennessee or UConn?"

"Huskies, hands down. And I guess we know who you like."

I just shook my head. "Lady Vols—all the way."

"How can you even say that? UConn has won more head to heads, more championships, and now that Summitt's gone …"

I gasped and pointed my finger at her. "Don't."

She put her hands up. Even Teesha—a UConn fan—knew that saying anything bad about Pat Summitt was sacrilegious in the basketball world. "Okay. You're right. I was sad when I heard about her Alzheimer's, too … but UConn is still the best."

"I can't even … I mean … argh …" I grabbed the pen in frustration. "Agree to disagree."

"I'm not agreeing to anything." Teesha read the next

question. "Where do you want to play in college?" She looked at me. "I'm guessing Tennessee?"

"No, actually. Stanford."

"Interesting. I guess you are a smarty pants."

"It's not about that. I like their program." Teesha nodded in agreement. "And you?"

"Notre Dame."

"Notre Dame?"

She shrugged. "My mom went there. And I like Skylar Diggins."

"Fair enough," I nodded. "You heard from them yet?"

"No. You heard from Stanford?"

I shook my head. We left it at that.

I looked for the next question. "Favorite song to listen to before a game?"

"Right now … either DJ Khaled, 'All I Do Is Win,' or Eminem, 'Not Afraid.'"

"'Rhythm is Dancer' by Snap!"

"Who?"

"It's a 90's song. But it's got an awesome intro and I just love listening to it right before a game." I quickly pulled it up on my phone and pressed play. I closed my eyes and started humming along to the intro, the way I almost always did before a game. When I opened my eyes, Teesha was staring at me like I was equal parts weird and crazy. "What?" I defended. "It's a good song."

"Please tell me that you didn't listen to *that* before beating us in the finals?"

"Before the game and at halftime," I smiled proudly.

"Oh, my God." She grabbed her phone and started to play "All I Do Is Win," turning it up louder than mine. "Now this is a pump-up song. Like, if my song and your song met in a dark alley somewhere, my song would kick your song's ass." She got up on the bed and started to dance and rap with the lyrics. I laughed.

I turned up my music as loud as it could go, got up on my bed, and started to sing along. Teesha sang louder, trying to drown me out. It was a "song-off."

After thirty seconds of yelling, we heard a banging at the door. We both turned our music down and jumped off the bed to answer.

Coach K stood behind the door with her arms crossed and an unimpressed expression.

"Sorry, Coach," we said in unison. She just shook her head and walked away.

As soon as the door clicked shut, we looked at each other and burst out laughing.

Then, at the exact same moment, we both realized we were laughing together and quickly stopped. We went back to our spots on the beds, back to hating each other.

"Whose question is it?" Teesha asked.

"Yours."

"Why do you play basketball?"

"Because I love it. I know that sounds simple but it's true. I love it. When I'm playing, I don't think about anything else but the game. And I just love the competition. Plus," I hesitated, "it reminds me of my dad."

"Is it true ... what happened to your dad?"

I nodded. "Yeah. He died in an accident."

"Sometimes I wish my dad had died, instead of just leaving."

"No, you don't," I muttered. "Trust me. You don't."

"At least your dad didn't choose to leave you for another family." I could hear the bitterness in her voice.

Neither of us said anything for what felt like a few minutes. "How about you?" I broke the silence. "Why do you play?"

"Because I'm good at it. I've always been good at it. And I like being with the team. Cruze, Tats, Monty... they're like my sisters."

"Next question," I said. "What are you afraid of?"

"What does she mean? Like spiders and stuff?"

"I don't know. I think she means with basketball."

Teesha thought about it for a minute. So did I.

"I guess ... I don't know ... it's stupid."

"What?"

"Not being good enough," she finally blurted out.

"Good enough for what?"

"I don't know. Just ... good enough. Letting people down. Until you got here, I was always the best. It can be a lot of pressure, you know?" I wasn't sure if it was a rhetorical question but I nodded anyway, because I did know. She went silent. Suddenly, I was seeing a whole different side to her, and I could tell she felt uncomfortable being that vulnerable, especially with me. "Whatever. This is stupid. What are you afraid of?"

I was going to say clowns just to be funny, but since she was being that honest with me, I felt like I owed her something. "I'm afraid of not being able to play."

"What do you mean? Like sitting on the bench?"

"No, like not being able to play ever. When it's all over. Or just if something happens, like an ACL or something." Teesha smiled in a way that made me feel like she understood me.

"What do you admire about the other player's game?" She looked up and waited for my answer.

I had to think about it. Not because I couldn't think of one, but because I couldn't narrow it down. "The first thing that comes to mind is your dribbling. You make it look so easy. And you've got that between-the-legs–crossover–pull back that's just deadly. Oh, and the crossover-spin at the top of the key. My best friend Brooke fell for that a couple of times."

"You never did," Teesha smirked.

"Well, that's because you usually go back to your right to finish."

"I do not."

"Like, ninety percent of the time," I confirmed. "Or you dish it to Monty or Oaks. And that's the other thing I love about your game—your passing. You see things others don't."

"You do, too," she said. "You had that one behind-the-back assist in the semi-finals last year. I have to admit, it was pretty awesome. And your three-point shot ... I don't know how you do it. Quick release and it's so smooth."

"Yeah, but your inside jumper is way better than mine. I couldn't defend it."

She looked unconvinced. "Please, you stopped me plenty of times. I hate it when you defend me. It's like Cruze. You're both so annoying to have as a check. You never give up."

I couldn't contain a huge smile. "You think I play defense like Cruze?"

"You're not as quick in the full court, but your half-court D is ... it's solid. You're pretty tough for a white girl. Coach K was all over me to shake you last year. It's like you know what other players are going to do even before they do ..."

"Well," I interrupted and then stopped myself.

"What?"

"It's just that sometimes ... you're easy to read. Especially when you're mad." She rolled her eyes like she had heard this speech a thousand times before. "Why do you get so mad?"

"I don't know. I just do. Sometimes I can't control it ... okay, most times I can't control it."

"This kind of goes with the next question," I said. "What would you change about the other player's game? I get angry, too. A lot. Especially when I'm around you." We laughed and the mood lightened. "It's just ... you play heavy sometimes. You stop talking, stop having fun, and let the game get to you or something."

"I let the game get to me?" she said in high pitch. "You're the one who plays with a stick up your ass."

"What?" I argued back.

"You do. It's like you think too much about the right footwork, the right play ... everything is so technical with you. Just have fun with it. It's okay if you make a mistake once in a while."

"Like you?" I said defensively. "And then get mad at myself?"

"That's not what I mean. I mean, you need to let loose sometimes. Smile more. Have fun with the game, just play it; don't let it play you."

I knew Teesha had a point. I envied players like her and Cruze who laughed and joked on the court. My old team was never playful like that. Winning was the only thing that mattered. Coach Paige used to yell at the bench if we even looked like we were having fun. Even if we were winning—by a lot—he would say it wasn't enough, that we had to play harder. One of the things he loved to say to us was, "Fun is for five-year-olds on the playground. The gym is for basketball, and in this gym we win." It didn't matter what gym we were in.

Intense, focused, hard on myself—I don't know another way to play.

After we finished with Coach K's questionnaire, Teesha and I ended up talking well into the night.

With lights out, sleep creeping over us, we argued about who would make the ultimate woman's dream team, and then argued whose dream team would win if it came to a gold medal game.

Then, just before I finally closed my eyes, I made up my mind to tell her something that I never thought I would say. I still don't know why I said it. Maybe I thought she was asleep, or maybe I thought she deserved to hear it.

"It was all ball," I whispered into the darkness. After a minute of silence, I thought she was either asleep or that she didn't know what I was talking about. I closed my eyes.

"I knew it!" she hissed. I heard her turn over in her bed. "You owe me a championship."

I smiled. "Are we besties now?"

"Goodnight, Bennett Ryan."

"'Night, Teesha Collins."

CHAPTER 19

True to her word, the next morning at breakfast Coach K quizzed us. She must have liked what she heard and saw because she let us start the semi-finals together. She also said she'd be watching us closely.

It took a little getting used to but, by the third quarter, Teesha and I started to find a groove together. I would steal the ball and send her for a fast-break layup. She would drive and kick it out to me on the three-point line. We combined for 39 out of 79 points that game—another decisive win.

I thought she would race to tell the team what I had said about her getting all-ball and not fouling me, but she never did. I guess she just needed to hear it.

In the finals, we played the host team, the Westview Wild Mustangs, and the home crowd had come out to cheer. The gym was packed and full of mostly green shirts and green painted faces. At one point during warm-up, a real horse walked through the gym and got the fans on their feet and stomping in the stands.

I spotted a lone blue face sitting near the bottom of the stands on our side. It took me a second to recognize that the grayish hair belonged to Mrs. Humphries. Like the girls had told me, she was holding a cowbell in one hand and a blue-and-white pompom in the other. It was awesome.

We had a slow first quarter and Westview jumped to a quick lead. They were a scrappy and fast team and we got into foul trouble early. Cruze had three fouls at the start of the second quarter and had to sit. Not long after, Teesha got called for her third, a borderline—could have gone both ways—loose-ball foul. She got up ready to argue the call but I got to her first.

I tried to calm her down but she angrily brushed my hand away. The Westview crowd "oooohed" like it was a major altercation. It didn't bother me. I knew she was pissed off. I would have been, too. Monty quickly stepped in and led her to the bench. She had to sit with Cruze for the rest of the half.

Going into the third quarter, we were still down: 28–38.

Coach K let Teesha start the second half; a gamble, considering her three fouls. But it was a gamble that paid off.

I hit two back-to-back threes to get things started. About a minute later, I stole the ball at the top of the key and went on a two-on-one breakaway with Teesha. I made a move on the defender and gave a no-look bounce pass to her. She went up for a layup but, with the defender recovering, made a behind-the-back pass that I caught mid-step and finished gently off the glass.

It was a perfect passing play that was so fluent it almost seemed scripted. Our bench went wild. Even the Westview crowd acknowledged how nice it was.

The whistle blew for a Westview timeout. I could hear the cowbell ringing loudly as I jogged to the bench, giving Teesha a high-five at half-court.

After that, something just clicked. We were unstoppable.

We went on a 16–0 run and ended up going into the fourth quarter up 19 points.

We won the Wild Mustang Tournament, beating the home team 75–59. I had my third ever triple-double—27 points, 12 assists, 11 steals. Teesha and I combined for 48 points and, for the first time in tournament history, they split the tournament MVP between two players.

Back on the bus ride home, we celebrated our victory with a team dance-off. Just for me, the team played "Rhythm is a Dancer," followed by a variety of 90's jock jams. I taught everyone to rap along with Tag Team's classic, "Whoomp! There It Is." Later, Cruze had a particularly hilarious dance to MC Hammer's "U Can't Touch This," and soon we had the song on repeat, with the entire team copying her moves. Even I got up and danced ... badly.

CHAPTER 20

I woke up the next morning feeling awesome. Really. Awesome. The best I had felt since we moved.

I bounded down to the kitchen to see that my mom had set out a bagel breakfast for both Prynne—who was still sleeping—and me. There was also a note that said she was out running errands and that she loved us. Underneath was a *P.S. ~nice pic!*

The *Oregonian* paper was left open at the sports section. There, in full color, was a picture of Teesha and me sharing a high-five after our passing play. We had big smiles across our sweaty faces. Mine, of course, looked goofy and crooked. The headline read: *Enemies—Frenemies—Friends?*

The article went into detail about the volatile playing history between Teesha and me. It compared our stats, our playing ability, our strengths and weaknesses, and then summed everything up by giving a rundown of our dominant tournament performance and shared MVP. It went on to say that by combining my finesse and her raw talent, the Riverside Storm should be upgraded to a Category 5 hurricane—Hurricane Beneesha—that other schools should take refuge from.

"Hurricane Beneesha?!" *Oh, no*. I already knew how much fun the team was going to have with that title.

Beside the article was a small credit-card-size paragraph—more of a side note—about how Lincoln had won their home tournament, narrowly defeating the Southlands Spartans 54–52 in the finals.

Somewhere between my question night with Teesha and the semi-final game, I had forgotten to wonder about how my old team was doing. I didn't think about them at all.

I thought about texting/calling Brooke to get the tournament details, but something stopped me and I put my phone down. Maybe I didn't need to know.

Prynne, still groggy with sleep, dragged herself into the kitchen and leaned over my shoulder. "Still can't take a photo, huh?!" She stepped back and tried to imitate my crooked half-smile.

"Hey," I laughed with her.

"You're, seriously, the least photogenic person I know." She yawned and stretched. "Where's Mom?"

"She left a note. Said she's running errands. And that she loves us."

"Good to know." Prynne put a cinnamon raison bagel—the only one left and the one I wanted, and she knew that—into the toaster. "The tournament must have gone well."

I nodded. "I got a triple-double."

"Oh. Awesome?" She raised her voice like a question.

"It is," I confirmed but didn't bother explaining why.

"So, are you and Teesha Collins, like, besties now?"

"That's what I keep saying. But no. Not even close. Coach Kelley made us sleep in the same room together. And we have to sit together, eat together, do everything together or else."

"Or else what?"

"She'll make us run or something not fun."

Prynne shook her head in disbelief. "You and this whole basketball thing are crazy to me. It's not some military dictatorship—you can do what you want."

"Never mind." I didn't expect her to understand. "So, why were you up so late?"

"I was running lines." She took her bagel out and started to spread it with cream cheese. "And I know to you that means something different but, in my world, that means I was reading lines. Like with words. For a play."

"Ha ha. Me and my basketball-playing brain get it," I said in my best dumb caveman voice. "What play? For what?" As she turned to put the cream cheese back in the fridge, I stole a half of the bagel.

"The school is ... HEY!" She reached for the bagel but I licked all of it before she could get to me. "Eewww ... fine, it's yours." With my mouth full of bagel, I smiled at my victory. "Anyway," she sat down across from me, "the school is putting on this classical storybook satire play. I don't totally understand it, but it has all the Disney princesses. I'm auditioning for Cinderella and Belle."

"Since when are you into drama?"

"Since Friday." I shook my head and rolled my eyes. "What? You don't think I can do it?"

"Actually, I think you might be perfect for it."

Prynne gave a contented smile. "You want to read lines with me later?"

"Sure, if you want to rebound for me later?" I said it, knowing what her answer would be.

"Pass—pun intended."

"I'll read with you when I get back from shoot-around."

"You will?" I nodded. Prynne looked skeptical. "Why are you in such a good mood? Is it because of that double-triple-quadruple whatever it is?"

"Triple-double, and no. I don't know why. I just am." My

phone vibrated on the table. It was a message from Matti—the picture of Teesha and me with #beneeshastormbasketball underneath it. Another text came through with a smiley emoticon that simply said:

That is so funny. Hahahahahahahaha.

Great, we have our own hash tag now.

I was in a good mood. Too good a mood. Things finally felt like they were back on track. That's why I should have known ... why I should have realized ... it wasn't going to last.

This was the calm before the storm.

CHAPTER 21

After the icebreaker tournament, the regular season began. And it started really well. We went 5 and 0, winning each game by more than 20 points—one game by a dominant 53. I had a career high—albeit a high school career—44 points that game.

More recruiting letters and phone calls from colleges and universities started to roll in—just not the one I really wanted.

Teesha and I continued to play well together. And it wasn't just in the gym.

Following Coach K's orders, we could always be found eating lunch and hanging out in the hall side by side. At first it felt forced. One of us would dutifully wait for the other outside a classroom or save a seat for the other in the change room. If we had a pregame talk or if a timeout was called, the girls would always leave the seat beside me open for Teesha and vice versa. They weren't being polite. In fact, at times they were downright pushy about putting us together. We all knew Coach K's threat of running was more than a threat, and no one wanted to run any more than we had to. After a couple of weeks, being with Teesha started to feel natural.

As forecast, the girls on the team had fun with the Hurricane Beneesha name. Cruze had the most fun, trying to come up with creative trash talk and things that rhymed with Beneesha. For the record, nothing does. But that didn't stop Cruze from trying.

"Best get out the way—Hurricane Beneesha is about to touch down."

"Have you met Beneesha? 'Cuz they're about to teachya."

"Storm warning! Hurricane Beneesha is about to unleasha."

I knew the team was going to have their fun. What I didn't count on was *#beneeshastormbasketball* becoming a thing. It went viral. Well, as viral as something can go inside a high school. Pictures taken at games started showing up on social media sights, and soon we had a mini following. Fans came to games with homemade signs and T-shirts—even Mrs. Humphries had a poster board she would wave whenever Teesha and I connected on a good play. I'd never seen anything like it.

As we headed into the winter break, I was playing the best basketball I had ever played. I was having fun.

And then this ...

Coach K entered the change room as we were getting ready for practice. We were excited about winter break and were talking about the upcoming Winter Ball–the biggest and most prestigious tournament of the year.

The week in between Christmas and New Year, sixteen of the best teams from across the state come together to battle it out for a large frosty-glass basketball trophy. The Winter Ball is my favorite tournament of the year. It's about bragging rights, and the winner usually, but not always, goes on to win the State Championship. Last year's final saw Lincoln and Riverside going into double overtime in a sold-out gym. Lincoln finally squeaked out the victory.

We were on opposite sides of the draw and, if things went the same way this year, it would not only be the match-up that everyone wanted, it would also be the first time I would get to face my old team.

Coach K never came into the change room before practice, ever. The troubled look on her face confirmed that something was wrong.

"Bennett, can you come to my office?"

As I walked out, a few of the girls started to "ooooh," but when Teesha gave a stern look and a shake of the head, they stopped abruptly.

Walking up to the office, I ran into Matti on the stairs. Her eyes were red from tears. "Matti? What's ..." She sprinted down the stairs before I could finish. That's when I knew that something was really wrong.

A familiar and uneasy feeling started to crawl through me. My heart started to thump heavily and it became hard for me to breathe. I had felt this before, and I grabbed hold of the railing to steady myself.

The night the officers—my dad's colleagues and friends—knocked on the door to tell us about the accident is the worst memory I have. I was usually in bed by that time, but it was New Year's Eve, and my mom had let Prynne and me stay up late to watch the countdown and fireworks. It was strange for someone to be knocking that late, but not that strange, because lots of people in the neighborhood were out in the streets and having house parties. I left my sister on the couch watching a holiday movie and went into the kitchen to get a refill of sparkling apple juice, our champagne substitute. I stopped in the hallway when I heard the mumbling of voices at the door. I couldn't hear the words—it was the tone that stopped me, and it was the look on their faces and my mom's when she turned and saw me, that made me realize something awful had happened to my dad, and that life as I knew it would never be the same.

A similar dread was coming over me now. First Coach K's ominous, "Bennett, can you come to my office?" And then the look and tears on Matti's face. My mind went to the worst-case scenarios. *My Mom? Prynne?*

My rational mind should have known that nothing had happened to either of them. I had just seen my mom in the hall on the way to practice. She smiled and waved at me. I knew that Prynne was in the drama room, rehearsing for the play. After her audition, the drama teacher said she was a natural for the stage and awarded her the role of Belle for the school production—a big deal, according to Prynne. So, rationally, I should have realized that nothing was wrong, but panic took hold and irrational thoughts started to cloud my mind.

With shaky legs, I barely made it up the stairs and down the hall.

"Close the door," Coach K said, looking at her computer. Then, looking up to see my pale face, "Bennett?! Are you okay?"

"Just tell me what happened. Is it my mom? My sister? Who?"

"What?" she asked, confused. Quickly realizing what I must be thinking, she waved her hands in the air. "Oh, God. Nothing like that. Nothing has happened to anyone. Everything is fine. Well, not everything."

I let out a sigh of relief and melted into a chair. My heart was still beating hard and fast. "I thought ... I thought ..."

"It's okay," Coach K said reassuringly.

When my breathing returned to normal, I sat straight and

wiped my sweaty hands on my shorts. "What's going on?"

"I'm just going to cut right to it. A petition has been filed against us. It involves you ... playing for Riverside."

"What?"

"It appears that Coach Paige, over at Lincoln, has a problem with you playing for Riverside. He's filed a petition with the League, accusing Riverside of foul play. Specifically, he's accusing the school of giving your mother the principal position on the condition that you would come and play for the school."

"WHAT?" I jumped out of the chair.

"I know," Coach K said calmly. "It's bullshit."

"So ... they're saying that my mom would have only got the job if I came to Riverside?"

"In a nutshell."

"That's ridiculous. That's not even ... I didn't even want to come here." I said it harshly, but I didn't mean it the way it must have sounded. Even though it was the truth. "What does this mean?"

Coach K let out a defeated huff of breath. "The League and Commissioner are going to investigate the allegations. I don't think they'll find anything to substantiate the claim. The problem is that it could take a while. In the meantime, we're going to explore our options."

"What does any of that even mean?"

"It means ..." she paused.

Oh, no. I already know what it means. Don't say it. Don't say it.

"You can't play."

I fell back into the chair like someone had pushed me down.

"I'm sorry, Bennett. It's just until they can investigate and figure this mess out. I don't know how long it's going to take and ..."

"What happens if they think that Coach Paige is right?"

"That won't happen."

"But what if it does?"

"Then you can't play. And we have to forfeit all the games that we've won so far."

"I don't understand. Can they even do this?"

"They can and they have. There are really strict rules about players switching teams during their senior years. Only a few exceptions can be made. Moving out of district is one of them, but if the League thinks that we got you to come here by giving your mom a job, or that she felt coerced to pull you here to accept the job ..."

"This is so stupid. Why would I come here after we beat you in last year's final? This is the team that I grew up hating ... that hates me! It doesn't even make sense."

"It doesn't have to. It has nothing to do with sport or you. It's purely political." Her words came out bitterly. "Like I said,

I think it's bullshit. And I think we'll beat this. But until we can figure this out, and believe me, this is the League's decision and not mine, you are officially suspended from play. You're not even allowed to practice with us or sit on the bench during a game. I'm sorry."

This can't be real. This can't be happening.

The heaviness I had felt in my chest earlier came back and uncontainable tears started to stream down my face. With my elbows on my knees and my head in my hands, I started to sob. I heard Coach K get up and walk around the desk. She put a hand on my shoulder.

"If you want to stay here for a few minutes, I can tell the team, or you can, or we can do it together ..."

"I'll stay here."

She gave a consoling squeeze of my shoulder. "Okay."

I was still crying when I heard the door to her office open and then click shut. Knowing I was alone, I let all of my emotions out. Actually I didn't "let" anything out. The tears were coming out whether I let them or not. And they came—hot, fast, and uncontrollably. I kicked the desk in anger. Then I got up and punched a wall, which hurt—a lot. But I did it again anyway.

How could they do this to me? My old coach? My old team? My old friends? I felt betrayed. Angry. Devastated. But mostly angry.

I looked out the window and saw the team huddled in a semi-circle around Coach K. I could see their confused and questioning expressions, and I knew she was delivering the news. All at once, their heads looked up in my direction and I quickly ducked, not wanting them to see my puffy tear-filled face.

After a few minutes of feeling sorry for myself, I got up, opened the office door, and punched the wall one last time on my way out.

I had walked up to the office feeling like someone I loved was dead or injured. When I left, I felt the same way.

CHAPTER

22

Principal mom was in the hallway when I left the change room. I was in no mood to talk or to see her, and she knew it.

Her hands were open in front of her like she was approaching a wild animal. "Bennett, I just heard."

"Mom, I just wanna go." I turned my head so she couldn't see how puffy my eyes were.

"Come to my office so we can talk about this."

"I don't want to go to your office!" I yelled.

"Honey, calm down. We'll fight this."

"I can't play basketball. They won't let me play ..." More tears came.

"It won't be for long. They don't have any proof. You know that none of it is true. I would never ..."

"It doesn't matter," I snapped. "It's still your fault. None

— 203 —

of this would have happened if you hadn't taken this stupid job. I would still be Lincoln. I would still be playing basketball. I would still be happy. I hate you."

My mom stepped back like I had slapped her.

I wanted to take it back the second it slipped out. But I didn't. Instead I turned and jogged toward the doors.

"Where are you going?"

"Nowhere."

"Bennett?" I didn't answer. "Bennett, don't leave angry. Bennett ..."

I could still hear her calling my name as the doors shut.

I wasn't "allowed" to be at practice and I definitely didn't feel like going home, so I got in my car and drove.

My phone vibrated wildly in my gym bag. There was a stack of missed calls and text messages from my mom and sister, desperately trying to get hold of me. I had told my mom I hated her, and I had broken the cardinal family rule and left angry without saying, "I love you." A part of me felt awful and wanted to turn around and apologize, but a larger part was still stubbornly fuming and wanted my mom to feel bad.

I turned my phone off and kept driving.

Thoughts ran through my mind, and I couldn't help but wonder if there was any truth to the allegations. She said there wasn't, and I didn't want to believe that she could sell me out like that. But she had always wanted to be a principal. *Would she have done this?*

It was no secret that she wasn't a fan of Coach Paige, and she'd shut down any idea or plan I had of staying near Lincoln. *Had she done this?*

She has never understood how important basketball is to me. Could she really have done this?

Eventually, my anger turned to another direction—where it belonged in the first place—Coach Paige. He had always been a hard ass. He was intense and he liked to win.

He didn't just like to win, he liked to destroy.

Other coaches in the league didn't really like him. In fact, nobody really liked our team.

We used to get evil glares from other teams when we arrived for a game or tournament. Some would say—many on Riverside have said—that we were arrogant, cocky bitches. I say: we were good, we were winners, and we knew it ... okay, we might have been arrogant, cocky bitches—but that's who we were. Players either hated us or they wanted to be us. We were "*that*" team.

Everybody knows "*that*" team.

At the time, I knew other teams didn't like us, but I didn't know they full-out hated us. You don't question much when you're winning.

It's a whole different view from the outside looking in.

Coach Paige used to tell us that basketball wasn't a popularity contest, it was just a contest—it was just basketball. Winners weren't winners because people liked them; they were winners because they won, period. His coaching philosophy—*winning isn't enough; records need to be shattered and names need to be recorded.*

With last year's season, we had shattered records: most points in one game—119; largest score differential—our victory over Saint Mary's 119–21 (Coach Paige was upset and didn't talk to us after the game because we didn't win by an even 100); most three-point field goals in one game—17. And it was an undefeated season.

Continuing from last season, Lincoln was currently on an unbeaten streak of 49 wins. The state record was 76, set by Southlands back in the 80's. I knew that Coach Paige had his sights on breaking that record. Only a few teams stood in his way, and Riverside was by far Lincoln's biggest challenge.

"What an asshole!" I yelled and hit the steering wheel in frustration. *How could Coach Paige do this to me?* I felt so betrayed. This wasn't about basketball. This was about winning, about Lincoln beating Riverside and continuing their unbeaten streak. I knew Coach Paige was capable of being a jerk, but I didn't think he was capable of this.

I kept driving, not realizing where I was going until—two hours later—I pulled in through the entrance to the cemetery.

The sun was setting and a light rain started to fall as I parked the car. I'd left the school so fast that I hadn't changed out of my shorts and reversible jersey. My breath escaped in white puffs and goose bumps jumped up all over my arms and legs.

I'm not sure what had pulled me here. I'm not particularly religious. God (or whoever/whatever) and I have had a rocky relationship since my dad's death, and I'm not sure where I stand on heaven and the whole spirit thing. Sometimes, I think I see or feel him in the gym, watching from the stands, but then I tell myself it's just wishful thinking.

I only come to his gravesite with my mom and Prynne once a year on his birthday. My mom and sister come every New Year's Eve, but I can never bring myself to join them. It isn't here where I feel closest to him, anyway.

My dad was the first person who told me that I could go far with basketball. And because I thought that my dad could do no wrong, I believed him. But there was a time, right around his death, when, for some reason, I wanted to hang out with my friends and go to the mall more than I wanted to be in the gym. I still can't explain why.

The day he died, he had asked me if I wanted to go to the gym and shoot around. I said no, but he didn't give up. He asked again, trying to goad me by saying I couldn't take him in a game of H-O-R-S-E. I said no again. I had better things to do, like shopping and catching a matinee of the latest Hollywood blockbuster with my friends.

He was never the kind of intense parent who pressures their kids to be dedicated and play all the time. He understood that I wanted to be a teenager and do regular teenage things. I think he always knew I would eventually return to the gym when I was ready. He wasn't mad that I didn't go with him, but I do think (even though my mom has told me countless times that I'm wrong) that he was disappointed. I went to the movies and he went to shoot around without me. That was the last time I ever saw him.

I turned my phone on and texted my mom:

Don't worry. I'm fine. I'm visiting Dad. I'll be home soon. I'm sorry. I love you.

She texted back instantly:

I'm sorry, too. We'll figure this out, I promise. Dinner will be ready when you get home. I LOVE YOU.

The rain started to fall harder. I tucked my hands under my arms for warmth. "Dad ..." I looked around to make sure no one else was around or listening. It felt strange to be talking out loud to no one ... to myself ... to him.

"Dad, if you are there, if you are listening ... you probably already know they won't let me play ..." and then it was like he responded. Not really, because that would be weird, but with those words—*they won't let me play*—a memory that I had long tucked away in the place where memories go was triggered.

I was ten, I think. My dad and our family were stationed on the east coast somewhere. I wanted to join a pick-up game on an outdoor court a couple of blocks from our house. I came home crying and when my dad, who was cutting the front lawn, saw me, he came running and asked what had happened.

"They won't let me play," I said through tears.

In retrospect, I was way too young, and the boys were way too old and big for me to play with, but my dad never mentioned any of that. Instead he said, "First of all, Sweetie, those boys are just afraid a girl will show them up. Secondly, the only person who can stop you from playing is you."

"What do you mean? They won't let me on the court," I sniffed.

"Do you have a ball?"

I showed him the one in my hands. "Yes."

"And do we have a driveway?"

"Yes," I said, confused.

"Well then, I think you're the only one who is saying you can't play."

"But ... but ..."

"No buts. There's always a way to get in the game."

He left the lawnmower in the middle of the yard and took me to buy a hoop for the driveway. In less than an hour we had it up, and he had even painted a regulation key on the ground.

Then I said I didn't have anyone to play against, and he responded, "What do you mean? You're playing against the best in the world." He stood up and pointed under the basket. "I see Jordan, Johnson, Bird ..."

"Swoopes," I interrupted him. "Lobo, Leslie, and Staley?"

"Absolutely, them, too." He leaned down and whispered, "Do you think we can take them all?" I nodded enthusiastically.

That day I played with my dad against my heroes ... correction, I played with my hero.

I was no longer ten, and I couldn't just imagine a dream team to play with, but my dad was right then and he was right now—I was the only one who could stop myself from playing. I could sit back and feel sorry for myself, or I could find a way to get in the game.

"Thanks, Dad."

CHAPTER

23

My mom and Coach K were optimistic that things would be resolved quickly. I'm not sure what "quickly" means to them, but we have different ideas concerning the matter.

Quickly to me meant that I should have been playing basketball the day after this whole thing started. But three days later, I still wasn't playing, and we had our final league game before the winter break against Westview. Of all the games for me to miss ...

We'd already beaten Westview in their own tournament. Since then we had gotten more solid, but so had they. Of the teams in our league, they were our toughest matchup. Going into this game, we were both undefeated; the winner would undoubtedly, barring any shocking upset, go on to win the league. The team who came first in the league had an easier draw going into playoffs, but in the long run, it was more about bragging rights than anything else.

Since the announcement about the allegations and my suspension, the team had kind of avoided me. They didn't ignore me, and they weren't mean or anything, but I felt like they were giving me awkward glances and keeping their distance, almost like my suspension was contagious and they could catch it next. I'd witnessed this kind of behavior before.

Two summers ago, I played on a select team. During one of our tournaments away, our starting point guard went down in a heap of tears and screams, grabbing her knee. It turned out to be what everyone suspected and everyone dreaded—the ACL. We were all concerned for her, but hardly any of the players, myself included, got close to her. Obviously, we all understood that a torn ACL was not contagious. But being around her, with her knee elevated and wrapped in ice, was a reminder of our own vulnerability, and that, in an instant, basketball could be taken away.

I wasn't allowed to be on the bench with the team, but there was no rule against my being in the locker room before the game. This was still my team and I was still a captain.

When I opened the door, I could hear Teesha's voice talking loudly over everyone else ... about me. I stood hidden behind the wall and listened in.

"We don't need Bennett. We were a team long before she came around and we're still a team now. Was she on our team last year when we went all the way to the state championship final?"

"No," Tats responded. "She was on the team that beat us." There was a grumbling of agreement from the group.

"So what?!"

"So, she's good. We need her."

"No, we don't!" Teesha barked. "We can win without her. We don't need her."

"T-time's right," I said, walking around the corner. In the middle of tying their shoes or putting their hair up, everybody looked at me and froze. Teesha's eyes widened like I had caught her ... well, like I had caught her talking behind my back, which I had. As much as it hurt to hear, I wasn't mad.

"She's right," I said again. "You've always been a good team. I used to hate playing against you. Tats, driving the lane and pulling up for an easy two, or kicking the ball out for a wide-open three. Oaks and Monty under the hoop, like two gigantic ogres with their ..."

"Ogres?!" Oaks and Monty erupted at the same time.

"Sorry," I shrugged. "That's the first thing that came to mind. It was like a gauntlet just getting to the hoop, and then you two were there, with your long arms and big hands, always stuffing me ..."

"Stuffing you like a Thanksgiving turkey!" Cruze chimed in and players giggled.

"And listening to Cruze's super-annoying trash talk before and after she stripped me of the ball." The laughter continued and the mood lightened. "And Teesha." She looked at me, worried what I was about to say. "You were the worst. I hated playing against you the most. You just never let up. I thought you were a mega bitch."

"Really?" Teesha asked with a surprised smile.

"You thought I was, too."

"Still do." She winked sarcastically ... I'm pretty sure it was sarcasm.

I looked over the team. "I absolutely hated playing against you, and that's why I love playing with you. This is a good team, a really good team, and you definitely do not need me to beat Westview."

"What's going on in here?" Coach K walked in with her whiteboard and marker.

Tats stood up and gave me a hard pat on the back. "Oh, Beaner is just giving us her 'win one for the Gimper' speech." Everyone started to laugh. "What?" she asked confused.

Coach K shook her head. Still laughing, she replied, "It's Gipper, not Gimper."

Tats sat back down and waved a hand in the air. "Whatever."

After Coach K gave a proper pregame talk, I ventured up to her office to watch the game with Matti. I couldn't be on the bench, and I didn't feel much like being in the gym—too many sympathy stares and glares coming my way.

The same sports writer who had written the "Beneesha" article got wind of the petition and my suspension, and called the house for a statement. I was in the middle of saying that I only want to play basketball, when my mom grabbed the phone, simply said, "No comment," and then hung up. Because this was an official legal matter, I wasn't allowed to talk to the press.

A legal matter? Talk to the press? This whole thing was being blown way out of proportion and starting to make me feel like it wasn't just going to "blow over."

With the article, the entire basketball world—my world—knew what was going on. I was getting sympathy text messages, Facebook posts, and there was even a new hash tag: *#savebeneeshabasketball*. The only person/people I hadn't heard anything from was Brooke/my old team—not really a surprise.

"Hey Bennett—double N, double T!" Matti opened Coach K's office door and eagerly waved at me.

"Hey Matti—double T with an I and no E."

She was wearing an all blue Riverside Storm tracksuit with her name stitched on the arm.

"I don't think I've seen you in that before."

"Really?" She looked confused. "I always wear it on game days."

At that moment, I realized that besides her face in the window at home games, I never saw Matti during a game day. Truth was, since the season had started, I hadn't seen Matti much at all.

When I came in, she handed me a bag of popcorn, closed the door, and then jumped on the couch. She had her own bag of popcorn and a bottle of orange juice on the windowsill. She even had her own coaching board and erasable marker. I noticed a very particular manner in which she carefully set her popcorn and juice—with the labels facing her. She propped the coaching board next to her.

"I saved you a seat. But try not to bump my board."

I nodded and knelt on the couch like she was, leaning with my elbows on the back looking out the window.

Warm-up was just finishing. I could barely hear the thump of the music but, in the gym, I knew how loud it was. "Why is it so quiet in here?"

"My mom had them soundproof the room for me."

"Oh." I couldn't help but stare at Matti. I'd never seen anyone look so intense when watching a warm-up. She was staring at Westview while they shot pull-up jumpers, keeping her eyes on them while she talked to me.

"Are you sad that you're not playing? Because I am."

"I'm a little sad ... a lot sad."

"I don't get it. My mom's tried to explain it to me but I just don't get it."

"I don't get it, either."

She mumbled something, sat back from the window, and wrote something on the whiteboard. "Number ten, Sage Walsh, is shooting eighty-four percent right now."

I looked down at the court and found Sage. I knew who she was—scrappy as hell and Westview's best player. She had a weird outside shot that almost looked two-handed; by all accounts, it was a shooting form that shouldn't work as well as it did. What bothered me the most about her was her nail length. She kept them painted green to match the team colors and just long enough to leave little red scratches on her check's forearms—something I knew firsthand. How Sage played, so went the team. And she looked focused and ready for a fight.

"What else do you see?" I asked Matti with genuine curiosity.

"Number fourteen, Grace Lee, she went five for five from the three-point line last week against Ellington."

"Really?"

Matti nodded. "If they play a five-out tonight, we could be in trouble."

"You think they'll play a five-out?"

"Against us, with you out and Monty and Oaks in the middle, I would. My mom doesn't think they will, but she said she'd watch for it. They'll also come out with a full-court press."

"We destroyed it last time."

"With you," Matti looked at me. "But with Teesha and Cruze, they'll press. Plus, they know their best defense is in the full court. They don't have an answer for Monty and Oaks but, if they keep the ball on the outside and force us to shoot, they might beat us."

"You really think so?"

"Yep," Matti said matter-of-factly.

"Huh." I was mesmerized by her pregame analysis.

The whistle blew and the teams came in for their huddles. I could imagine what Coach K was saying: Come out fast, box out, talk on D ... the usual. I ached to be down there, ready to yell out "*STORM!*" with the team.

Almost as if she knew what I was thinking, Matti turned to me. "I know you'd rather be playing, but I'm happy you're here watching the game with me."

"Thanks, Matti—me, too ..."

"Just don't talk a lot, okay?" She looked back out the window. "I have to focus."

"Okay."

The teams cheered and took to the court.

As the ref was about to toss the jump ball, I felt a set of eyes on me and scanned the crowd. Up at the top of the stands, across the gym, Coach Paige was sitting with a clipboard, scouting the game, and he was staring straight at me. I clenched my jaw and tried to keep my focus on the game.

Like they had in our first game, Westview jumped out to an early lead. Matti had been right. They came out with a stifling full-court press that had Cruze, Tats, and Teesha struggling to get over the half-court line. We had eight turnovers in the first quarter. Coach K was jumping wildly on the sidelines.

"Pushing left ... giving her that ball and pushing Teesha left every time. Double team in the corner." Matti was mumbling to herself what she was seeing. Every now and then, she scrolled something on the whiteboard. I got the sense that this was how she watched every game.

I looked down and saw what Matti was seeing. After we inbounded the ball, the defense pressured Cruze but left Teesha open to get the ball. Then they pushed Teesha left and led her into a double, sometimes a triple team. Teesha was one of the best dribblers I had ever seen, but her skills also made her cocky and too proud to give up the ball ... and Westview was taking advantage. I could see Teesha getting frustrated, and I knew it meant that silly fouls were coming.

Sure enough, at the start of the second quarter, Teesha picked up two quick fouls, for a total of three, and was subbed off.

Watching Westview on offense, Matti continued to mumble. "Don't leave her open ... don't leave her ..." Sage Walsh drained a three. "I told you not to leave her open." Matti shook her head in disappointment. Down on the court, her mom was doing the same thing.

Like Matti had said, Westview had gone to a five-out offense, pulling Monty and Oaks out of the key and into the perimeter. Oaks was a little faster and more comfortable than Monty playing out, but neither was faster than their smaller checks, who drove by every chance they got. It was killing me to watch and not be in there playing.

Matti leaned back. "We should go to a three-two zone."

"Your mom hates zones."

"I know. But she also hates losing. A three-two would be more effective against Westview."

The buzzer finally signaled for halftime: Riverside 18, Westview 35—our lowest halftime score this season.

I got up to join the team for the halftime talk. "Why don't you come with me?"

Matti shook her head. "No, thanks. I'd rather stay here."

"But your mom should hear some of the stuff you've told me. The whole team should hear it."

Matti's eyes widened in nervous terror. "No way. They don't care what I have to say."

"I do."

Matti continued to shake her head. "No. I don't want to."

"Fine ... but I'm going to tell your mom we should go to a two-three and ..."

"No! Not a two-three ... a three-two."

"Well, you better come, because I'm probably going to get it all wrong."

Matti sat on the couch, biting her lip. "You'll stand beside me?"

"Right beside you."

She thought for a few seconds, looking down at her coaching board. "Okay. But only for a minute."

We snuck into the locker room and stood at the back of the room, listening to Coach K berating the team. She was digging into Teesha for losing her cool and picking up dumb fouls. As Coach K started talking about the second-half strategy, I kept looking at Matti and nudging her to step in and say something, but she just kept shaking her head and mouthing the word, "No."

The halftime talk was over quickly and the team put their hands in for a cheer.

Storm!

As everyone filed out, Coach K stopped at us. She looked questioningly at Matti and then me. "Everything all right?"

I looked at Matti and raised my eyebrows, trying to signal for her to say something.

"I have to get out on the court so ..."

"Matti thinks we should go to a three-two zone," I blurted out. "That, and you can't let Teesha bring the ball up. It's what they want. You should use her as a distraction but send it back to Cruze."

"So you're a coach now?"

"No ... but Matti is. She sees a lot." I looked at Matti. "What is Sage Walsh's shooting percentage right now?"

"For the game? Seventy-one. And I don't think you should use Teesha as a distraction. I think you should pull Monty up and use her height to break the zone. Throw it to Monty, have Teesha on the left, and send Cruze running up the right."

Coach K was about to step in and say something, but she stopped and thought about Matti's suggestion. "Interesting." The buzzer went and Matti dropped her board to cover her ears. "You better get back to the office. I'll think about the zone. Bennett, how are you doing?"

"I'd rather be in the game."

"You and me both."

Coach K ran out the door and Matti and I made our way back to the office.

"Bennett?" A familiar voice made me freeze in the hallway.

"Isn't that your old coach?" Matti asked loudly.

"Yes," I replied coldly.

Coach Paige continued toward me. Teams cheered in the gym; there was a whistle, yelling ... the game was back on.

"How are you doing, Bennett?"

Like you care. "I'm good." I wanted to run ... or punch him in the face. Maybe punch him in the face and then run.

"Who's your friend?" He looked at Matti.

"I'm Matti, double T with an I and no E. And you're Coach Paige of the Lincoln Lady Lions. You're a jerk."

I choked on a laugh.

Coach Paige was not amused. "Is that what the kids are saying about me these days?"

"No. My mom said it." There was a loud cheer and a sharp whistle. Matti looked apprehensive. "Should I stay with you?"

"No, it's okay. Go. I'll be up in a second." Matti sprinted up the stairs like she was running from a fire.

"I have to say I'm impressed with how well you've adjusted here."

"Impressed or scared?" He smirked. "What do you want?" I snapped.

"Whoa. You go to Riverside and now you don't like me?"

"No. You filed a petition so I can't play basketball and NOW I don't like you."

"Look, I just came to say hi, and to let you to know that what's going on isn't personal. I just want to make sure things are fair."

"Isn't pers ... You didn't come to say hi, you came to scout the game. And fair?! Are you for real? I can't play basketball because of YOU."

"You, your mother, and Riverside are the reasons you can't play basketball. Rules are rules."

I shook my head in disbelief. "I used to think you were a good coach." I paused. "All you care about is winning. Matti's right, you're a jerk. And you're a liar. You know that none of those allegations are true."

"Is that what your mom said?" He crossed his arms. "You should ask her if they talked about you during the interview, because I have it on good authority that they did."

"My mom didn't get this job because of me. And you know that I didn't want to come here, but now that I am here ... I love it. And I can't wait to take you down."

"If you play again."

That was a low blow. "They don't need me to beat Lincoln. But I hope I'm on the court, because I want a shot to play against you." I started to walk away.

"I hope this gets sorted out, too, and soon, for your sake. I heard that Stanford will be scouting at the Winter Ball."

I stopped. My fists and jaw clenched. "I'll see you on the court."

"We'll see."

Reeling from the exchange with Coach Paige, I went back to the office and joined Matti. With him sitting in the stands, every now and then glancing and smiling my way, it was difficult to focus on the game.

Coach K made some adjustments and we did better against their full-court press. Teesha picked up a fourth foul and, letting her temper get the better of her, eventually a fifth, leaving the game with seven minutes left to go. Sage Walsh took advantage and got fourteen points in the fourth quarter. She had a game-high 30 points, while we had a game-high 26 turnovers.

When the final buzzer went, it was Riverside 49 and Westview 71.

"If it makes you feel any better," Matti said, "we probably would have lost with you in the game, too."

It didn't make me feel better.

CHAPTER 24

The night of our Westview loss, I confronted my mom about what Coach Paige had said.

"Mom, be honest with me. Did your getting the job have anything, *anything*, to do with my going to Riverside?" I expected her to just say no—I was sure (semi-sure) it was just a bluff from Coach Paige—but instead she hesitated. "Mom?"

She shuffled a stack of papers on the table. "I didn't think it did, but now I'm not so sure."

"What do you mean?"

"We've been going through our case and there was a conversation after I got the job ... it was a follow-up interview ... a formality." She drank a sip of wine. I noticed half the bottle was empty—a bad sign.

"And?"

"We did talk about you—and Prynne. It was just a light conversation about the family and how I thought you girls would adjust here. I didn't think anything of it, and I have no idea how Lincoln knows about it."

"But they still don't have anything."

She took another sip. "They might." I waited for her to continue. "We did talk about you, about your final game. Someone casually asked if I thought you would play for Riverside, given the rivalry. I said, of course you would. That basketball means more to you than a rivalry. It means everything to you. Then someone commented that maybe this would be Riverside's year. And that's all."

"But they didn't hire you because of me!?"

"Honestly, I don't know what to think anymore."

"So what happens now?"

"The case is going before the basketball commission in the first week of January. There'll be a decision that same week."

"The first week of ... that means I'm missing the Winter Ball."

"I'm sorry, Sweetie. I know what this means to you ..."

I stormed off—mad at Coach Paige, mad at my mom, mad at basketball, mad at the world.

CHAPTER 25

On the last day of school before winter break, while everyone was joyfully sucking on candy canes and excitedly talking about their holiday plans, I was a "mopey asshole"—an exact quote from my sister Prynne. And she wasn't far off. My attitude would have scared away the Grinch. I had convinced myself that this was going to be the worst Christmas ever, and I was determined to take others down with me.

When the final bell went, I took my "mopey asshole" self into the gym and started dribbling and shooting. Basketball workouts usually made me feel better. But no matter how much I dribbled, or how many shots I hit, this one didn't.

I stayed in the gym until it was well after dark and the janitor came in to kick me out.

As I was driving home, still feeling mopey but a little less like an asshole, the headlights of my car picked up a weird wet lump on the side of the road. It was raining and hard to see but, as I got closer, I realized it was a person struggling to carry three massive recycling bags ... and then I realized I recognized the lump–Cruze.

I drove by, pulled the car over, and hopped out. "Cruze?"

"Shit." She dropped the bags. "It's you, Beaner. I thought someone was coming to snatch me."

"Snatch you?" I laughed. "If they could catch you."

"You know it," she said proudly.

"What are you doing?" The rain was starting to come down harder.

"Nothing."

"Do you want a ride somewhere?"

"No. I'm good."

She was soaked and looked anything but good. I popped the trunk open. "Cruze, get in the car."

I could see her thinking about saying no, so I grabbed two bags from her and threw them in. She reluctantly stuffed the last one in and got into the front seat.

"How come you're out here so late?" she asked me.

"Coming back from the gym. I needed a workout."

"You mean you needed to work it out?"

"Something like that. What are you doing? What's with the

recycling? For a second I thought you were one of Santa's elves, carrying bags of presents around."

"An elf?"

"Well, you are the same size ..."

She punched me. "Does an elf hit like that?"

"Ouch! Maybe a mean one," I said rubbing my sore arm. Cruze got quiet. For a minute, all we could hear was the rain and the windshield wipers.

"Can you take me to the grocery store?"

"Sure."

I took Cruze to the nearest store and helped her unload and sort the bags of recycling. It became clear, by how well the workers in the store knew her, that this was a regular routine. Then I remembered the three bags of recycling that Matti always left behind the container, and everything started to make sense.

Cruze collected the money, bought some milk, eggs, and cereal with it. She kept telling me that I could leave at any time but, when it became evident that I wasn't going anywhere, she got back in the car and gave me directions to where she lived.

She was usually full of energy and spunky one-liners but, in the car, she seemed reserved. "Don't tell anyone about this, okay?"

"I won't."

"I mean, some already know about it. It's not a secret but, like, don't talk about it."

"Cruze, I promise."

"Okay," she said, relieved.

We drove away from the main suburb and then down a dirt road that took us to an area with small dilapidated houses and rusted trailers, a part of the city I had never been before.

"You can drop me off here." She motioned to a tiny yellowish house decorated with a few strands of red Christmas lights. There was a beat-up truck propped up on cement blocks in the driveway.

"You walk all the way here?" I asked in disbelief.

"Why do you think I can run so fast?" she smiled. "Gotta be quick or the wolves will get me." My smile faded. "Just kidding." She punched me again. "They've only come at me once."

There was a wrinkled face peering out the window at us. "Who's that?"

"Oh, no. Well, you're going to have to come in now. That's my *abuelita*, and if you don't come in, she's going to think that I got a ride from a pedophile. And even if I can convince her it's you, she'll be mad that I didn't invite you in. Can you come in for a minute?"

I looked at the time. My mom would be starting to wonder where I was. Soon the texts would come. "Sure," I said, and quickly texted my mom, telling her where I was and that I'd be home later.

Walking into Cruze's house was an assault on the senses. As soon as the door opened, little voices yelled, "Cee Cee," and five tiny bodies came bounding at the door like little Mexican jumping beans. The smell of baking and cinnamon was intoxicating. A mini version of Cruze leaped into Cruze's arms and kissed her on the cheek. In the room we were standing in, there was a sparse Charlie Brown tree covered in lights. On the wall behind it, there was a cross, a picture of the Virgin Mary, and a framed photo of Cruze playing basketball, with her second-place state medal hanging beside it.

A miniature wrinkled and gray-haired woman—I assumed Cruze's abuelita—walked into the room, and there was an exchange of rapid talking that, with my few years of high school Spanish, I had no hope of translating. She kissed Cruze on both cheeks and then immediately came at me to do the same. I had to lean way over to accept.

"Beaner, this is my abuelita. Abuelita, this is Bennett."

"*Hola,*" I smiled.

Cruze went back to speaking Spanish. There was a quick exchange between the two, and then the rest of the kids still standing around us started to get excited and speak Spanish, too.

"Ay, no. Abuelita!" Cruze rolled her eyes, but the finality in the way that her abuelita moved her hand in the air told me that whatever the exchange, Cruze had lost. She rolled her eyes and looked at me. "My abuelita wants you to stay for dinner. Beaner, when it comes to Abuelita, you don't really have a choice."

"Does dinner have anything to do with the cinnamon I smell?"

"Those are Abuelita's *empanadas*!" the mini-Cruze spoke up. "They're soooo good."

"They are," Cruze agreed.

"I'm in," I said to a roar of cheering.

Cruze pointed to a girl at her hip. "Beaner, these little minions are Amelia, Miguel, Josephina, Diego, and ..." she hugged the mini-Cruze in her arms ... "I forget who you are."

"Cee Cee," the littlest one laughed, "Soy Mila."

"Oh, right, Mila," she winked. "These are my brothers and sisters."

"Wow. I thought one sister was enough."

"One sister is enough," she joked.

"Hey!!" The group erupted. It was obvious by the way they looked up to her, literally and figuratively, that they adored their big sister.

"*Ella es giganta,*" Mila said to Cruze. The others laughed.

"She said ..."

"I got that one. She thinks I'm a giant."

They all laughed.

"Sorry," Cruze apologized. "I don't have a lot of guests come over. Watch yourself; they love to play pranks."

"Oh, so they're mini-you's."

"In every way ... I mean it, though. Watch yourself."

Over dinner, I was bombarded with questions about basketball, and a few asked for my autograph.

"Sorry," Cruze said. "They've seen your picture in the paper and think you're some kind of superstar."

"Cruze is the superstar," I countered. "I've never seen anyone play defense like your sister." I was waiting for Cruze to back me up with some quick-witted comment of her own but, in front of her family, she turned red and went quiet.

Even with Cruze's warning and my vigilant eye, someone—I think it was a team effort—managed to put some extra hot sauce in my rice when I wasn't looking. A whole glass of milk couldn't cool the fire in my mouth. At least everyone, including Abuelita, got a good laugh.

I never got to meet Cruze's parents because they were working the night shift at a packaging factory. It was a second job for both of them. Amelia said it was their favorite because they got to work together.

The house only had one bathroom and two bedrooms. I didn't ask where they all slept, but blankets folded up on the couches and a stack of Cruze's textbooks in the living room told me that she and at least one other slept in there. With the kitchen table just barely able to fit everyone around it, it was hard for me to imagine how everyone lived in this one little house. Prynne and I argued over the bathroom constantly, and we only had to share it with each other.

Despite the tight space, the entire family seemed happy. I had played against Cruze for years, been teammates with her for over two months, and only now was I learning about who she really was.

At the end of night, with my tummy full of food and arms full of empanadas to take home—I objected; Abuelita insisted—Cruze walked me to my car.

"Thanks for the ride ... and for staying for dinner."

"Are you kidding?" I said. "I loved it. Your family is ..."

"A handful?!"

"Awesome."

"They can be kinda awesome." Cruze smiled and looked back at the house. Five little faces were spying on us from the window.

"How come they're never at a game?" I asked.

"With my parents working ... it's hard for them to come."

"Do you walk home all the time?"

"Not always. I can usually hitch a ride from some stranger passing by." She waited for the look of horror on my face. "I'm kidding, Beaner."

"Okay, well, I can drive you home from now on."

"Beaner, I don't need your pity. My family is doing just fine."

"It's not pity ..."

"Besides, you might not even be on the team anymore ... sorry, I know it's not funny. If I were you, I'd be going *loco*. I don't know what I'd do without basketball. I'd have to be around this craziness all the time."

"I don't know how you *do* do it. Where do you even study?"

"At school, before or after practice."

"Is this why you usually shower at school?" She nodded. Even though the school had showers, no one really used them except Cruze. I shouldn't have asked the next question, but curiosity got the better of me. "Is your family ... are you all ..."

She laughed. "We swam over the Rio Grande. And I only lost one sibling."

It was obvious she was messing with me.

"Both my parents are legal; me and all of my brothers and sisters were born here. My Abuelita ... well, I'd like to see the *migra* try and take her away."

"Me, too."

We hugged, wished each other a Merry Christmas, and I left ... feeling nothing like the mopey asshole I had been for the past few days.

CHAPTER 26

The Christmas after my dad died, my mom started a tradition that every year we would choose a charity or help out a family in need. Yes, it was a way of giving back, but it was also a way of helping us focus on something other than the fact that we were down a family member.

After I brought back the empanadas and told my mom and Prynne about Cruze's family, it was a unanimous decision.

We ventured to the mall together and each headed into the shopping craziness with a set amount and specific family members to buy for. I had Cruze, Mila, and Abuelita. Prynne had the rest of the siblings, Amelia, Miguel, Josephina, and Diego. And my mom was assigned Cruze's parents. My mom also gave us the task of looking for something we wanted for our own presents and reporting back to her ... but to be honest, I had way more fun looking for Cruze.

I was perusing an electronics store when a store worker, wearing a green elf hat and bopping along to some unknown beat under a set of earphones, approached me.

"How's it going?"

"Good," I gave the obligatory answer and head nod that I thought meant *now leave me alone and move on*. But he stayed.

"Have you tried these new headphones yet?"

"Nope."

"You have to give them a try. It's a total listening experience. They cancel out all ambient noise and only let you listen to the music in its purest form."

I shrugged. "I have some like those already."

"But not *these* ones. These ones are the best. You've never heard anything like them."

I thought if I gave in and listened for a few seconds, he would eventually move on. "Okay."

He slipped the earphones over my head, and the buzzing of chatter, the beeping of registers, and the hum of Christmas was immediately replaced with some classical music. I was surprised to hear the music selection; the way he was bopping when he approached me suggested something a little more hip-hop. But then I started to recognize the beat; I couldn't name it, but I knew it was a popular song on the radio.

"Is this classical pop?" I pulled an earphone up.

"Yeah. The store manager won't let us play anything else." He said it apologetically, like he would much rather be listening to something else. But to me, it was perfect. An idea was stirring, and I couldn't believe I hadn't thought of it before.

"What do you think?" the clerk asked as I took them off and handed them to him.

"They're perfect."

The earphones were ridiculously expensive—more expensive than the ones I already owned. But I knew when I told my mom that they were all I wanted and why I wanted them—combined with her guilt over basketball, which I may or may not have used to my advantage—she would give in and let me get them.

I was right.

On Christmas Eve, my family and I went to Cruze's house and dropped off two boxes full of food and gifts. With all the gifts, I slipped in an old but relatively new (because I treat all my basketball shoes like gold) pair of basketball shoes that I had grown out of. It wasn't that I didn't want to get her a new pair; I just knew she wouldn't accept them.

The lights were off and we assumed they were at church—I was secretly glad no one was home, especially Cruze. I wasn't sure how she was going to take it, and it's easier to accept things when there is no one to say no to.

I didn't hear anything from Cruze that night but, on Christmas Day Prynne found a plate full of homemade empanadas and churros on our doorstep. There was no note. There didn't need to be. Some things don't need to be talked about.

All through Christmas and the following days I was antsy. The closer the Winter Ball got, the more anxious I became. My mom and sister thought it was because of basketball, and it was, just not why they thought it was. No decision was going to be made about my playing status until the holidays were over, and I had come to terms with that ... as best I could ... really ...

Okay, I'm still unbelievably fucking pissed-off about the whole thing and, every now and then, when I think about not being able to play in the Winter Ball, I want to scream (I have screamed—into my pillow, in the shower, at breakfast when I read an article about the upcoming tournament with the prediction that Lincoln was going to win it all ... that scream made Prynne spill her Cheerios). I'm trying.

I was anxious because I had convinced Matti to come with the team to the Winter Ball. I couldn't play, but I was going to travel with the team and I wanted Matti to be there. It was an away tournament. We'd be staying in a hotel. It was completely out of her comfort zone but I had a plan. When I pitched it to

Coach K, she was a little skeptical, but still willing and happy to have Matti come with the team ... if Matti wanted to.

It took some convincing (a lot of convincing) but she finally agreed to join, under the conditions that she could bring her own bedsheets and that we room together. I wouldn't have wanted it any other way.

CHAPTER 27

We hadn't been at the hotel for more than five minutes when, sitting with the team in the lobby, waiting for Coach K to check us in and assign us our room numbers, I saw the elevator doors open and a familiar purple and gold start walking my way—four members from my old team and the Aussie twins. Brooke was at the front of the group.

I knew I would run into them eventually; I just wasn't ready for it right then ... or ever.

Brooke and the others stopped when they got to where I was sitting. Teesha, Matti, Cruze, Jess, and Oaks were sprawled out beside me with their bags. Everyone got quiet, except for Cruze, who decided it was a good time to whistle and hum the western showdown tune from *The Good, The Bad, and The Ugly*.

I gave Cruze a nasty look and stood up so I was face to face with Brooke. We hadn't talked since the start of the season. It felt strange and awkward to see her now. Everyone else was watching us while sizing each other up.

"Hey," she said casually.

"Hey," I said back.

"How's it going?"

"Good. You?"

"Good. So ... did you have a good Christmas?"

"Yep. You?"

"Yep." She glanced around me. "So ... this is your new team."

"This is my team."

"I heard you guys had a pretty big loss to Westview."

"They got lucky."

"They got lucky?" one of the Aussies spoke up. "I heard they whipped ya."

Teesha jumped up beside me. "They didn't whip us."

"This your new best friend?" Brooke brought her fingers together to make a hash tag symbol. "Hash tag Beneesha basketball," she said sarcastically. The rest of Lincoln started to laugh. Brooke's bitchiness surprised me. *Or had she always been like this?*

Cruze, Oaks, Monty, O ... almost the entire team got up.

We stood for a few seconds, silently staring at one another.

"Fight, fight, fight, fight ..." Cruze started to chant.

"Cruze!" I shook my head at her and she stopped.

I felt Matti squeeze in beside me. "You're Brooke Hastings. Number 8. You and Bennett—double N, double T—are best friends and used to play together. Or you were best friends. You don't play together anymore so I don't know." She looked at me. "Are you two still best friends?"

If it wasn't awkward before, it was now.

"Okay." Brooke looked at Matti, confused. "And who are you?"

"I'm Matti, double T with an I but no E. I don't like E's. Nice to meet you." She held out her hand for Brooke to shake.

"Who's this chick?" Brooke looked at me.

I started to open my mouth ...

"I just told you. I'm Matti. And it's not nice not to shake someone's hand."

"Don't you guys have a game or something?" I asked Brooke, hoping she'd take the hint and leave.

"Yeah. And don't you play after us? Well, not you, but your team?"

"Oh, snap!" someone behind her said.

I stepped toward Brooke. "You know this whole thing is bullshit."

"You mean, do I know that you didn't want to go and play for Riverside? Who would?"

— 244 —

"WHAT?" Cruze jumped in front of me. "Chica, you better back it up."

"Or what?"

"Ladies!" Coach K called to us. "I hate to interrupt this ... whatever *this* is. But I've got your room keys and, Lincoln, I believe your team bus is waiting."

"See you later," Brooke said as she and the others started to back away.

"Yeah. See ya," I said.

"Wouldn't wanna be ya," Cruze added.

Teesha playfully punched her. "Good one," she said sarcastically.

"Good luck in your game!" Matti called out genuinely.

We got our room keys and, as we made our way to the elevator, all I could hear were mumbling comments about Lincoln.

"Man, those girls are bitches."

"Those Aussie twins are bigger than I thought they'd be."

"We'd better get to the final because I can't wait to kick their ass on the court."

"I've got a special box-out waiting for that Hastings chick."

"I can't believe Beaner used to play for them."

A part of me wanted to speak up and defend Lincoln, say that's not what they're really like, but I kept my mouth shut because another part of me couldn't believe I used to play for them, either.

We arrived at the gym in time to watch the second half of the Lincoln game. This was the first time I'd be watching my old team in action. As we sat down, I could hear Coach Paige's voice barking orders from across the gym. A familiar set of nerves started to tingle in my stomach.

"How are you doing, Matti?"

Matti was sitting wide-eyed beside me. She was glued to my side and her hand was gripping my thigh as she took in her surroundings around the gym.

Coach K was watching her. "I don't know if this is going to work, Bennett."

I wasn't sure my plan was going to work either, but I was determined to try. "Matti?" I called to her. She was distracted by everything going on in the gym, and I could feel her starting to pull away. "Matti?" She looked at me. I handed her the earphones that I had bought at Christmas. "Put these on."

She followed my directions and, when the earphones were on, I hit play. The tension and apprehension was instantly released from her body. I felt her grip on my leg loosen and a big smile formed on her face.

"CLASSICAL POP!" she said loudly and everyone turned to look at us. I nodded at her and put a finger to my mouth, signaling for her to talk quieter. "Oh, sorry," she whispered.

I had spent most of Christmas Day searching the Internet for a selection of classical pop songs and putting together a playlist for Matti. So far, it seemed that she liked what I had chosen.

As the game continued, Matti's smile got bigger. She was watching basketball, in the gym, with the team.

Coach K leaned over to me. "It looks like it might work. How did you think of this?"

I couldn't take my eyes off Matti's smile. "How did I or anyone *not* think of this sooner?"

"I never thought I'd see my daughter in the gym like this." Coach K patted me softly on the back. "Thank you."

I went back to watching the game and felt someone nudge me from behind. Teesha looked at Matti and then gave me an approving nod. She held out her fist and we hit knuckles, pulling our hands back like an explosion—it was what we did after a particularly good play to say (without words) that the other had done well.

"WHY HAVEN'T LINCOLN PULLED THE PRESS?" Matti yelled, loud enough for half the gym to hear. The team all turned and told her to talk quieter. Then we all started laughing.

Matti was loud and she was also right. Lincoln was up forty points and was still in their full-court press.

How very Coach Paige, I thought.

There is no rule against it, and every team handles it differently, but general basketball etiquette is to pull the press when your team is up twenty. Even Coach Paige usually, not always but usually, followed the unspoken rule. I had a feeling he was putting on a show for Riverside. He wanted to show us just how dominant Lincoln was.

Watching my old team was a bit like déjà vu. I knew what they were going to do before they did it. Coach Paige had changed the offense—slightly—but it still didn't stop me from knowing their next step. I had spent the last four years playing with most of these girls and I knew their moves in and out.

Brooke caught the ball on the wing.

She'll fake a shot, drive middle, spin dribble at the junction of the key, and finish with bank shot.

I had everything right but how she finished—she went with a reverse layup. Brooke had been working on her game.

The two players I couldn't predict were the Aussie twins. They were better and faster than I thought they'd be. Brooke had undersold them.

Number 9, Hanna, was a little better than her sister Hayley, number 10. Hanna played stronger, more confident. She wanted the ball in her hands and she liked to drive. Hayley didn't shoot much, but what she lacked in offense, she made up for on defense. She was smart, knew where to stand, and where and when to cheat off her check.

In the small amount of time I had been watching the game,

Hayley had made five steals and, of those five steals, she had sent the ball up the court for her sister to make an easy fast-break layup four times.

The twins are going to be a problem.

Lincoln appeared stronger than they were last season. Looking around at the intimidated faces watching the game, I'm pretty sure I wasn't the only one who felt that way.

Like Lincoln, we won our first two games with little effort. Unlike Lincoln, we pulled our press after we went up twenty.

The first day of the tournament was over and, as predicted, we and Lincoln were advancing to the semi-finals. Lincoln was to face off against Westview, while we were to play Ridgemont, a visiting team from California that no one knew anything about. We had seen the end of their quarter-final game against Southlands, a game they won by fifteen. They looked big. According to the program, four of their players were over six feet, with their center post hitting six foot five.

Usually coaches fiddle with the size in tournament programs to make their team seem bigger than they are—coach Paige had me at a generous six-foot in last year's Winter Ball program— but I walked by Ridgemont on their way to the locker-room ... the program didn't lie. The Ridgemont girls were giants. The semi-final was going to be a battle.

CHAPTER

28

Every Winter Ball tournament included a banquet night. Teams dressed in their warm-ups or team gear and gathered together in a decorated hall for a celebratory dinner. The idea is to bring all the teams together and show that even though we play for different schools and come from different walks of life, we are all here because we love basketball and we are all the same. It's a nice idea ... in theory.

Before the actual dinner was served, there were welcome speeches and acknowledgments given to the sponsors and those who helped make this—the 21st annual—tournament happen.

As the speeches commenced, there was a running slideshow showing photos from the previous year on a big screen behind the stage. Photos of me in a Lincoln jersey flashed by ... then a photo of me with Brooke, hugging each other after the double

OT win. I looked across the room and locked eyes with her. We both turned away quickly. I glanced back up at the screen just in time to catch another photo of me, this time holding the Winter Ball trophy with the rest of Lincoln at center court. I felt the eyes of my Riverside teammates on me and decided not to turn around.

Teesha leaned over to me. "Tell me, what's it feel like to win?"

"Why don't you just find out for yourself?"

She leaned back in her chair. "Like I said before, you owe me a championship."

The speeches finally ended and it was time for the entertainment, provided by the teams. It was tradition. Every team had to put together a lip-sync routine. It was up to each team how "into it" they got. Some went all out, dressing in outfits to match the song choice, or putting together a choreographed dance. Others got up on stage and just tried to get through it with as little embarrassment as possible.

To encourage us to put some effort in and have fun with it, the top team performances, as selected by the referee committee, got to go to the banquet table first. Food! The extra incentive that many teams needed.

Last year, Lincoln ate last. We felt we were "too cool" and too good to care about some stupid lip sync, and also, Coach Paige gave us a speech about how we were at the tournament to win on the court and not on some silly stage. We ended up standing together and swaying back and forth to some song I don't even remember.

Riverside approached things differently. As I was learning, the lip-sync battle was just as important as the tournament. Last year they came second but this year, with Cruze and Tats organizing things, we were determined to win it. Even Coach K got in on the action, buying us all matching fluorescent wrist and head bands.

Like I suspected, Lincoln put in a half-assed effort, standing around while the majority of the team mouthed the wrong words to Katy Perry's "Roar"—which, now that I think about it, was the same song we did last year.

Westview, however, came ready to play. They lined up on stage and, just before the music started, simultaneously ripped off their tear-away pants. Each girl was wearing a pair of colored basketball boxer shorts that spelled Mustangs on the back. The banquet hall erupted with laughter and cheers as Westview started a hip-hop routine set to the *Space Jam* movie theme song. I have to admit, their performance was pretty good.

As we took the stage and got ready for our routine, I could hear soft boos and laughter coming from the Lincoln tables. Someone called out, "I thought this banquet was for players. Why is Ryan here?" I did my best to ignore them.

We got into our positions and waited for the music to start.

It wasn't planned but Cruze jumped to the front of the stage and said, "This performance is dedicated to our close friends, the Lincoln High Lady Lions." We all had to stifle our giggles.

The first notes of Tag Team's, "Whoomp! There It Is" started, and as Cruze sang out, *"Riverside back again ..."* we all zipped down and pulled off our hoodies to reveal florescent T-shirts with *Storm Basketball* written on the front and *#kickinyourass* on the back. Our 90's-themed wrist and sweat bands were a nice touch. Cruze and Tats led the routine, rapping along like a mini Tag Team while the rest of us danced (badly) behind them. Westview was good, but we were better.

Cruze and Tats ran around the banquet room getting everyone on their feet and singing with us. Within a minute of the song's starting, almost the entire room was waving their hands in the air ... everyone except (of course) Lincoln.

Up on that stage, dancing with Riverside, I didn't miss my old team at all anymore. I didn't even care—well, I cared a little less—that I wasn't playing in the tournament. I was having too much fun.

We were all still laughing and dancing as we grabbed our plates and went to the buffet line first. A huge spread of salads, pastas, and roast meats awaited our hungry stomachs.

In the middle of the buffet table, there was a giant ice sculpture of a basketball going through a hoop. In front of that was the Winter Ball championship trophy and a large trophy with a girl shooting a basketball on top—the coveted Belle of the Ball trophy that went to the MVP of the tournament. I was familiar with it.

"Hey." Oaks bumped me as we passed by the trophy table. "Weren't you the Belle of the Ball last year?"

"Yep," I nodded. And I was hoping to be the first player to win it twice. *So much for that.*

I really should have been ready for what happened next. I'm a little disappointed in myself that I didn't see it coming. Maybe there was a part of me that didn't think Lincoln was capable of it.

Walking back to my table, balancing a plate full of food in my hands while talking with Oaks, something—not something: a foot, a foot belonging to Emma Finnerty—stuck out from the table and took me down ... hard.

Like I said, I should have been ready for it, but I was chatting with Oaks, unaware of where and who I was walking by and BAM! I tried to catch myself but it was too late. My plate went flying into Oaks and the next thing I knew I was eating carpet while a room full of players erupted in laughter. Flat on my face, I seriously contemplated crawling under the tables and out of the room.

"Beaner! Are you okay?" Oaks reached down to help me up.

"I'm fi—"

"What the hell was that?" Cruze and Teesha, who had been walking behind me, confronted an entire table of laughing Lincoln players. Monty, Jess, and the rest of the team joined them. The banquet hall fell silent.

"Whoa, whoa, whoa!" Emma threw her hands in the air. "It was an accident."

"Maybe it'll be an accident when my dinner roll stuffs your mouth shut." Cruze held a bun in her hand, ready to throw it at the first person that made a move.

"Cruze! Put down the bun." Coach K had seen the altercation from the coaches table and came running over. "Is everything okay over here?"

"Everything is fine," I said. "I just tripped. Klutzy me." I looked directly at Emma.

"You didn't trip," Oaks objected. "I saw—"

"Oaks!" Coach K snapped. "Leave it. Everyone, leave it and go back to your table."

"Yeah, we'll leave it," Cruze glared at the entire Lincoln table. "Leave it for the court." She jerked her arm like she was going to throw the bun. Emma flinched. Cruze took a bite of her bun and with a full mouth said, "It's called a fake, chica."

"Cruze!" Coach K shook her head and pointed us to our table. "Go!" Her word was final.

Once we got to our table, the conversation quickly turned to talk of revenge.

"Lincoln's going down!"

"There's no way we're going to let them get away with that."

"YES, you are." None of us had seen Coach K follow us back to the table. "If I hear anything, ANYTHING, about any of you doing something to Lincoln, then our next few practices won't require basketballs. And if you need a translation—you'll be running till you die. DO YOU GET ME?" We all nodded, reluctantly. "GOOD." She leaned over and whispered so only we could hear her. "But you better beat Ridgemont tomorrow, because I want nothing more than to kick Lincoln's ass right now. Hash tag, kickin' *their ass.*"

We were all so shocked to hear Coach K say something like that, it took us a second to register.

Tats jumped up and cheered. "Oh, no, she didn't!"

Cruze jumped up next. "Whoomp—there it is!" she yelled. "Say it with me ..."

"Whoomp—there it is!" the team chanted.

"What?"

"Whoomp—there it is!"

"LOUDER!"

"WHOOMP—THERE IT IS! WHOOMP—THERE IT IS! WHOOMP—THERE IT IS!"

As the team chant-rocked through the banquet hall, I glared over at the smug Lincoln table. *Please, please, basketball gods or dad or anyone who's listening ... please let me play basketball soon. PLEASE!*

CHAPTER 29

The semi-final game against Ridgemont was every bit the battle for the boards that I thought it would be.

Lincoln, fresh off their victory against Westview (Lincoln 63, Westview 57), was seated in the packed stands, watching and waiting in anticipation to see which team they would play in the finals.

I was seated across the court at the bottom of the stands, directly behind the team bench—where I was "allowed" to sit—watching the game with Matti. She had her coach's board out and was making notes as she watched the game.

As the battle continued, I did my best to focus my thoughts on the game and not think about the fact that I wasn't playing and couldn't help my team, or that Lincoln was watching on the other side, or that there was a group of college scouts—Stanford included—watching the game from high in the bleachers. There was a lot *not* to think about.

On the court, we had gotten out to a quick start and took an early lead. Ridgemont was taller than us, but we were faster and took advantage of our speed in transition, where Teesha, Cruze, and Jess connected for a few easy layups.

Breakaway transition layups seemed to be the only way we were going to score inside the paint. The guards tried to get the ball into Monty and Oaks but were denied more times than they succeeded. Teesha tried attacking, but her go-to pull-up jumper had been blocked three times. Cruze made a nice in-and-out move to beat her check, only to get rejected so badly that the ball was cleared out into the stands. The crowd watching—myself included—responded with a collective "OOOHHHH!" For the first time ever, Cruze went silent.

Partway through the second quarter, Matti asked me if I was okay. With the headphones still on, she was doing a much better job of keeping her voice at an acceptable level.

I nodded at her and mouthed the word, "Why?"

She took off her earphones. "Because you won't stop bouncing your legs and you keep biting your fingernails."

I pulled my hand away from my mouth and looked at my gnawed digits. "Oh."

"Here." She handed me her earphones.

"What?"

"Put them on. It's cool. You'll like it. But you have to put them on to see."

"What about you?"

She plugged her ears with her fingers. "I'll be okay for a couple of minutes."

I slipped the earphones over my head. The cheering, yelling, buzzers, and whistles were replaced with violins, cellos, and a piano. The play on the court continued but, with the music in my ears, it was like I was watching another game, or another sport. The pace slowed down. I relaxed. Everyone relaxed. The ball bouncing on the court, flying through the air, going through the hoop, even the players running, weaving, cutting in and out ... there was a rhythm to everything. I'd never looked at the game this way before. It was kind of beautiful.

I watched for a couple more minutes and then gave the headphones back to Matti. "Thank you."

"Feel better?"

"A little bit."

"Now you know how I see the game."

"I like your world, Matti."

She smiled. "Me, too."

Halftime score: Riverside 34–Ridgemont 25

The second half felt like a different game from the first. Ridgemont slowed the play and switched to a half-court zone to suit their big style inside the paint. They collapsed in the middle, forcing us to shoot from the outside and letting their bigs clean up the rebounds.

Teesha and Cruze, frustrated with not being able to attack the middle, started shooting outside jumpers that were rimming in and out. The offense looked scattered and rushed. We were no longer playing "our" game.

Slowly, Ridgemont started to claw back.

Defensively, Monty and Oaks were doing everything they could to stop the six-foot-five monster under the hoop. The girl was huge and deceptively fast. She looked like she should have been a starter in the WNBA, not playing on a high school team.

With six minutes left in the fourth quarter, Ridgemont had tied the game: 47–47. Monty had four fouls and was in trouble, which meant that we were in trouble. Coach K had no choice but to sit her for a couple of minutes and hope that Oaks could hold off the monster.

"OAKS!" Coach K yelled as she paced in front of the bench. "FIGHT. GET AROUND HER."

Oaks was doing everything she could, but Ridgemont took advantage and kept pounding the ball into the monster every chance they got.

The monster got the ball and made a quick drop-step to the hoop. She missed the shot but got her own rebound and made no mistake the second time. Ridgemont took the lead: 47–49.

Coach K erupted. "BOX OUT! OAKS! REBOUND!" A few girls sitting at the end of the bench had to duck out of the way as a flying whiteboard marker flew over their heads.

"My mom's not very happy," Matti said to me.

"No, she's not."

The play went back and forth for a couple of minutes. Tats got fouled during a shot and hit both foul shots to tie the game back up: 49–49.

On the next Ridgemont possession, Cruze got one of her stealthy steals. She and Teesha took off up the court and it looked like it was going to be an easy basket. Cruze hit Teesha with a pass. Teesha caught the ball on the run and went up for a layup—BAM!

Out of nowhere, the six-five monster's long arms stretched out and stuffed the shot. The gym went wild. Ridgemont saved the ball from going out of bounds and went on their own breakaway, hitting a streaking guard for their own easy layup. Just like that, the score was 49–51. The momentum started to shift for Ridgemont.

Teesha yelled out at the court in frustration. She wanted a foul on the last play. There was no foul. Everyone in the gym could see that the block was clean ... everyone except Teesha's bruised ego. She continued to complain. A whistle was blown ... technical foul. *Oh, T-time!*

Ridgemont hit both shots and went up: 49–53.

With under three minutes left, Coach K called a needed timeout. I leaned as close as I could in order to hear everything she had to say in the huddle.

She told everyone to calm down and reminded the team that there was still a lot of game left. She told Teesha to cool off and shake off the technical. It was her fourth foul and we couldn't afford for her to get a fifth. Then she laid into Oaks about boxing out and denying the monster the ball.

"She's too strong. I'm doing everything I can," Oaks responded.

"Do MORE!" Coach K yelled.

"I CAN'T!"

"What did you say?" Coach K's voice came out like ice.

"I said, I can't ... she's too ..."

"You're out, Oaks."

"What?" Oaks looked shocked. I was shocked. The whole team was shocked.

Coach K ignored our shocked faces and grabbed Monty. "You're in. Do what you can ... try not to get a foul. But don't make it easy." Monty gave an acknowledging nod. "WE DON'T SAY CAN'T ON THIS TEAM. EVER. YOU GOT THAT!" Everyone nodded. Oaks looked sheepish. "GOOD! Now let's cheer it up ..."

A whistle was blown. The team put their hands together.

"Number four is the worst shooter on the team," Matti said before anyone could cheer. She had somehow pushed her way into the huddle and stood in between everyone, her coaching board in her hands and her earphones around her neck.

Coach K looked back at me like it was my fault Matti had left the stands and joined the team. I gave her a shrug.

Matti continued, "Number four is only shooting about twelve percent for the game. Tats, she's your check. You should leave her space and drop to double-team the monster with Monty."

Another whistle was blown. Ridgemont was on the court waiting.

Everyone looked to Coach K. "Matti's right, Tats. Give four some room ... but not too much." Tats nodded.

"STORM!" The team cheered and the game was back on.

Matti climbed over the bench and took her seat beside me. She saw the stunned but impressed expression on my face.

"What?" she challenged.

"Nothing ... Coach."

Matti smiled and put her earphones back on.

Coming out of the timeout, it was Ridgemont ball. The ball was at the top of the three-point line as they set their offense. Tats dropped off number four and helped Monty to deny the monster.

Four cut and received the pass. Tats gave her room to shoot and stayed with Monty.

The gamble paid off. Number four looked uncomfortable to have so much time with the ball. She looked to get it into the monster but we had her closed off. With the shot clock winding down she took the shot ... air ball.

Teesha got the rebound and wasted no time getting up the court for an easy pull up. We were down by two: 51–53.

On the next play, Ridgemont fumbled the ball getting it up the court. Cruze pounced on the loosed ball, flicking it back to Jess as she fell out of bounds.

We took our time. Set up the offense.

The ball went in to Monty, but she was covered by the monster and kicked it back out to Teesha. Teesha looked to shoot, but Cruze ran off a screen by Tats and was wide open. Teesha hit her and Cruze made no mistake, connecting for a three and putting us up by one: 54–53.

The gym went wild and the momentum shifted back for us.

With 1:04 left on the clock, Ridgemont called a timeout.

Coach K tried to calm everyone's nerves. "Tats, continue to drop off four and double with Monty. Keep up the pressure in the full court. When a shot goes up, BOX OUT. This game is going to be won or lost on the boards. A minute four is a long time, so if they score, just stay calm and set up the offense.

Cruze, if you get another open look like that, take it ... and everyone CRASH THE BOARDS!"

I took a sip from my water bottle and listened intently, like I was in the game with them. *I'd give anything to be in the game right now.*

Oaks wanted to be back in the game, too. As the team went to cheer, I saw her say something to Coach K, but Coach K responded with a shake of the head and pointed for her to sit down. Oaks went back to the bench, looking completely deflated.

I was sure that everyone in the gym was starting to question why Oaks—our second biggest post—was out of the game. Some fans in the stands, including Mrs. Humphries, were calling for Oaks to be back in.

Stubbornly standing with her arms crossed, focused on the game, Coach K acted like she didn't hear any of it.

On the next Ridgemont possession, the point guard ran a pick-and-roll play with the monster. Monty did everything she could without committing a foul, but the monster got the ball and finished with a power layup ... it was almost a dunk: 54–55.

We countered with a pick-and-roll play of our own. Monty got a pass off Teesha and was fouled by the monster mid-shot. A whistle went. The gym went silent and everyone watched as the ball rolled agonizingly slowly—sloth movement slow—circling around the rim ... and ... finally ... dropping ... in.

I jumped in the air. Matti jumped up. We hugged.

Teesha and Monty hugged.

Our whole bench was on their feet for the AND 1.

Monty set up at the foul line. Half the gym, including all of Lincoln, were yelling, banging, and waving their arms in the air to try and distract Monty from her shot.

With no more fingernails left, I had switched to chewing on the drawstring of my hoodie. *I hate being a spectator.*

Monty was not the best foul shooter. Some of the girls liked to call her Shaq—referring to the infamously bad foul shooting of Shaquille O'Neal.

I couldn't watch ... I had to watch ... I couldn't watch ... but I had to watch ...

"Toss the ball around your hands, dribble twice, toss the ball again ..." Matti was beside me, commentating Monty's shooting routine a split second before she did it. "Now breathe and release ..."

Ssswwwiiissssshhhhh.

Monty iced the shot. Half the gym went wild.

00:28 on the game clock. Score: 57–55.

Ridgemont got the ball, went up the court, shot, miss ... there was tussle for the rebound and the ball went out of bounds. From where I was sitting it could have gone off Ridgemont, it could have gone off us.

00:07–the referees conferred about which team the ball went out off.

My heart was in my throat. *I hate being a spectator. HATE IT.*

Whistle–Ridgemont ball. They were out of timeouts.

PLAY-BY-PLAY

00:07–Ball in.

00:05–Quick shot. Rebound Ridgemont.

00:03–Pass out to Ridgemont #4 on the three-point line.

00:02–#4 has room to shoot.

00:01–#4 shoots a three ...

The ball flew through the air.

The buzzer sounded.

The ball banked hard off the backboard, hit the front of the rim, bounced high in the air, and dropped (with my heart) into the net.

Game Ridgemont: 57–58.

There was a lot to register in the split seconds following number four's miraculous buzzer-beating banker three. It all came in flashes.

The fans in the gym–yelling, cheering, and going crazy.

Ridgemont–rushing the floor in celebration.

Teesha, Monty, Cruze, Tats, Jess, Oaks, Nikki, O, Taya, Jaz,

Sierra, Maya, and Coach K—looking at the hoop in utter shock, disbelief, and heartbreak.

Lincoln—celebrating on the other side of the court.

Matti—shouting, "NO, NO, NO," then pushing me aside and running out of the gym.

"Matti! Wait!" I took off after her, hopping over the stands, weaving around fans and players, and sprinting out of the gym. Outside the gym doors, I saw her blue tracksuit disappear around a corner and down a hallway. I could hear her footsteps slapping the linoleum and her shouting, "NO, NO, NO, NO ..." over and over again as she ran.

"MATTI!" I ran a maze through the school hallways, listening to her yell, finally catching up with her in a dimly lit alcove beside a set of locked doors that led to the outside and God knows where after that. She was stuck with nowhere else to run.

"Man, you can run fast," I said while catching my breath.

She either didn't hear me, or pretended not to. Her earphones and iPod were lying on the ground. "NO, NO, NO ..." she kept repeating, stomping back and forth and hitting her head with her fists.

"Matti, stop." I reached out to grab her arm but she hit me away. She paused to look at me, but not really look at me; it was like she was looking through me. "Matti?" I waited for her to say something.

"No, no, no ..." She looked away and continued with her rant.

I didn't know what to do so I just stood there and watched, like a spectator—again, a spectator—completely helpless to do anything.

After a couple of long minutes, she finally started to calm down and breathe.

She began talking, not to me, not to herself, just talking. And in typical Matti style, she was talking fast. "She wasn't supposed to hit that shot. Number four was shooting twelve percent. She only had two points in the whole game. Zero for three from outside the three-point line. I checked. I read the program. Ridgemont Ramblers, number four, Elena Erickson, first and last name starting with an E. I don't like E's. Fifth letter of the alphabet. I don't like them." Her forehead furrowed and she shook her head like she was trying to figure out a difficult calculation. "Zero for three. Should have been zero for four. She shouldn't have hit that shot. It doesn't make sense ..."

"Matti," I said softly, carefully. "It's sports. It doesn't always make sense."

"But the numbers ..."

"The numbers don't always add up. They're not *always* right ..."

She clenched her jaw. "Numbers are always right."

"Okay." I put my hands up in defeat. "Numbers are usually

always right ... in math. But this is basketball. Nine times out of ten ... ninety-nine times out of a hundred ... heck, even nine hundred and ninety-nine times out of a thousand, number four might miss that shot."

"She didn't miss. She hit it. I said she would miss. She should have missed. I said ..."

"Matti, no one is blaming you for what happened in the gym. Shots like that happen. They're not supposed to go in but they do. Sometimes it can work for you, other times ... it's why I love this game."

"You love that we lost?"

"No. I hate to lose. I really hate to lose." I had run out of the gym after Matti so fast that it was just now settling in that we had actually lost. No Winter Ball final. No game against Lincoln. I tried not to think about it. "What I love is that sports are not about the numbers. You can't really predict anything. Things happen that are unexplainable, even unbelievable, but they happen. I don't know why. Maybe she ate her Wheaties this morning and she shot farther than she normally shoots. Maybe someone opened the door and a gust of wind blew into the gym at that exact moment and propelled the ball the exact amount it needed. Maybe the basketball gods looked down and agreed that this was going to be number four's one moment in time. Maybe she just shot a good shot ..."

"It wasn't a good shot. She had no arc and it bounced off the backboard—"

"Okay, I agree. It wasn't a good shot. It was a lucky shot."

"Basketball gods?" She looked at me skeptically.

"I don't know. Maybe. The point is, she shot it and, for whatever reason, it went in. Numbers had nothing to do with it. It's just basketball." I could see Matti contemplating my logic. "Did you get this upset when Lincoln beat Riverside last year?"

"No. Because I knew you were going to hit that shot. That made sense."

"But were you still upset that Riverside had lost?"

"I didn't like it. But then you came to Riverside, and I like that."

"You see, things happen that we don't like, that we can't explain, that are out of our control. But they can lead to other things that we do like. We can never know what's going to happen."

"Are you still talking about basketball?"

I started to laugh. "I don't even know anymore." I picked up her earphones and handed them to her. "Are you feeling better?"

"No. I still don't think she should have hit that shot. It doesn't make sense. It doesn't add up." We started to walk back to the gym. Matti stopped, grabbing my arm in realization. "Maybe that was her nine hundred and ninety-ninth shot."

"What?"

"Out of a thousand. Like you said. Maybe that was her one shot."

I knew it would make Matti feel better if I just went with it. "Maybe."

"Yeah," she smiled. "Maybe. And hey, maybe Ridgemont will beat Lincoln in the finals."

"Maybe," I nodded as we kept walking. "Maybe."

Lincoln beat Ridgemont 55–49. I had all kinds of mixed emotions as I watched Brooke, the team, and Coach Paige hoist the Winter Ball trophy at center court. I wish I could say that I'm a big enough person to be happy for her and Lincoln. But I'm not. Of all my mixed emotions, the one I felt the strongest was rage. Hanna Taylor, the better of the Aussie twins, was awarded the Belle of the Ball. I saw the Stanford recruiters talking with her. More rage.

At one point during the Lincoln celebration, Cruze asked me if I wished that I were out there with them. My answer came quick and honest. "Do I wish that I were out there hoisting that trophy? Yes. Do I wish that I were out there with *them*? No."

No, no, and no.

The mood on the bus ride back to Riverside was somber. Oaks sat in the back, as far away from Coach K as she could. Some girls were sleeping. Others were tuned out listening to music. No one was talking.

I wanted to talk to Oaks about the game and about Coach K. I wanted to put music on, start a dance party, and cheer everybody up. I wanted to do something, say something ... but I hadn't played in the tournament—I didn't even sit on the bench—and it wasn't my place to do or say anything. I hadn't earned the loss like they had. I wasn't on the court when that buzzer beater ripped their hearts out. It feels different on the court. And I wasn't on the court.

I was a spectator.

CHAPTER

30

Two days after the Winter Ball, on New Year's Eve, the anniversary of my dad's passing, I drove with my mom and Prynne to the cemetery.

On the way there, we didn't say much. My mom and I listened to the radio; Prynne had her head buried in a script, going over her lines. With the upcoming play and her role as Belle, she was more dedicated to the play than to anything I had ever seen her do. I'd even helped her go over her lines a couple of times ... she was actually pretty good. For the first time ever, it felt like I was seeing the real Prynne, not the imitation version.

My mom was quiet and looking troubled. Normally I would say that her mood had something to do with the anniversary, but she had been like this since the day we found out about the petition. It was bothering her as much as it was bothering me.

We each laid a flower at my dad's headstone. And for a couple of minutes we all just stood there, looking down at the ground, listening to the wind.

"I think I'm going to hand in my resignation to the school board," my mom blurted out.

"What?" Prynne and I spoke at the same time.

"I've been thinking about it. A lot. And I've spoken to the lawyers. If I quit, Coach Paige's allegations won't hold as much weight. The Commission will have to rule in your favor. You can play basketball again."

"Mom, you can't quit because of me."

"Yes, I can."

"No, I won't let you."

"And I won't let them use me to punish you."

"Well, I could say the same thing. I won't let them use me to punish you. You can't quit your job. You love it."

"I can find another job. I can even go back to teaching. This is your senior year."

"But being a principal is what you've always wanted."

"What I want, and always wanted, is for you and Prynne to be happy. It's what your dad and I wanted together. And you're not happy. Not without basketball. I made a mistake taking this job and moving you two here ..."

"No! I'm glad we moved."

"Me, too," Prynne added.

My mom looked doubtful. "You're glad that I picked you up, moved you away from all your friends, your basketball team, your chance to win the Winter Ball, to be the Belle of the Ball for a second time ... you're glad you're not playing basketball?"

"Okay ... I'm not *glad* about all that. But I do like it at Riverside. I like the team. I really do. I wouldn't change anything ... except maybe the basketball-playing part."

"Then let me do that for you."

"You should let her," Prynne chimed in. Mom and I both looked at her. "What? I should get a say in this, too."

"You're right," my mom nodded.

Prynne turned to me. "It's just ... don't get me wrong, I love that you've helped me run my lines for the play and had this whole helpful, attentive, nice sister act thing that you've had going on the last couple of weeks. But ... you're not you."

"Thanks. Are you saying I'm usually a bitch?"

"Bennett!" my mom scolded. "Don't say that here."

"Sorry."

"No, I'm not saying that you're usually a ... the B-word. I mean, sometimes you are, but no, what I'm saying is that you're not yourself. You're like this shell version of yourself. I used to hate basketball because it's all you did. You were never around.

You were always in the gym or on some court somewhere. It's all you cared about ..."

"I ..."

"No," she snapped. "Let me finish. This is my time."

"Okay."

"I *used* to think basketball was all you cared about. I even tried to play it, make myself like it like you, so I could be like you, so I could share what you and Dad had, but ... I just didn't get why you liked it so much."

"Prynne ..."

"Anyway," she continued, "I still don't get the basketball thing, but I get your passion. That's the thing I admire about you. Why I've always looked up to you ... my big sister. Not because you play basketball and you're amazing at it, but because you love it. And I never had anything like that. You've always known exactly who you are and what you want, and I never have."

My mom and I just stared at her. I don't think either of us knew what to say. Prynne had never opened up like this before.

"Prynne's right," my mom said. "You're not our Bennett without basketball."

"In fact ... you're kind of boring without it," Prynne added.

"Hey!" I knew she was kidding—sort of—but I punched her arm anyway.

After a long group-hug, we each said a few words to my dad.

We ended up talking all the way home. I filled them in on all the details of the Winter Ball, giving a play-by-play account of the games. My mom and Prynne surprised me by how into it they were ... at least they seemed like they were into it, even asking legitimate basketball questions.

I had always assumed they just weren't interested in basketball, so I never talked to them about it. When they asked me about games or practices, my stock one-word answers were usually, "Good. All right. Okay. Fine. Fun. Hard. Tiring." But in the car, they told me that they thought it was *me* who didn't want *them* around—in my basketball world. Secretly they kept every program that I was in, read and cut out all the articles that mentioned me in the paper, and even watched highlights of me on YouTube—some that I didn't even know existed.

"Bennett," my mom said, "don't you know?—we're your biggest fans."

We celebrated that New Year's Eve like we had every New Year's Eve post Dad—together. My mom made tacos and had all the ingredients for root beer floats. We put our PJ's on and settled in to watch the various televised countdowns.

This New Year's Eve felt different than the others, less sad, and we were closer than we'd ever been. With everything that was happening, I felt hopeful for the year ahead. There was no way

I was going to let my mom quit her job for me. I just knew there had to be other options. Maybe the Commission would side with us. Maybe Coach Paige would grow a heart and drop the petition. Or maybe the doorbell would ring and Teesha would be standing on my front porch with the best news ever ... (that last one surprised the heck out of me as well).

"Teesha?" I must have looked as confused as I felt. "What are you doing here?"

"I'm here to give you a belated Christmas present."

"What do you mean?"

"The petition's been dropped. The League Commissioner didn't feel that Coach Paige's accusations had enough evidence ... that's the official statement. Unofficially, I think my mom scared the crap out of him."

"What?"

"Like I told you. My mom's a lawyer. A good one."

"But ... but ..."

"Look," she huffed. "I admit that when Coach K told us that you couldn't play, I was happy at first. I thought I was going to get my team back and it would be like it was before you showed up. But, umm ... it's like you said to me, this team is better with you than without you. With you in the stands, it just wasn't the same on the court."

"Are you serious right now? This isn't some joke? Some team prank?"

"I'm serious. I never ask my mom for anything, but I asked her for this. She said she'd see what she could do and she did it. It's no big deal ... you stuck your neck out for me at the start of the season, and I heard what you and your family did for Cruze."

"She told you?"

"She tells me everything. She likes you. Matti likes you. Everyone likes you. You might have been a Lion but you're Storm now."

"Wait. Does this mean *you* like me? Does this mean we're besties now?"

"Don't push it." She smiled. "Really, I asked my mom to do it because you still owe me a championship. And I'm going to make sure you deliver."

I still couldn't believe this was happening. "I can play?!"

"You can play."

I jumped through the door and into her arms. "OH, MY GOD, I LOVE YOU!"

"Whoa, whoa, okay." She pushed me back. "That's enough of that."

"What's going on?" Prynne's face rounded the corner.

I jumped and hugged her next. "I can play. I CAN PLAY! Mom doesn't have to quit ... I CAN PLAY!"

"Your mom was going to quit her job?" Teesha asked in shock.

"Now she doesn't have to." I was so excited and relieved that I started talking as fast as Matti. "It's New Year's Eve. What are you doing right now?"

"Umm ..."

"Come inside. Can you spend the night? We've got root beer floats, popcorn, gummies ... come celebrate with us. Or do you have plans with your mom or someone else?"

"No, my mom is out at a work party, but I don't want to bother ..."

"Okay, great. It's settled. I've got some extra PJ's." Before she could come up with some excuse not to stay, I pulled her into the house.

At first Teesha seemed really uncomfortable, like a really awkward guest at a really awkward party, but when my mom and Prynne heard what she had done, they stuffed her with tacos, loaded her up with a supersized scoop of ice cream, and I gave her an extra pair of PJ's. My favorite pair—a bright orange Tennessee Lady Vols onesie. She refused to put them on ... but I tried.

We spent the night playing board games and watching the countdowns. After the ball dropped and we were sugared out, Teesha and I went up to my room. I pulled out a foamie and made her a bed beside mine. We talked about basketball, about the Winter Ball, about the rest of the season ...

As we were all talked out and falling asleep, Teesha told me one more surprising thing in a day full of surprises.

"Just so you know, my mom said that the silver bullet in getting them to drop the petition was a statement from Brooke Hastings."

"Brooke said something? Really?"

"She said that she didn't believe that your mom got the principal job because of you or basketball. She said that you didn't want to come to Riverside but that you had to, not for basketball, for your family."

"I can't believe Brooke said that."

"Well, she did. It shocked me, too."

"Wow."

"Yeah. Goodnight, Bennett Ryan."

"'Night, Teesha Collins." I couldn't resist. "Hey, we besties *now*?"

"Shut up and go to sleep."

And I did ... with a big contented smile on my face. That night I dreamt about playing basketball, and beating Lincoln in the state finals.

CHAPTER 31

In one second I had basketball taken away from me, and in one second I was given it back. That's how it felt. No, you can't play. Oh ... wait ... yes, you can. Of course, there were about a million seconds—1,468,800 seconds according to Matti—where I wasn't allowed to play, but that was over, and now it was time to focus on the rest of the season.

If Coach Paige's plan was meant to break us, it backfired. My first practice back, we felt stronger, more united than ever.

Coach K started the practice by giving us a speech about losing, and how we can learn far more about ourselves from the losses than we can from the wins. "A win is a win. A win makes you feel good and focus on the next game. A loss can be hard to take, but it makes you focus on the last game. Examine it. Study it. Dissect it. Why did we lose? What could we have done differently? What will we do differently next game? We learn by losing. Losing doesn't feel good but it's how we grow, as individuals, as a team."

Coach K's words made the Winter Ball loss sting a little less. But it still stung. *And I still hate to lose.* A picture of Lincoln hoisting the trophy made front page of the sports section. Even though the image was burned in my mind, I cut it out and taped it up in my locker to give me extra incentive.

It felt good to be back. Really good. I didn't even mind running lines. And I beat Cruze in a couple of sets, although she was quick to give me some excuse that she was going easy on me, trying to help boost my confidence.

Like I did before the winter break, like I usually do, I stayed an extra hour after practice to put up some shots. This was normal for me, routine. What wasn't normal were the twelve team members who stayed to shoot with me. Sometimes one or two stayed. Teesha usually stayed. But not twelve. Not the entire team. It was like we had made an unspoken pact: to do everything we could, as a team, to be the next State Champions.

I left practice sweaty, happy, and grateful. For days I had debated contacting Brooke to say ... something. But I usually stopped mid-text and turned my phone off, too stubborn or too scared to go through with it. Sitting in the change room, I finally gave in.

Hey. I just wanted to say thank you for ... you know.
So ... thanks.

Brooke didn't text back until much later that night, when I was already in bed and almost asleep.

I still hate Riverside. But I hate seeing you on the sidelines more.

I responded instantly:

I hope you didn't get in trouble with Paige.

I could see her typing.

He didn't say anything but I know he's pissed. Whatever.

After a couple of minutes, I finally wrote:

See you in the finals?!

Brooke's reply was quick:

You better.

CHAPTER 32

Our first league game after the winter break was a home game. The day of the game, the social mediaverse within Riverside was buzzing with a new hash tag: *#beneeshasback*.

The game was against the Alder Bay Buccaneers. It wasn't forecast to be a very good game. Alder Bay had only two wins on the season. Regardless, the gym was almost full. Mrs. Humphries was in her usual spot, decked out in Storm wear and ready to wave her signature cowbell. My mom and Prynne had come out to witness my return. Matti was on the bench, whiteboard in hand, taking notes on the Alder Bay warm-up with her earphones in place. She had a seat next to her mom, and looked like a mini-version of Coach K. They were even wearing the same collared coach's shirt. It was Matti's first time sitting on the actual bench. She glanced over at me and gave her usual thumbs-up.

Everything felt right again.

I got to start the game. And when I hit my first basket—after receiving a pass from Teesha—the gym ignited with cheers, drumming, and "beneesha" chants.

Everything *was* right again.

We ended up hammering Alder Bay 88–31. I didn't have a particularly good game—5 turnovers, 12 points—but I didn't care; the entire team got on the scoreboard. It was like we were exorcising the demons left over from the Winter Ball.

The rest of the season played without any allegations or petitions. We went undefeated, having good games and bad ... but mostly good.

Monty suffered a minor concussion and was out for two weeks. Jess and Tats both sprained their ankle in the same game. Jess was out for a week; Tats was out for three.

Oaks, one of the nicest people on the team, one of the nicest people I had ever met, continued to battle with Coach K, especially the weeks that Monty was out with a concussion and we relied on her to be our main big on the inside. During one particularly heated altercation at practice, Oaks ended up walking out. I went to go and get her but Coach K instructed me to "leave it." Coach K was constantly riding her. She never seemed to think Oaks was trying or doing enough. Oaks was constantly defending herself. She always felt like she was doing her best, doing everything she could. For whatever reason, these two could not see eye to eye.

Matti continued to wear her earphones, taking part in practices and sitting with the team during games. She excelled in her new and official role as assistant coach. She even came up with a couple of set plays for us to run. One of them was a special play called "Swish;" she had designed it just for me.

We won two other tournaments. Neither one had Lincoln in it.

If I was going to get my shot at them, I was going to have to wait until the playoffs.

On their side of things, Lincoln was doing equally well, winning two out-of-state tournaments and putting their win streak at 69. Hanna Taylor continued to dominate the court, winning tournament MVP's and getting a full-page article/interview in the paper. The article, about her and her sister Hayley, but mostly about her, was titled "Down Under Domination." It talked about her success in America, about her committing to Duke (she was pursued by others but chose Duke to be with her sister), and it also talked about her rivalry with me. Hanna and I had barely shared a few sentences; we hadn't even played each other on the court, but, according to the paper, we were in a "bitter rivalry." The article ended with the prediction that our rivalry would play out in epic fashion, on the court, during the State Championship. I highlighted the last lines and taped it up in my locker next to the Winter Ball picture. Hanna and I weren't in a rivalry before, but we were now.

As for me, my game continued to get better. I had Teesha to thank for that. We trained together before and after practices, issuing shooting and dribbling challenges to the other person, then trying to one-up each other.

Challenge: How many pull-up jumpers can you hit in three minutes?

Challenge: How many foul shots can you hit until you miss?

Challenge: Who can hit twenty-five three-point shots first?

Challenge: Who can hit fifty three-point shots first?

Challenge: How many three-point shots can you make out of one hundred?

Challenge: Who can hit one hundred three-point shots the fastest?

Our challenges went back and forth. As they evolved, so did we. We invited others to play with us, but the rest of the team chose to rebound or watch instead. Even some random fans started to come out and watch us. Cruze started taking bets on the side, not for money, for something much more valuable—sets of running suicide lines.

Trying to one-up the other person stayed in training and at practices. In games, we played as one. We were better together. The team played better when we played together. At times we felt unstoppable. We created passing plays that made other teams look like their feet were stuck in cement. By the time they knew where the ball was, it was already in or on its way into the net. Sometimes, we just had fun with it—making extra passes, no-look passes, Harlem Globetrotter-style passes—because we wanted to, because we could, because it was easy. Matti even made a YouTube highlight reel of our best plays—*#beneeshapasses*. In two days, it had over four thousand hits and counting. Passing became the favorite part of our game.

Off the court, we started doing a lot more together. I went over to her house to play some outdoor hoops; she came over to mine for dinner. Sometimes others joined us. No one said anything—no official invite was put out—but after certain practices or games, we all just hung out, watched some college ball and ate pizza, usually at Teesha's house or mine.

Stanford still had not come calling. I was starting to lose faith they ever would. This far into the season with no scouting calls or recruitment packages was a bad sign. While I was holding out for them, other schools were holding out for me. I had gone on a couple of recruiting trips. USC, Penn State, Oregon, Maryland, and even Notre Dame had offered me a full scholarship. I didn't tell Teesha about Notre Dame because I didn't want to make her feel bad. I knew she was fielding recruiting offers, but we had an unofficial "don't ask don't tell" policy. I think we both wanted to keep it quiet, because talking about it just made us feel like we were in competition again.

Outside of my basketball world ... *okay, nothing exists outside of my basketball world* ... but in my family life, we were closer than we had ever been post Dad. We talked more. Prynne and I fought less. My mom loved being a principal even more now because Prynne and I (more me) took away the guilt and were letting her love it. I got used to seeing her around the halls. I kind of enjoyed watching her do her thing and lay into students who were caught cutting class or smoking up.

Prynne's play, and her role as Belle, was a success. Cinderella was supposed to be the star but I thought—and I admit to being biased—that Prynne stole the show. The entire team came out to watch and, when the curtain rose, we all jumped up, cheered, and chanted her name.

I went to find her after the play, to tell her how awesome I thought she was, and that's when I caught her kissing Prince Charming in the costume room.

Prince Charming—aka Adam Parker—was cute, in the tall, geeky, drama-guy way. He hung out in the hipster crowd. I suddenly understood why acting in the play was so important to Prynne. I was actually really impressed. And I liked this version of my sister the best. I hoped that she had finally found her passion—acting, not Adam. I came to tell her how awesome she was in the play, but instead I took a picture of her and Prince Charming mid-kiss and used it to threaten and tease her for weeks after.

CHAPTER

33

A familiar edgy nervousness set in the day of the Zone Finals. We had won the cities, coasted through the Zone Playoffs, and we were now set to play Westview in the Regional Final ... in their gym.

Clinching a spot in the finals secured a spot in the State Championships, but there was still a lot at stake in the final game. The winner would be Regional Champion and, as champion, would be put on the opposite side of the draw from Lincoln in the state playoffs.

Coach K stressed that we all needed to focus on one game at a time, but I couldn't help thinking about meeting Lincoln in the state finals. That was the game I wanted, the game I thought about every time I opened my locker and looked at their smug faces.

But first, we had to take care of the Westview Wild Mustangs.

The newspaper called Westview the "scrappy team with heart," and said that while most were expecting another Lincoln vs. Riverside state final, Westview was the dark horse team that could upset either of us.

During the season, we had split with Westview. Granted, we weren't a full team, and I was not playing when we lost to them in league, but they had gotten better. As Coach K told us in her pregame speech, Westview was not a team we could take lightly. We were in their gym and this was playoff basketball.

Anything can, will, and does happen in playoff basketball.

I threw up just before we took the court for warm-up. No one batted an eyelash as I ran into the bathroom stall and chucked up what little I had in my stomach.

"Feel better?" Teesha asked me when I emerged.

"Yep. Feeling great."

"Good."

I wasn't the only nervous one. As we waited in a line to take the court, no one said a word. There was a lot of bouncing up and down, moving of heads, and shaking our arms out. I felt like throwing up again.

"Whoomp, there it is!" Cruze's voice broke the silence.

"Whoomp, there it is!" she said louder and turned to the team. "WHOOMP, THERE IT IS! WHOOMP, THERE IT IS! WHOOMP, THERE IT IS!" She was dancing now, getting the rest of us to smile, laugh, and chant with her. *Whoomp, there it is* had somehow stuck with the team from the Winter Ball banquet to become our unofficial team cheer.

"WHOOMP, THERE IT IS!"

"WHOOMP, THERE IT IS!"

"WHOOMP, THERE IT IS!"

Our chants echoed off the tiled change room walls as we took to the court.

The Westview gym was standing room only. On one side, there was a sea of green—painted faces, flags, drums, pompoms, posters, fans in spandex onesies, and a real horse. On the other side, pretty much the same thing, except in blue, minus the horse. Our mascot was a Grade 11 kid dressed in a fluffy gray storm cloud, carrying a lightning-bolt staff. The horse may have been a little cooler, but at least we didn't have to worry about our mascot crapping on the hardwood.

REGIONAL CHAMPIONSHIP
Westview Wild Mustangs vs. *Riverside Storm*

1ST QUARTER

The tone for the game was set before the referee could even throw the jump ball. As we walked onto the court and took our spots around the center circle, Cruze and Westview's top three-point shooter, #14 Grace Lee, bumped into one another.

"Watch yourself, *Empanada*." Grace gave Cruze a shove.

Cruze stepped up, nose to nose with Lee. "You watch yourself, *Spring Roll*."

"Hey!" the referee shouted. "That's enough of that, ladies."

Cruze and Lee obeyed. But when the ref turned her back, I saw a couple of unnecessary elbows flying.

The whistle blew. The ball was tossed. The game was on.

Some games start slow with the teams trying to feel the other team out, but not this one. This game started fast and stayed fast. The ball transitioned up and down the court so quickly that the heads of the fans were turning back and forth as if they were watching a tennis match.

In five minutes of play, the score was 17–12 for Westview, and I don't think either of us had set up our offense yet.

All week long, we had practiced our press break in order to be ready for the stifling Westview press. We pulled Monty up and set her in the middle of the court to take advantage of our height. For the most part it worked, but Westview countered by applying more pressure on the inbounds. When the ball was entered, they pounced and swarmed us like hornets. Some fouls (not nearly enough) were called but, for the most part, the ref allowed Westview's aggressive style of play.

Teesha was stripped of the ball by Sage Walsh, Westview's

best player. Sage slapped Teesha across the arm when she went in for the steal. It was a clear foul—at least clear to the Riverside fans, as they booed their dislike of the non-call. From across the court, I knew Teesha was going to retaliate.

Oh, no, Teesha. Don't ...

She ran Sage down and hacked her as she went up for a layup. It was a bad foul, a dumb foul.

Both sides of the crowd were booing now.

"Are you kid ..."

Teesha started to argue the call, but I ran over to her before she could get her third word out. "Let it go, T. Let it go."

"But she ..."

"I know what she did. It was a foul. But leave it. It's not worth it." Teesha nodded and walked away. She actually listened to me.

2ND QUARTER

Westview continued to press us hard. In one minute, we had three turnovers—one of them was mine. Westview converted our mistakes into seven unanswered points. And we were getting into early foul trouble. Cruze, Oaks, and I each had one, but Monty, Teesha, and Tats each had two. It was starting to look like a replay of our league game against them.

Grace Lee hit a three to make it ten unanswered points and make the score 35–18 for Westview. As the ball went in the net, I heard her say something to Cruze. "How you like that, *Churro*?"

Cruze bumped her as she went to collect the ball. "It's on, *Wonton*."

The next time Westview came down the court, Cruze got her revenge by picking a steal off Lee and sending me a pass for a fast break. I went for a layup, colliding with Sage Walsh on the way up. A whistle blew.

Foul. That was a foul. Had to be a foul. She fouled me. Right?!

The ref punched a fist through the air. "CHARGE!"

CHARGE?! Are you fucking kidding me?

The gym exploded. Westview fans were cheering. Our fans were yelling, irate with the call. Even my mom and Prynne were arguing the call. I wondered if they actually knew what they were arguing about.

Okay, maybe ... maybe, it could have possibly, depending on the angle, been a charge. A little one. But for the record, when you're the one going in for the layup, it's NEVER a charge.

Coach K called a timeout. I thought she was going to rip into us—rip into me—but instead she took a breath, instructed us to do the same thing, and tried to calm us down.

I leaned in, attempting to listen and watch as she drew up a variation of our press break, but my focus was still on the last play. I went over the layup in my mind. I should have pulled up. I should have attacked the left side. I should have stuttered or crossed over or ...

"BENNETT?!"

I snapped out of the replay running through my mind. Coach K was looking at me. Everyone was looking at me. *Uh-oh.* She was obviously waiting for me to ... acknowledge I was listening? Respond to a question? Say something? I had no idea what she was waiting for.

"Jess," Coach K turned to Jess, "you're in. Bennett, have a seat."

I nodded, tucked my tail between my legs, and sat down.

"Bennett, you need to get your head in this game." Coach K stopped as she walked by me. "Don't think about the last play, focus on the next one."

"Sorry, Coach."

The game started back up. Matti came over and sat down beside me. "How's it going?"

"Oh, great. Best game ever," I said sarcastically, forgetting that Matti didn't really get sarcasm.

"Really? Because you're not playing very good. You missed that shot in the corner that you usually hit, and that charge was ..."

"Matti, I was kidding. It's not going great at all."

"No. It looks crazy out there."

"It is."

"Here." She took off her earphones and handed them to me.

"Matti, now is not the time ..."

"Just do it." She plugged her ears and waited for me.

I was in no mood, but I knew she wouldn't give up until I did it, so I slipped the earphones over my head. Instantly, I understood why she had been so persistent. The violins, the orchestra, the music took away the yelling, the chanting, the drumming ... it was calming. I had forgotten how calming it could be.

With the music in my ears, I watched the game from the bench. I don't know if it was the music or not, but I started to see the game differently. I saw a pattern to the frenzied zone that Westview kept throwing at us. I saw holes in it, too.

I took the earphones off my sweaty head and passed them back.

"You see?" Matti asked me.

I smiled. "I see."

"Good." She ran back to her assistant coach's chair.

I spent the remaining minutes on the bench. We managed to slow the bleeding but Westview kept their lead. Going into halftime, things did not look good.

Halftime score: Westview 44–Riverside 27

3rd Quarter

We weren't down by much. We had half a game left to make a comeback. We needed to chip away at their lead. We needed to stop letting the fans affect us. We needed to start playing our game. We needed to stop whining about the non-calls and start fighting back ... just a few of the things we already knew, but still needed to hear from Coach K during her halftime rant.

Our plan was to come out strong, to take it to the net hard, to take care of the ball, and to shut down Sage Walsh and Grace Lee. It was a good plan ... in theory. But Westview would not let up and we could not buy a basket.

Ten seconds after the third quarter started, Grace Lee hit a banker three to put Westview up an even twenty. Our fans were silenced.

After the halftime chat, Coach K pulled me aside and told me that when she used to have a bad game, she would choose one thing, and only one thing, to focus on. Forget the rest.

I chose to focus on shutting down Sage Walsh.

I didn't care what else was happening in the game, or that the Westview fans had come up with a "*hash tag Beneesha sucks*" chant. I put my full attention on Sage. I was her shadow. Where she went, I went. I was in her face and on her back, denying every single pass. I wanted to make her life a living hell. When she cut, I cut. She zigged, I zagged. Westview did everything they could to get her the ball. They knocked me as I ran by and hit me with off-ball screens. When she did get the ball, I closed out tight, forcing her to dribble. I could sense her getting frustrated. I was in her head.

I was so focused on Sage that I didn't think about my offensive game; I just played.

When the third quarter ended, I looked up at the scoreboard. We held Westview to seven points and had started to climb back into the game: Westview 51–Riverside 43

4TH QUARTER

I don't really know what or how it happened. I was under the hoop. I had just boxed Sage out from a shot, went for the rebound and, the next thing I knew, something hit the side of my face and I was on the ground. My left eye was throbbing and, when I pulled my hand from my face, there was blood ... a lot of blood. *Sonofabitch*. My irrational mind thought that my eye had popped out. It hadn't.

The noise in the gym was disorienting. Hands hooked under my arms and helped me to stand. Someone—I think Oaks—asked if I was okay. I nodded. I heard Teesha yelling. I looked up to see her walking straight into Sage. Monty was running and pulling her back.

Sage put her hands up in defense. "It was an accident."

Now I understood. Sage had elbowed me.

The refs called a timeout to get the blood cleaned up off the floor.

As Cruze and Oaks led me to the bench, I first heard and then saw Coach K yelling at the referees about the hit. I guess no foul had been called because the refs said they didn't see it happen.

"Do you think she did that to herself?" Coach K screamed. I had never seen her so angry before. She got mad and yelled a lot, but that was at practice when we didn't run a drill right— this was pure anger. The refs gave her a warning, but she continued to rant about how the game was out of hand from the beginning and ...

A whistle blew and a technical foul was issued. They told her that if she didn't stop, they would kick her out of the game. She came back to the bench in a huff. "Are you okay?"

"I think so," I said, sitting down.

"You have a pretty nasty cut under your eyebrow. Probably going to need stitches ..."

I started to panic. "I'm not leaving the game ..."

"Bennett, it looks ..."

"I'M NOT LEAVING. Can't the medics put some special tape on it or something?"

"Fine. But if they think you should come out of the game ..."

"I'm not," I said defiantly.

The tournament medic met me at the end of the bench.

"That looks pretty nasty," he said, kneeling down and opening his medical kit.

"How fast can I be back on the court?" I looked up at the game clock. There was 6:32 left.

"Two, three minutes?"

"Hurry."

As the medic tended to my eye, I watched the game. The referees had given both Teesha and Coach K technical fouls for their outbursts. Westview didn't get anything. *Bullshit!*

For the technicals, Westview got four foul shots and the ball. BULLSHIT!

Our fans yelled and stomped on the benches as Grace Lee stepped to the line. Mrs. Humphries was the loudest, yelling and wildly waving her cowbell.

Lee hit the first two, missed the third, and nailed the fourth. With the three points, the score was now: Westview 62–Riverside 54.

"Come on, come on ..." I pleaded with the medic.

"Almost done. Hold still. This might hurt ..."

My eye was throbbing and, even though I couldn't see it, I knew it was swollen, but it didn't hurt. The whole area felt numb.

"Okay," the medic looked at his work. "Now, that should

hold, but you need to get some ice on it pronto and you will need stitches ..."

I stood up. "Yeah, yeah, yeah ... am I good?"

"You're good."

"Thanks." I ran back to Coach K. "I'm good. Get me in." She looked at my eye. "I'm good, honest."

"Fine. Go for Jess. But if that starts to bleed again or you get dizzy ..."

"Okay!" I ran over and knelt in front of the scorer's table.

The medic had said two to three minutes but, when I finally stepped back on the court, there was only 3:14 left on the clock. Score: Westview 67–Riverside 60.

My first run down the court, we set up our offense and I received a kick-out pass from Monty at the baseline. I faked a three, Sage jumped, and I drove to the hoop, finishing with a reverse layup.

Westview threw the ball in and, on the return, Cruze poked the ball out of Grace Lee's hand. It was a foot race to see who would get to the ball first. My money was on ...

Cruze picked up the loose ball and went in for a layup. Grace Lee fouled her on the way up and Cruze finished the shot for an AND 1 play.

"Yeah, baby! That's right." Cruze celebrated, jumping antagonizingly close to Lee. "That's how I like it. In the net, deep-fried, with a side of sweet and sour sauce."

"That doesn't even make sense," Grace responded bitterly. "And I'm Korean, not Chinese."

"You don't make sense," Cruze mumbled on the way to the foul line.

"Ooh, ouch, that the best you got?"

"No, this is ..." Cruze held her follow through and iced her foul shot. We were within two: 67–65.

On the next play, Westview got Sage the ball. I closed in but they hit me with a pick. Sage attacked quickly. She drove at the hoop, Monty went up for the stuff, but Sage made a fancy move and drew the foul. She missed the shot but the damage was done. It was Monty's fifth and final foul. Westview cheered.

Coach K used the timeout to talk to Oaks. "Oaks, that's your net and your key. Do you understand?"

"It's my key," Oaks repeated.

"You have to rebound hard. No second-chance shots, you got that."

"I got it. I can do this."

With 1:44 on the clock, Sage hit both foul shots to put Westview back up by four: 69–65.

The next play down, Teesha hit a quick pull-up jumper.

Westview got the ball in and ran the clock down as much as they could. They sent the ball inside to the post. Oaks did what she could, but their post shot up an off-balance hook shot that bounced off the backboard and in. It was a lucky shot, but Coach K was yelling at Oaks to deny the pass. By the look on Oaks's face, I could tell that she was way angrier with herself than Coach K could ever be.

Less than a minute left and we were still down by four.

"You got a three in you?" Teesha whispered as we brought the ball up.

"Yep."

"Be ready."

And I was. Teesha drove, sucked in the defense, and pulled up for another jumper—a replica of the shot she had just hit—but this time she made a no-look pass back to me. Sage had dropped down to give extra defensive help with Teesha, and it gave me just enough room to take the shot ... I held my follow through. I knew it was in the second I released it.

Swish.

Our fans went crazy.

Westview called a timeout—0:44 on the clock: 71–70.

After the timeout, Westview ran a play, trying to get Sage the ball. She made a cut, and attempted to run me off a double screen, but I jumped over top of both and denied any pass attempt. With time running down, Grace Lee put up a quick shot. She missed and Oaks came down with a HUGE rebound.

Coach K called a timeout with 0:18 remaining.

She wanted us to run Swish—Matti's play for me.

We set up with me on the sideline. I threw the ball in to Cruze and then ran to the hoop, setting a screen for Teesha. Then I ran off Oaks and popped out at the side. It had worked. I was open.

Cruze passed me the ball.

With six seconds left, I took the shot ... everything went into slow motion ... the ball arced high ... it came down ... and ... hit the rim.

I missed.

I missed.

But Oaks didn't. She jumped up, caught the rebound in the air and, before coming back down, released the ball.

The buzzer went.

REGIONAL FINAL

Westview 71 – Riverside 72

CHAPTER

34

"Let's watch it again," Matti said eagerly.

Fourteen of us—the team plus Matti—were crowded around Teesha's computer, watching the end of the game.

Teesha replayed the final seconds—for the tenth time that night.

I cringed, watching the ball release from my hand. I was ecstatic that we had won—I really didn't care how, why, or who had won the game—but it still stung, watching myself miss the final shot over and over and over again.

Cruze saw the pained look on my face. "Hey, if you hadn't taken the shot, Oaks wouldn't have gotten the rebound."

"I know. I'm glad it was Oaks." And I really was glad. Given the turbulent season and relationship between Oaks and Coach K, it was awesome that Oaks got her moment to shine. Coach K gave her a big hug after the game.

Cruze was close to my face, squinting at my eye. "Stop looking at it."

"I can't help it. You look like Rocky." She started to hum the Rocky theme as she poked the fleshy area.

"OUCH!"

"Sorry. It's just so squishy looking."

Right after the game—after a recruiting agent from Stanford (FREAKING FINALLY!!) cornered me on the court, talked about how she loved my tenacity, and made plans to fly me out for a campus visit—my mom whisked me to the hospital and I got five stitches under my left eyebrow. While I was in the waiting room, I got a text from Teesha to come over to her place for a celebratory pizza/sleepover night. Her mom had missed the game due to an out-of-town meeting. Letting Teesha host a team party was her mom's way of saying, "Sorry I couldn't be at the game, but I still support you"—I think.

By the time I arrived at the house, my eye was almost completely swollen shut, with a black/purple/green bruise circling the area. The team had already eaten, but they saved me four slices of Hawaiian, which I was currently chowing down on.

"Let's watch Beaner get beaned again," Cruze said.

"Okay," Teesha answered. She scrolled back to the "hit." I don't know who was filming, but they had a better angle than any of the refs who missed the call. Teesha slow-moed the video.

The ball was shot. I boxed Sage out and we both looked up and went for the rebound. She stepped in front of me. An elbow was thrown at my face and ...

"OoooHHHHH," the team called out as we watched my head snap back and my body hit the floor.

Most of the talk, actually, *all* of the talk that night revolved around the game—Coach K's technical—the Westview mascot that did end up crapping on the floor—my eye—Mrs. Humphries and her cowbell—Oaks's rebound and then game-winning shot.

We reminisced, laughed, and reenacted everything. Tats gave a particularly good impression of me grabbing my eye and falling to the floor in pain. Matti even got in on the mix and pretended to be her mom, yelling at the refs. But we had the most fun reenacting the trash-talk banter between Cruze and Grace Lee.

"She's my nemesis," Cruze growled. "The Riddler to my Batman, the Lex Luther to my Superman, the Voldemort to my Harry Potter, the Darth Vader to my ..."

"CRUZE ... sit down. We get it." Five people threw their pillows at her.

"Fine." She threw the pillows back. "Haters gonna hate, players gonna play."

A little later the doorbell rang.

I went with Teesha to see who it was. She looked out the peephole. "What the ..."

Behind the door stood a group of students from our school. Most were wearing blue and some still had their faces painted. More were getting out of their vehicles. Prynne was with them.

"What's going on, guys?" Teesha asked.

"We heard there was a party here."

"What?" She leaned her head into the house. "Which one of you morons said there was a party here?" The whole team came running to see what was up. Teesha looked at me.

"What are you looking at me for?"

"Isn't that your sister?"

"I didn't tell her to come over."

"Cool!" Tats yelled. "Party, party, party ..."

"What do you think?" Teesha asked me. "Should I let them in?"

"It's your house."

"Yeah. My mom would kill me." She took a couple of seconds to think and then shrugged. "Oh, well. We should celebrate. We did just WIN THE REGIONAL CHAMPIONSHIP!"

"YEAHHHHH, WE DID!!!"

The team stepped aside as people flooded through the front door. Within minutes, music was blaring and drinks were flowing. I don't know how or who brought the alcohol, or if it was already in the house. I do know it was there, and we were drinking it.

Cars kept pulling up and full loads of our peers—fans who had been at the game—piled out. There were so many people that the party spilled out from the main floor, into the backyard, and onto the backyard basketball court.

Every person who saw my eye—*every person*—made a comment about how nasty it looked, called me Rocky, and then thought it would be funny to throw a fake punch at it. It got old fast.

At the start of the party, I asked Matti if she wanted me to drive her home. It's not that I didn't want her to stay, I just wasn't sure if a loud party with music was really her scene.

"Home?" she asked. "Why would I want to go home?"

"Well, there's a lot of people coming in and this could get kind of loud."

"No," she said, wide-eyed, and pushed me aside. "I want to stay."

"Are you sure? What would Coach ... I mean, your mom ... say?"

"What would *your* mom say?" She pointed her finger into my chest.

"Fair enough."

"I won't say anything to my mom, if that's what you're worried about." She seemed annoyed.

"No, that's not what ..."

"I'm a part of the team, too. I want to party."

"Okay, but tell me if you want to leave ... or go upstairs if you need some space."

"Bennett!" she yelled. "I'm sixteen; I'm not a child ..."

"I know ..."

"I can do what I want. And I want to party." She grabbed a sparkling peach cooler off the counter, opened it, and took a big sip right in front of me. "See."

I put my hands in the air. "Okay, Matti." I grabbed my own cooler and took a sip. "Then let's party."

I really should have driven her home.

Three sparkling peach coolers and one shot of tequila later, I was out on the basketball court playing night hoops with some members of the boys' basketball team. We had invented our own version of H-O-R-S-E and altered it into a drinking game. I was about to take a granny shot from half-court with a drink in my hand—first rule of the drinking game was *no spilling*; if you spilled, it was considered a party foul and you had to drink—when Teesha came running into the court, looking for me.

"Hey, what's up ... watch this shot ..."

"Beaner, you need to come. It's Matti."

I dropped my drink and went running up to the house. I could hear one of the boys yelling behind me that I had just committed a major party foul and would have to drink when I got back.

"What's going on?" I asked Teesha.

"You'll see."

She took me to the bathroom, where a couple members of our team were already crowded around the door. When they parted to the side, I saw Matti, sitting on the tiled floor with her head leaning against the toilet. She waved at me.

"Hey, Bennett—double N, double ... something," she giggled.

"How many drinks did she have?" I looked at the team.

Monty shrugged. "I don't know ... only two, I think."

"Two point seven," Matti chimed in. "That's almost one thousand and ..." she hiccupped, laughed, and then mumbled, "... and something millil ... millilil ... milliliters."

"She's drunk," I said, stating the obvious.

"Coach K is going to kill us," Oaks said, also stating the obvious.

"What do you think we should do?" Teesha asked me. "I can put her in my room to sleep it off or ..."

"Hey, hey ..." Matti whispered. "Don't worry about it. I already talked to my mom. She's on her way to pick me up."

If my left eye hadn't been swollen shut, it would have opened as wide as my right ... as wide as every eye in the bathroom. "You phoned your mom?!"

"Well, actually, she phoned me, if you want to get technical about it. Ha! Technical!" She pointed at Teesha and laughed at her own inside joke.

"She's actually pretty funny when she's drunk," Cruze laughed.

I turned to Cruze. "Seriously?"

"What?" She looked at all our faces. "Right ... Coach is going to kill us."

I looked back at Matti. "What did your mom say?"

"Umm ... not much. She asked what all the noise was. I told her it was a party, then ..."

"We're dead."

"Let's get her downstairs."

Teesha and I helped her to stand and stood by each side to make sure she was stable. When we got her to the front door, Coach K was already there, standing with her arms crossed and with a super-unimpressed/angry/disappointed face.

As soon as they saw her, the rest of the team scattered, leaving only Teesha, Matti, and me.

"Mom!" Matti called out. "Hey!"

"Coach ..." Teesha started to explain.

"No." Coach K shook her head. "Just get her to the car."

"Mom, you look ... *maaaddd*. Don't be mad. Hey, guess what? I threw up. It tasted like fuzzy peaches. Some came out of my nose. It made me sneeze and then ..."

We hurried Matti and her big mouth past Coach K as fast as we could.

I helped her get into the car and buckled up her seat belt. "Are you mad, Bennett?"

"No."

"Really?"

"Really." I smiled.

Matti smiled back. "Do you want to hear a secret?"

"Sure."

"Okay," she whispered and signaled for me to lean closer. "I like you, Bennett, double N, double T. I think *you* are *in the swish.*"

"I think you're in the swish, too, Matti, double T with an I but no E."

"No E. I don't like E's. Eeeeeessss ..."

I closed the car door while Matti was still sounding out E's, and then went to face Coach K with Teesha.

"Coach, we know you're mad but ..."

"Oh, I'm not mad." Clearly, she was mad. "I was just thinking, since we just won the regionals and have less than a week to prepare for the State Championships, I've decided to have an extra practice ... tomorrow morning ... 8 AM. In the gym. Shoes on, ready to go."

"What? But it's Sunday tomorrow."

"You're right. Seven it is." She walked around her car and opened the door. "Make sure you tell the team. And, girls," her voice sounded like ice, "don't be a minute late."

Teesha and I stood together and watched her drive away.

"We. Are. Dead."

"Yep," I nodded. "Super, super, one hundred percent, dead."

CHAPTER 35

Since everyone had slept over at Teesha's, it was easy—as easy as pulling blankets off and pouring ice water on sleeping heads— to make sure that we all got up and got to the gym on time ... actually, we were fifteen minutes early. And so was Coach K.

She was standing in the middle of the gym, arms crossed, smirk on her face, waiting for us. There were six big garbage cans strategically placed throughout the gym—one on each corner and two at half-court.

That can't be a good thing.

We threw our bags down and walked to the baseline. None of us was brave enough to step on the court.

It took me a second to notice Matti. She was curled up on the bench with a hood over her head, wearing sunglasses and earphones. I think she was sleeping.

"Good morning, ladies," Coach K said, far too loud for 7 AM, if you ask me.

"Morning," we mumbled collectively.

"Great win yesterday," she slow-clapped. "Regional Champions ... Wooooo!" She was far too peppy for this early in the morning. "I trust you all slept well last night." We all gave quick sideways glances at one another.

"I think I'm still drunk," Cruze whispered.

"What's that, Cruze?" Coach K yelled.

"Uh ... I said, I can't wait to practice." She gave thumbs-up to emphasize her enthusiasm.

"Great. Let's get started." She picked up a basketball by her foot and started walking toward us, bouncing it. The *BANG BANG BANG* echoed off the gym walls and into my head. "I know how much you girls love the Storm Target Drill ..."

The Storm Target Drill was a full-court running and shooting drill that combined layups and outside shooting. It had taken half the season to start hitting our target—fifty baskets in three minutes. We did like the drill ... when it wasn't 7 AM and we weren't hung over.

"... but you know, fifty baskets in three minutes has gotten a bit easy for you, so I think we should shoot for sixty. And since we need to up our conditioning before the State Championships, every layup you miss, and every basketball under the target, you'll run the length of the gym—there and back. Sound good?"

Sounds grrreeeaaattt.

"Here we, go!" Coach K blew her whistle. Our hands shot to our ears and we all groaned at the piercing sound.

I'm not sure how everyone else was feeling, but I was hurting. Every part of my body, including my hair, felt like it was sore.

We didn't run it at our usual pace, but we started the drill okay. Then our passes started to go everywhere but where they were supposed to go; the ball bounced off our hands and out of bounds, and our shots ... well, we were lucky when they got near the net.

Two minutes into the drill, it became painfully clear why the garbage cans were so strategically placed. O, Jess, and Tats stumbled to a can and started to puke.

I'm pretty sure I saw Coach K smiling. "If any of you makes a mess on my gym floor, we'll be running suicides the rest of practice." She blew her whistle.

In three minutes, we managed to get 42. Not bad, considering, but not good, either.

"Forty-two and four missed layups. Let's see, that's ..."

"Twenty-two!" Matti shouted from her spot on the bench.

"Yes, twenty-two full there-and-back lengths of the gym." She could see the terror in our eyes. "But okay, you did win the regionals yesterday, so maybe I should go easy on you." There was hope. Then she snapped her fingers and our hope snapped with them. "But then, you did have a party, with alcohol, and got my daughter drunk. So, twenty-two it is." She looked at her watch. "Better get started."

No one moaned, groaned, or said a peep as we set up on the baseline and started our punishment.

"Is it possible to sweat alcohol?" Oaks asked me on the run. "Because I think I can smell tequila coming out of my pores."

"Don't mention tequila," Monty complained and grabbed her stomach. One by one, girls starting dropping like flies, running to the nearest garbage bin to toss whatever they had left in their stomachs.

The only one running like it was any other practice was Cruze. She seemed light on her feet as she sprinted by me.

"Cruze, how are you running like that?"

"Like I said, I think I'm still drunk."

Coach K blew her whistle. "Let's go, ladies. These lines aren't going to run themselves. Pick it up. We still have to hit our target." We responded with a collective groan.

I was on my eighth length of the gym when a cold sweat broke out over my face, and my stomach felt like a mini tornado. I sprinted to the nearest bin. If I wasn't already going to be sick, the sour stench from the bucket sealed the deal. I was still hugging the bin when Teesha joined me.

"It does taste like fuzzy peaches," she said in between heaves. I threw up again.

"Hey." Teesha patted my shoulder and I looked up. "I think I can say, since we're sharing the same puke bin and everything, that we might be besties now."

I smiled. And then I threw up.

CHAPTER
36

So, here we are. One year later. Same gym. Same teams. Same faces in the stands. Same Championship Final. If I weren't wearing a different color, I would think I was having déjà vu.

True to the predictions, it was another Lincoln vs. Riverside final showdown.

On our side of the draw, we coasted through our first round and quarter-final games, and then faced the Southlands Spartans in the semis. With their six-four post, Annette Walker, they were good. But with Monty and Oaks, we were better.

Since the regional final, Oaks had been playing with a newfound confidence. While Monty and Annette went head to head under the hoop, Oaks was free to go off, and go off she did. With 5 blocks, 17 rebounds, and 19 points, she was deservedly the game MVP.

We ended up winning the game 65–52. It was a comfortable victory, but Southlands proved to be a strong team, and with Annette Walker only in Grade 11, I predict Southlands will be in the final next year. That's the way basketball works: some seasons are yours and sometimes you just have to be patient and wait your turn.

Opposite us, in the other semi, Lincoln had a tougher time beating Westview. They played after us and we all stayed to watch the game. Going into the fourth quarter, it was tied 47–47. I was conflicted about who I wanted to win. It would be nice to see Lincoln go down, but I wanted to be on the court when that happened. Even though I was going to have a scar, my eye was healing nicely, and I wasn't thrilled about the prospect of playing against Sage Walsh again. Deep down, although it's difficult for me to admit, I still cared about the girls wearing the purple and gold. Once you play on a team together, laugh together, cheer together, bleed together, those connections are there forever. That little lion that I had silenced when I stepped on the court in Riverside was still there, meowing quietly for Lincoln to beat Westview.

In the final minutes, Hanna and Brooke took over the game. It was Brooke who made a nice steal off Sage and sent a breakaway pass to Hanna for an easy basket, which turned the momentum Lincoln's way.

I can't explain it; it was an uncontrollable reflex, something that just happened, but I cheered and clapped for Brooke (not Lincoln) after the play. I got evil glares from a few of my teammates and quickly shrugged an apology. I made sure to keep my hands in my hoodie pocket and my mouth shut the rest of the game, a game that ended: Lincoln 62–Westview 58.

The article that came out in the sports section the day of the state finals was simply titled: "Here We Go Again." It painted a detailed analysis of our two seasons, making sure to highlight the "Bennett Ryan Riverside controversy." The journalist made the game sound like it was going to come down to a battle between Hanna Taylor's offense and my defense. Even though we hadn't played against each other, I had been studying Hanna in every game that I could watch, and I knew she was doing the same thing with me. I wish I could say that I found flaws with her game, but the girl was solid; she didn't make a lot of mistakes. She could drive just as easily as she could shoot a three and take a pull-up jumper.

Coincidentally, Lincoln was tied for the all-time unbeaten streak. If they won the championships, Lincoln would overtake Southlands with 77 wins (and counting). Coach Paige was quoted as saying: "If we beat Riverside and set a new record—that would be great, but I don't focus on things like that." *Yeah, right.* Then he talked about his thoughts on the game: "… the one advantage we have is that we know how Bennett plays. There are few things she can throw at us that I haven't seen before. My team understands who they are facing." *Smug asshole.* Like the article said, this was going to be a battle. And I was more than ready for the challenge ... with a few things to throw at Lincoln that I was sure they hadn't seen before.

On the way to the game, I rode the hotel elevator by myself. I was listening to my 90's Jock Jams when the doors opened and Mrs. Humphries stepped in.

She was wearing her old Riverside Storm coaching tracksuit, her hair was completely colored blue, and her face was painted white with blue lightning bolts on each check. In her hands was a bag full of blue and white pompoms and her signature cowbell.

"Mrs. Humphries?!"

"Oh, hey, Bennett." She looked at my face. "How are you feeling? That eye has healed nicely. I still can't believe they didn't give that girl a flagrant foul. And in my day, I would have met her outside the gym later to give her a black eye of her very own."

I giggled at the thought of Mrs. Humphries punching someone ... although, thinking about her in her younger days, I wouldn't have put it past her. "I feel good."

"Good? Or Great?"

"I feel ... ready to play."

"That's what I like to hear. It's time to take those sheepish

Lincoln Lions down a peg."

"That's the plan."

The elevator doors opened in the main foyer and we stepped out. "Well, good luck today, Bennett."

"Thanks."

"And hey, I'll make sure you get an A on your Lit final if you can pull off a win." She laughed. "I'm just joking ... but I'm not really. Just beat them, okay?" She walked out the door, waving her cowbell. "See you in the gym."

My mom and sister were waiting for me in the lobby. "Was that blue-haired woman Mrs. Humphries?" my mom asked.

"Sure was."

"She looks ready for the game."

"You have no idea." I looked at Prynne. Her face was also painted with lightning bolts; her hair was up in a ponytail, and she was wearing some of my Storm warm-ups. I had never seen her look this athletic, ever. I laughed. "And what's this version of you I'm looking at?"

"I thought today I'd be Bennett Ryan's sister."

I stopped laughing. "And just when I was going to make fun of you, you go and say something like that. Where's Adam?" I didn't find out till after but, at Teesha's party, Prynne and Prince Charming officially made things official.

"He's driving to the game with a couple of friends. We're

meeting at the gym." She surprised me with a hug. "Good luck today."

"Thanks." I was starting to feel like I was shipping off for war.

My mom hugged me next. "I wish your father was here. He'd be so proud of the woman you've become. I'm proud of you."

"Thanks, Mom."

She nodded and wiped away a tear. "Now, go out there and make some swishes or put it in the net with a swish. Isn't that what your dad used to say?"

"Something like that," I smiled.

We had a final family group-hug and then I boarded the team bus. As I stepped on, I heard the familiar beginning beats of Tag Team's "Whoomp! There it is."

Cruze was standing on her seat. "Here she is now, ladies and gentlemen, team captain, number six on the court but number one in our hearts, Bennett, the Beaner, Ryyyaaaannnn!" My face went flush as everyone stood up and started cheering me on, while I walked the gauntlet of players to the back of the bus. "Beaner, this one's for you. Riverside back again, shoot it to make it, let's begin ..." The entire team, including me, joined in to sing along. We ended up singing all the way to the gym.

Lincoln Lady Lions vs. *Riverside Storm*

We gathered in a giant circle with our arms around each other in the middle of the locker room. Outside the doors, we could hear the loud thumping of music and the cheering of expectant fans, waiting for us and Lincoln to be introduced.

Coach K addressed the team. "Ladies, I don't have to tell you all the cliché lines about what this game means. You already know. Everything we've worked for, every practice, every drill, every suicide you ran, every line you touched, every drop of sweat that fell from your body, every time I yelled at you, every time you thought you hated me and wanted to walk out of the gym (she glanced at Oaks), all of it has led to this moment, to this game. This hasn't been the easiest season. But it certainly has been the most memorable, and we've gotten through it together ..."

"Can I say something?" Matti interrupted. Coach K nodded. Matti never said anything during a pregame talk. She was usually too shy and nervous. "I just wanted to say that Lincoln may have Hanna Taylor, and she may be really good, but we have something they don't ..." She looked around the circle at everyone. "We have Bennett Ryan ... and Teesha Collins and Camila Cruze and Georgia Oaks and Tatiana Smith and Montana Dunkin and Jessica Randall and Nikki Michaels and Taya Owens and Olivia Franklin and Jazmin Johnson and Sierra Hampton and Maya Hernandez ..."

"And Matti Kelley," I said. The team nodded with me.

"And me," Matti said, red-faced. "Oh, yeah ... and my mom. You see, we have each other, and that's something Lincoln will never have."

"Hands in," Coach K said. We all piled our hands in the middle.

"Who are we?"

"THE STORM."

"What are we?"

"WE ARE ONE. WE ARE A TEAM."

"Storm on two. One, two ... STORM!"

As the team ran into the gym, I quickly turned for a bathroom stall and threw up. When I came out, Matti was waiting for me. She had a smile on her face.

"Did you know that in the games where you throw up right before, you average about seventy-two percent shooting?"

I rinsed my mouth out. "Did you really do a calculation for that?"

"Well, only for the last part of the season, so my numbers could be off."

I put my arm around her shoulders as we walked out of the locker room together. "Matti, you're a little weird, and I like that."

"You do?"

"And you gave a pretty good pregame speech. I think you're going to make an awesome head coach one day."

"You really think so?"

"Yep. I'm ninety-nine point nine percent sure of it."

1ST QUARTER

"So, here we are," Brooke said to me as we took our spots for the jump ball.

"Here we are," I said back to her. "You decide where you're going yet?"

"Oregon."

I knew Oregon was where Brooke had hoped to go. She wanted to stay close to home. "Good for you. That's awesome."

"How about you?"

"Still undecided."

"After this is all over ... whatever happens, you want to grab a bite or something? Hang out sometime?"

I looked at her like it was the strangest yet most perfect thing she could be saying to me at that moment. "Sure." We both smiled. Then the whistle blew, our smiles faded, and we pushed for position. *Game on.*

We won the jump ball. Monty flicked the ball to Teesha. She hit me with a quick pass and I put it in the net with an easy layup.

The ball never even touched the ground. I winked at Coach Paige as I ran back for defense. *That one's for you.* I knew how much he hated not scoring the first points of the game.

I quickly found Hanna Taylor and settled in on defense. Now it really was game on.

She made a cut and got a pass on the wing. With a quick between the legs crossover, she got by me and attacked the middle of the key. *Shit, she's fast.* Oaks blocked her shot and half the crowd cheered.

"Nice block," I said, running up the court.

"I got your back, Beaner."

On defense, I was checking Hanna, but on offense, Hayley was checking me. She was all over me. Each time I touched the ball, she pushed me into a double team. On my next two possessions, I coughed up the ball and Lincoln capitalized on each turnover. This was their strategy, to take me out of the game.

Coach K was yelling for us to get the ball into Monty and Oaks. We needed to use our size against them. Each time we got a pass in, their defense collapsed and smothered the ball. In response, Monty and Oaks started to take quick off-balance shots that rimmed in and out. Lincoln boxed out hard—being a little smaller than most teams, it had always been a strong part of their game—and it worked. They got rebounds.

Hanna got the ball and made another move on me. I got sucked in and reached for the ball—foul. *Shit.*

I could hear Coach K yelling at me not to reach in.

The next play down, Lincoln ran a similar play. Hayley set a screen for Hanna. I jumped under and tried to catch Hanna on the other side, but she had already committed to the shot. In my mind, I knew I was going to get a foul even before the whistle blew—another foul. *Fuck.* And she hit the shot. *Double fuck.*

The horn sounded and I was subbed out with two fouls. If this was a battle between Hanna's offense and my defense, I was losing. Coach K grabbed my arm and whispered into my ear, "Don't play the game they want you to play." I nodded, grabbed a towel, and slumped into my seat to watch the rest of the first quarter play out.

At the end of the first quarter, it was Lincoln 18–Riverside 11. The only points I had were the two I had put in at the very beginning. Going into his huddle, Coach Paige looked over at our bench and winked at me. *Asshole.*

2ND QUARTER

Coach K kept me off for the first four minutes. Every minute I wasn't playing felt longer than the next.

Hanna took advantage of my being off and went on a run, hitting three quick jump shots. Teesha switched with Tats and tried to shut her down, but Hanna went at her and she reached in for a steal, picking up her second foul.

Offensively, we couldn't find our groove. Lincoln's defense made us rush our offense, and we started to put up quick shots in an attempt to get something going. Lincoln went up 27–14, and it started to feel like the game was getting away from us.

"Bennett?" Coach K called me up. She looked frazzled. "You're back in. You take Hanna, but don't reach. I see you reach and your ass is right back on this bench. I don't care what game this is."

"I got it."

"And Bennett! We need some offense."

"I think I have a plan." Matti grabbed her mom and showed her something she had drawn up on the whiteboard.

Coach K looked it over. "Okay, I'll try anything. This is your timeout to run."

We called a timeout and I subbed in.

Everyone waited for Coach K to say something, but it was Matti who knelt down in front of us. "Okay, okay, I think ... I'm pretty sure ... Lincoln is running a zone but they're adapting it to Bennett. Hayley Taylor is the only one playing man. So here's what I think we should do." Matti proceeded to draw out an altered offense, using me as a decoy.

"Welcome back," Hanna greeted me as I stepped onto the

court. "You here for a while this time?" I wanted to smack her cocky smile and cool Aussie accent right off her face.

The next time she got the ball and tried to get by with a double crossover, I reached again but, this time, I poked the ball out cleanly at the top of the key and sprinted down the court for a wide-open breakaway layup.

"Thanks for the welcome. It's good to be back," I said as I ran by Hanna.

Matti's alterations to our offense seemed to work. Hayley and the team were so focused on where I was running that they opened up holes for us to attack. Teesha took advantage and hit an easy pull-up jumper. Then Oaks and Monty both hit jumpers from the middle of the key.

Coach Paige was yelling at his team to play better defense. They started to yell at each other, putting blame on the other person.

Like Matti had shown us, the defense collapsed on Monty; she kicked it out to Cruze, who hit back-to-back threes, pulling us within three points. Cruze's family screamed and hooted with delight and then started dancing in the stands. Her five siblings were each wearing a shirt with a letter on it spelling out C-R-U-Z-E. It was her own mini fan club.

As the clock wound down on the half, I had barely touched the ball on offense, but Hayley never left my side. Even with Coach Paige yelling at her to "stay with her," I could tell she felt useless and wanted to leave me, cheat in, and help her teammates—I would. Then, on the last play of the half, Teesha sent a pass in to Oaks. Hayley couldn't resist. She dropped down to double. Oaks saw I was finally open and hit me with the ball. I've never been more ready to shoot. I sent up a three, my first shot in I don't know how many minutes. For a brief flash of a second, with my follow through still hanging in the air, I closed my eyes—*Swish*. It was solid *swish*—not just a sound, but a message to Coach Paige that my game was on.

The shot tied the game going into halftime: Lincoln 34–Riverside 34. Even better, Coach Paige was losing it on the bench. As we made our way into the locker room, I saw him kick a water bottle and rip a strip off Hayley for leaving me. Lincoln was starting to unravel.

HALFTIME

Having come from behind and found our groove, we felt more relaxed going into halftime. Coach K reminded us that this was the championship and we still had a whole half to play. Lincoln's strategy was failing them, but if I knew Coach Paige, he was going to stick with it. He was so focused on me that he underestimated my team.

The one thing Coach K asked us to focus on was "playing our own game." We had spent the first half letting Lincoln decide the pace, adjusting to their defense, and worrying about Hanna Taylor. We forgot to have fun.

I was just as guilty as anyone else. I had gone into the game focusing on playing Lincoln, instead of focusing on playing basketball.

Teesha took a sip from her water bottle and bumped her sweaty arm against mine. "You know what I think?" I shook my head. "I think we should introduce them to hash tag Beneesha." I smiled and bumped her fist with mine.

The warning buzzer went, signaling us to get back on the court. We got up and put our hands in. Coach K looked intently at each of us. "This is your last twenty minutes together. How do you want to spend it?"

Cruze spoke first. "Kicking some Lincoln ass." No one needed to say anything else. We all agreed.

3RD QUARTER

Coming out of the locker room, the feeling from Lincoln was different—less arrogant, more serious. Brooke didn't even return my smile when I saw her walk onto the court. Even in the tight games, I think they always believed they would win. For the first time in a long time, we had planted a seed of doubt.

Lincoln's first run down the court, they gave the ball to Hanna. She did exactly what I expected, putting her head down and driving as hard as she could at me and the hoop. This time I was quicker. I got in front, planted, and braced for the hit.

She went into me so hard that my breath was knocked out of my chest and I flew back, skidding right off the baseline.

Whistle. *CHARGE!*

"WHAT?" I could hear Coach Paige complaining in vain from the bench as Teesha and Monty helped me up.

"Yeah, Beaner! Well done." Teesha smacked my back.

Coach Paige continued to stomp and yell at the call. Hanna was shaking her head, but not at me, at herself. She knew what she had done.

"Hey, T," I whispered to Teesha. "Next play down, look for me on the back door." She nodded.

Hayley was back playing defense on me. I set up like I had the first half and made it seem like I was just going to stand outside and be a decoy.

Cruze started the offense by passing the ball to Teesha. Teesha started to drive. As soon as Hayley turned her head, I snuck behind her and Teesha hit me with a no-look pass under the hoop for an easy layup.

As Lincoln prepared to inbound, I heard Cruze doing what Cruze does best, trash talking to Hayley. "Oh, hey, I see you just met my friend Beneesha. I'm not sure what they call it down under, but here we like to say, you just got schooled."

"Stay out of my face." Hayley deliberately bumped into her as she went by.

The crowd "oohed."

"Ladies, keep it clean," the ref warned.

We went on an 8 and 0 run. Lincoln responded with their own 11 to 2 run. Much of the third quarter went back and forth like this.

I had done a pretty good job of containing Hanna Taylor offensively, but with three minutes left, she drove to the hoop. I tried to get in front to take another charge; we collided—hard—and the whistle went. Both of us were on the ground looking up at the ref to see what the call would be.

The three refs on the court got together to talk about the call. To be honest, I wasn't sure if I got in front in time. It could have gone either way.

And I guess the refs agreed, because they came out of their huddle and gave a double foul—one to each of us. It also came with a warning to "take it easy."

It was the third foul for each of us. At that point, we were up six: 48–54. To be safe, Coach K subbed me off. But Coach Paige kept Hanna on, gambling with her foul count and hoping she could do some damage with me on the bench.

I wanted to stay on. I asked to stay on. But Coach K was having none of it. "Sit. Rest. Teesha can take her."

Before the play started up again, I grabbed Teesha by the jersey. "Play off her a bit. Her first step is quick. She'll want to drive, but I don't think she can risk another charge, so be ready for some pull-ups ..."

Teesha didn't object to my advice. She listened intently, as if I were telling her how to dismantle a bomb, and nodded that she understood. We gave each other a high-five, and I sat on the bench to watch the third quarter tick away.

Teesha did a great defensive job. Lincoln caught up, but not because of Hanna. At the end of the third, we were tied again: 57–57.

4TH QUARTER

It was our ball to start the quarter. I was throwing it in but, on the way to the sideline, I told Cruze to make sure to give the ball back to me. She nodded.

Ball in. I passed to Cruze and she passed back. With Hayley playing defense on me, I casually dribbled up to the three-point line and took what I knew was a ballsy shot. But I also knew that Hayley wouldn't be expecting me to do it, and I wanted to send a message to Paige.

I let go of the ball about four feet behind the three-point line—message sent.

Swish—message received.

On the very next play, Hanna did the very same thing. Another message sent. Another message received.

Both sides of the crowd were going crazy. Our mascots started a mock fight on the sideline. We were giving them everything the rivalry promised and everything that they came to see.

When a loose ball hit the floor, so did a pile of bodies. Rebounding under the net should have come with signs saying, "Watch for flying elbows," and "Enter at your own risk."

Hanna Taylor and I went toe to toe and shot for shot.

I hit another three—my fifth—and everyone on the Riverside bench jumped in the air, waving towels, and pumping fists in the air.

Coach Paige was irate, yelling, "ANYONE, SOMEONE, GET ON RYAN."

Lincoln didn't waste any time. Brooke made a long full-court pass to a streaking Hanna. She was just out of my reach but, as she went for the layup, I went for the ball.

I got the ball ... I also got a little bit of her hand. Any other ref, any other game, it might have been a block. But not today. A whistle blew—my fourth foul.

No!

I turned around, ready to argue with the ref, but Teesha was in my face. She guided me away. "No, no, Beaner. Don't worry about it. Leave it."

"But ..."

"I know. Trust me ... *I know*. It's not worth it."

With 4:44 on the clock and Hanna set to shoot her foul shots, Coach K called a timeout. She switched Teesha on Hanna, told me to be careful, and let me stay in.

Hanna hit both her shots, putting Lincoln behind by one: 72–73.

We were well aware that time was winding down. Both teams started to play careful and tense up a bit. For a couple of minutes, neither of us could score.

There was 2:13 on the clock and Hanna drove to the hoop. Teesha managed to just touch the ball with barely the tips of her fingers, but it was enough to knock it loose, causing a loose ball. I dove, just as the ball was about to go out of bounds, and managed to flick it up the court to a running Cruze. With defenders closing in quickly, she finished with a layup. But something happened when she came down ... and from all the way on the other side of the court, I was sure I heard a *SNAP!*

I ran over and pushed through the circle of players around her. Teesha was already kneeling beside her and I joined in, kneeling on the other side. "Cruze! Are you okay?"

"No, Cruze is definitely not okay." She was on her back, grabbing at her ankle and grunting in pain. "Cruze is down ... Cruze is hurt ... Owwww ..." She squeezed my hand. "Did it go in?"

"Yeah, Cruze," Teesha smiled, "it went in."

She winced a smile. "Oh, good. Cruze is happy then."

I laughed. "Do you know you're talking about yourself in the third person?"

"Can't help it. That's what Cruze does when she's in pain. That's how Cruze deals."

Teesha and I looked up at one another and started to laugh.

"Cruze is not impressed. She's mad you two idiots are laughing ..."

"Sorry."

The medics and referees pushed in behind us. "We got this, girls. Go to your benches."

"Hey," Cruze called to us. "I didn't go down for nothing. You better win this game." We nodded and went to our bench.

As the medics attended to Cruze, everyone was sullen, including the fans in the stands—all of them. For such a little person, Cruze was a big loss.

Coach K started talking to us about the final minutes of the game, trying to get us to focus, but our attention was pulled back to Cruze.

A small hand giving a thumbs-up emerged from the group of medics as they picked her up and carried her off the court. The entire gym started to clap and chant her name. "Cruze, Cruze, Cruze ..." Up in the stands, I could see how worried, but also touched, her family was.

We cheered Cruze's name before going back on the court. All of us were resolute that we were going to win this for her. It was a nice thought, a gesture that might have worked in the movies but, in reality, we weren't ourselves without her on the court. Lincoln quickly took advantage of our disjointedness and got the next seven points to go up by four: 79–75.

Monty got a crucial offensive rebound and put us back within two: 79–77.

00:37 on the clock–Lincoln possession. They called their last timeout.

"They're going to put the ball in Hanna's hands," I said.

"Are you sure?" Coach K asked. "They know that's what we'll expect them to do."

"It doesn't matter. I know Paige. He'll want the ball in Hanna's hands, and only Hanna's hands. Let me take her."

"You've got four fouls."

"I know."

"It's okay, Coach." Oaks put her hand on Coach K's shoulder. "Monty and I will have Beaner's back." Monty nodded in agreement.

"When we get the ball back, I think we should run Swish," Matti said. "We need a three. Bennett's shooting a hundred percent from the three. Swish will get you open."

"Matti ..." I started to object.

"I know you missed last time. But maybe this time you won't. *Maybe* this time you'll make it. *Maybe* this is our turn to have a moment."

"Okay, let's do it."

PLAY-BY-PLAY

00:37—Ball in to Brooke Hastings.

00:33—Pass to Hanna Taylor. (Taylor runs the clock down.)

00:19—Facing pressure from Bennett Ryan, Hanna Taylor dribbles off a screen and drives to the hoop.

00:16—Hanna Taylor shoots. BLOCKED by Georgia Oaks.

00:13—Riverside on the attack. Tatiana Smith passes to Teesha Collins.

00:07—Teesha Collins drives to the hoop—she passes out to Bennett Ryan.

00:04—Ryan shoots for three ...

An entire season was about to come down to one last shot.

As the ball left my hand, I wasn't thinking *maybe*, I wasn't thinking anything. I was the only person in that gym (except for maybe my dad, if his spirit was there) who knew where that ball was going...

... *Swish.*

My three put us up by one: 79–80. The noise in the gym was deafening. Riverside fans were on their feet. Hands were in the air. There was cheering, shouting, hollering ...

And then ...

Lincoln passed the ball in.

I tried to get to her, but Hanna Taylor took one dribble and threw a Hail Mary from five feet behind the half line ...

An entire season did come down to one last shot ... it just wasn't mine.

STATE FINAL
Lincoln 82 – Riverside 80

POST
SEASON

Weeks after the championship game, I still close my eyes in bed at night and see the ball leaving Hanna's hands, flying through the air, hitting nothing but net as it falls through the hoop. I can still feel the metaphorical punch to my gut, the air leave my lungs, and the hot tears running down my face, as my brain registered what my eyes had seen but refused to believe. I can still hear the shocked silence from one side of the stands and the equally shocked roar from the other.

It wasn't supposed to happen that way.

We—Riverside—were supposed to win that game. We were supposed to be the State Champions. Us, not them. We were the "good" team, the fun team, the nice girls with the nice coach. Why did Lincoln get to win it … again? Why did they get to set the new state record for an undefeated win streak? Why did they get their happy ending?

Why them and not us?

Because this isn't just a story, it's sports.

We sat together in the locker room after the game—after we had high-fived and congratulated Lincoln, after we accepted our second-place medals, after Coach Paige told me I played a "great game." *Asshole.*

Even though I was wearing the same uniform, had gone through the same season, suffered the same loss, and was crying the same tears as everyone else, I felt like an outsider. I felt guilty. I still had something that my teammates didn't.

"I know you might not believe me, and it might be too soon to say this, but I want you all to know," I said amongst the sniffles, "that this team, this season, even without the championship banner ... is still the best season I've ever had. Ever. Lincoln can have their banners. Losing with all of you is far sweeter than winning any championship with anyone else." It was cheesy, but I meant it and I needed to say it.

My little speech prompted others to start speaking up. We went around the room recounting our favorite moments from the season. Eventually our tears turned into laughter, and then Cruze—still mad at us for not winning it for her, and with her ankle wrapped in ice and propped high on a chair—initiated a dance party that lasted well after Lincoln and most fans had left the gym.

Life after any sport season can be difficult to adjust to. After months of following a schedule, living in the gym, being with the same girls almost every single day ... it feels kind of hollow when things end. And yes, there will be other teams, other seasons, and even other sports, but that doesn't make it any easier to let it go and move on. For some players, it is harder than others.

Teesha was alone in the gym when I walked in. She was focused on practicing her pull-up jumpers and didn't see me standing in the doorway watching. After a couple of minutes, I threw my bag on the court and started to bounce my own ball.

"Your follow through is off to the right a bit," I said.

She took another shot, adjusting her follow through, and hit a swish. Then she turned to me and we bumped fists. "I thought you were in California?"

"I just got back. I went to your house but your mom told me you were here." I passed her the ball and went underneath the hoop to rebound, while she took another shot. "You have your own court, so why do you come here?"

She shrugged and shot again. "I guess I miss the gym."

I understood.

"So," she asked, "how was Stanford?"

"It was okay."

"Just okay?"

"Just okay," I repeated. "I was more enthusiastic about them than they were about me. I guess sometimes the team you think you're right for is not the team that is right for you."

"Sorry."

"It's okay, really."

Teesha moved under the basket and started to rebound for me. "So, what now?"

I stopped mid shot and pulled out a T-shirt I had tucked behind my back. I threw it at her and watched her unravel it. The look of shock on her face was exactly the look I was going for.

"Notre Dame," she said, confused. "Notre Dame?" I smiled and nodded. "But ... but I ..."

"You're going there, too. You committed over a month ago. I know."

"How did you know?"

"That night you had the big party at your house. I saw the envelope on your dresser. I couldn't resist. What I can't believe is that you kept it a secret this long."

"We said we wouldn't say anything. I can't believe you cheated." She looked back at the T-shirt and then at me. "But for real? We're both going to be playing for the Fighting Irish?"

I took another shot. *Swish.* "Well, I do still owe you a championship."

"Yeah, you do. I guess this means hash tag Beneesha lives on."

"Hash tag yeah it does."

She threw the T-shirt down and sent me another pass. "You want to see who can hit one hundred threes the fastest?"

"Game on." I took my first shot.

Swish.

Storm Standards

We are one.
We are a team.
We are defense.
We are tenacious.
We are dedication.
We are hard work.
We are boxing out.
We are forty minutes.
We are your worst nightmare.
We are full-court press, in your face, relentless.

There will be no warning. There will be no shelter.
We are the Storm, and nothing can stop a storm.

SHOUT
OUTS

Like winning a championship victory, writing a novel and seeing it published is a team accomplishment, and there are more than a few people I would like to give a shout-out to for inspiring and helping me to complete this project.

I dedicated this novel to all the coaches in my life, individuals who have taught me incredible lessons, and that list includes people who have coached me, those I have had the pleasure of coaching with, and some I have never met and just look up to.

Neuf, thank you for not only inspiring me but hundreds (maybe thousands) of others with your love and passion for this game. Tenacious forever! Cannon and KJ, I am so thankful that young me was coached by you two. You taught me the importance of goal setting and I try to bring your focused yet fun attitude to every team that I coach. Graves, as "shrill" as you are, the game is better when your energetic spirit is in the gym. Dani, it was after coaching with you that I was motivated to write this story. The girls and women you coach need your passion.

Coaches everywhere, from icons like Pat Summitt, Tara VanDerveer, and Kathy Shields, to those giving up their weekends in a community gym, you are an inspiration. To ALL the players that I have coached, thank you; I may be the coach but it is you who teach me something every day.

Wanda, if only our sixteen-year-old selves (the two who snuck into the arena change rooms, met the 1996 US Olympic Women's Basketball Team and got autographs from Sheryl Swoopes, Rebecca Lobo, and Jennifer Azzi) could see us now. We may not get to see each other very often these days, but I value our friendship tremendously and would not have achieved the goals I have without it. You are one of the most amazingly fierce females that I know.

The publishing team at Red Deer Press—Peter, Richard, Winston, and others that I have not met—thank you for believing in the potential of a girls' sports story from the very beginning. I am forever indebted to all of you.

To the most important team of all – my family and friends – your support and encouragement is invaluable. Like a true team you are there to cheer me on when I rise and help pick me up and dust me off when I fall. In no particular order I have to give a personal-shout out to: Munro, Jen, Jackie, Robynne, Nichelle, Tracey, Sarah, Kimmy, Maya, Celine, Bree, Chanelle, Roland, Shelley, Greens, Mom, Grandma (you may be gone but I know you are forever cheering from the stands), Grandpa (my first coach ever, thank you for saying "I could do anything" enough times that I started to believe it).

There is not enough space to thank all the coaches, players, friends, and family that have impacted my life. To those not listed here, know that I am truly grateful to all of you.

Sports have an amazing ability to bring people together, and every now and then a team comes along (sometimes unexpectedly) that, for some reason, seems more special than others and leaves a lasting impression. I hope that all young athletes get the opportunity to play with a team that forms lifelong bonds, helps to shape them, and most importantly, is fun.

INTERVIEW WITH DAWN GREEN

What made you decide to write a story about girls' high school basketball?

I love sports. I was raised playing multiple sports and, as a teenager, I was obsessed with anything sport related. I feel like I am dating myself when I say this—or maybe not, because times haven't changed too much—but as a teenager, it was difficult to find sport-related items geared toward girls. I had Michael Jordan and Magic Johnson on the walls in my room, but what I craved were female role models. When and if I did find something girl related, it was gold, and I took care of it like a prized possession.

I dedicated this book to my fifteen-year-old self because she really did look for something like *In the Swish* on every bookshelf in every bookstore. I can still remember one titled *In These Girls, Hope is a Muscle* by Madeleine Blais. It is a true story about a high school girls' basketball team in the U.S.—I must have read it five times, because it is good, but also because there was nothing else like it to read ... and (sadly, almost twenty years later) there still isn't much out there.

Female teens that love their sports really LOVE their sports. They search for interviews, record games, watch movies, pin up posters, and tape ripped magazine articles in their locker ... I should know. Girls play sports, girls love sports, and they should have items and access to role models geared toward them. With professional basketball and soccer leagues in the U.S., the success of North American female athletes and teams at the Olympics, and the rise of players like Christine Sinclair in Canadian soccer, there is a boom occurring in female sports. I can feel it, and I could not be happier. My hope for *In the Swish* is that it finds itself in the hands of that young girl who, like me, has been looking for it.

I could have written this story about soccer (a sport I also love, and maybe one day I will write about) but I chose basketball because this is the story I've had inside me for almost twenty years. I am passionate about basketball, but I was never talented or driven enough to play further than high school. Over the years I have coached many girls' teams at multiple levels of the sport, but I have always felt like I had something bigger to give back to the game that truly has given me so much ... I hope *In the Swish* is it.

Do you think there are important differences between basketball as it's played by boys, and basketball as it's played by girls?

Yes.

My grandfather, who coached both boys' and girls' baseball teams, once told me that there is a difference between coaching boys and girls. He said, "As a coach, when you yell at a boy, you only yell at the boy. But when you yell at a girl, you yell at the team." And, from my experience, although this is not always the case, he was right. Something beautiful about a girls' team is their emotional connectedness and cohesiveness. Some of the bonds formed on a sports team are some of the strongest bonds I have experienced, as a player and as a coach. I am not saying that doesn't exist on boys' teams, because I am sure it does, but there is something in the nature of girls that truly can make for the best "team" atmosphere.

Why did you decide to set this story in the U.S. rather than Canada where you live?

I love that a Canadian invented basketball, and I love that Steve Nash is from Canada, but when it comes to the game, I think it is fair to say that almost all people associate basketball with the U.S. I have played at and coached tournaments in the U.S. and there is a tenacity for the game that we lack up here. Most of Canada's best high school girls aspire to play in the States because the level of play, the fans, and the passion for the game are much more intense. I hope that's not always the case.

What is it about sports that allows a storyteller to explore the world of contemporary teens, their aspirations and struggles?

I think the realm of sports can make normal everyday things seem more epic than they actually are. A team is like a microcosm of the real world. Relationships can feel stronger, victories, whether they are personal or team, can feel that much sweeter, defeats are felt with more disappointment, and grudges can be held longer. As in the relationship between Bennett and Teesha, there is more drama when sports and team members are involved.

In the end, Bennett's joining the Riverside Storm doesn't work out as she hoped—i.e., her new team doesn't defeat the Lady Lions. Why did you decide the story should end in this way?

As I was writing this novel, the one thing I wrestled with was how it was all going to end. I had multiple conversations with friends about what I was going to do, and I had people asking me how I finally decided to end it … but the truth is, I didn't know how it was going to end until I wrote it. And ultimately, I didn't decide it. I know an author holds the storytelling power, but sometimes we don't. Sometimes the characters and the story tell the author how it should end. Of course I wanted the Storm to win, I was cheering for them, too … it just didn't feel right. This story is not about winning or losing. It's about making connections, learning about self, learning about others, and learning about self through others. I wanted this to be about a team and the lesson that sometimes, at the end of a season, win or lose, what you gain/learn from that team can be much more valuable than a championship. Some of my most memorable seasons and most memorable teams didn't even make it into the playoffs.

I think Bennett sums it up best in the book ...

> *We—Riverside—were supposed to win that game.*
> *We were supposed to be the State Champions. Us,*
> *not them. We were the "good" team, the fun team,*
> *the nice girls with the nice coach. Why did Lincoln*
> *get to win it ... again? Why did they get to set the*
> *new state record for an undefeated win streak?*
> *Why did they get their happy ending? Why them*
> *and not us?*
>
> *Because this isn't just a story, it's sports.*

Even though the movies like to have the happy underdog victory, real sports don't always work out that way. At the end of a season, there are always more players crying than celebrating.

You have been a basketball player and coach. As you were writing the story, did you find yourself modeling some of your characters on young women you have played or coached with?

Absolutely—sometimes intentionally, and sometimes unintentionally. Coach K is modeled after two women that I have coached with ... both amazing, highly respected (although sometimes known to be "shrill") coaches. And I have been coached by or coached against a few "win-at-all-costs" coaches like Coach Paige.

I am pretty sure that if some of the players I have coached ever read this novel, they will be able to identify some of the characters or characteristics of the players with certain players on their team. In fact, I think it's safe to say that most girls who read this book have a player(s) on their team like Bennett, Teesha, Cruze, Oaks, Matti, etc.

I mentioned the relationship between Bennett and Teesha in an earlier question and I know there are many girls out there who will relate to the mutual "despise yet respect relationship" between these two talented players. Many top athletes have a nemesis on the other team: someone who pushes them, forces them to up their game, and ultimately makes them a better player.

Though this is, in a narrow sense, a sports story, you are interested in much more than the game itself. Special needs kids, race, social inequity, sibling tension—they're part of the fabric of the narrative. Why was it important to explore these areas?

Sometimes, in sports, I think it is easy to get caught up with the competition and the idea of winning. Tournament programs list players by their name, position, size, and number, and it's easy to see a player by these constraints—easy to see them as the "other." In writing *In the Swish*, I wanted to explore the lives of the players because players on teams are people, and people come with lives that are complicated and, at times, messy. The most beautiful thing about making a team come together is that you are connecting different lives, races, religions, backgrounds, and beliefs into one cohesive unit ... and it's not easy to do.

Any successful coach will tell you that the tactical technical sport side of the game is only a small part of creating a winning program. At the beginning of the novel, when Bennett first comes to Riverside, she only knows the girls by what she knows of them on the court. I wanted her journey to include learning about the lives of her teammates off the court, to demonstrate to her, and to those reading, that as wrapped up as we can get in playing, cheering, and wanting to win, at the end of the day, it's just a game. The most important things that should be taken away from sports and teams have everything to do with the connections we make and the lessons we learn. Sometimes those lessons happen on the court, but usually they happen off and come to us from unlikely places and unlikely sources, much like the relationship between Bennett and Matti.

This is a very different kind of story than your previously published *When Kacey Left*. Why is it important for you to explore such different worlds in the stories you write?

Why not? I usually like to write whatever is "speaking" to me at the time, and I don't have a lot of control over what that is. I like to challenge myself as a writer, and I never want to be known as writing one particular type of story or genre. I think writing different things and exploring different worlds is what keeps a writer on their toes ... or their fingertips.

Thank you, Dawn, for the insights.